A DANGEROUS QUESTION

All at once I realized with panic that he didn't yet know that I knew; and yet his expression, when he was near enough to have smiled a greeting, was grave. The moment had come. Now at once I must ask him. The question, unconsciously rehearsed, sprang to my lips—no more than half a dozen words.

I didn't wait until he came up to me. He was still a few yards from the gatepost. And although it was more than a personal need—it was a duty to ask: "Where is she? What have you done with her?"—in the event I could not say those words. They formed not only a question, but an accusation I couldn't bear to make.

The question that actually passed my lips took a different form: a feeler feebly extended, not without hope.

"How well did you know Celia Mond?"

He had stopped half-way up the path. His answer took my breath away.

Also by Anna Gilbert

The Long Shadow
Miss Bede Is Staying
Flowers for Lilian
The Leavetaking
Remembering Louise
A Family Likeness
The Look of Innocence
Images of Rose

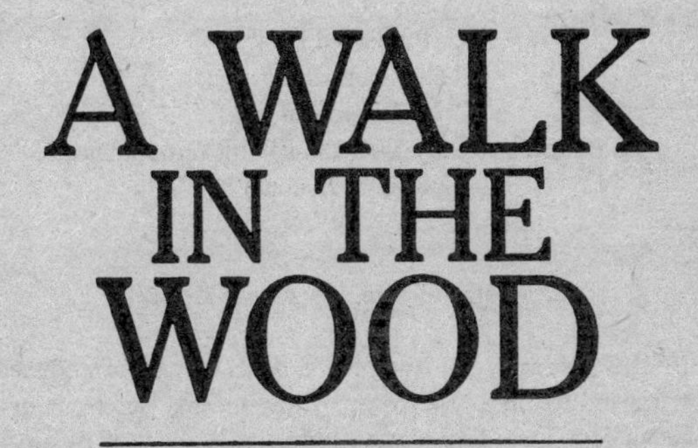

Anna Gilbert

A DELL BOOK

Published by
Dell Publishing
a division of
Bantam Doubleday Dell Publishing Group, Inc.
666 Fifth Avenue
New York, New York 10103

ISBN: 0-440-20655-3

Reprinted by arrangement with St. Martin's Press
Printed in the United States of America
Published simultaneously in Canada

July 1990

10 9 8 7 6 5 4 3 2 1

RAD

1

"You said you would never go back," Cressida reminded me.

"So I did."

"And now you've changed your mind. That's a good sign, isn't it? To be able to go back deliberately, of your own accord. It means that you've got over it—at last." Across the breakfast table our eyes met. "Oh, Kate, you have, haven't you? Got over it, I mean."

I reached for the butter dish, remembered that I hadn't brought an emergency ration card, and bit bravely into a piece of dry toast.

"You can't eat that. Here. There's more in the larder, honestly."

"No, really. Oh, well." I yielded to her offer of marmalade. "I shouldn't have landed on you like this, only it's so much easier to get to Kinning for the day from here. But that wasn't the only reason. I was longing to see you and talk things over."

"Well, here I am. You're getting off to a very slow start. You didn't breathe a word of this last night."

"They say one never should go back, don't they?"

"Never? Not anywhere? Must we forever press forward and upward without a backward glance?"

"Never go back to places where one has been happy, I suppose—or unhappy."

"That must rule out a lot of places. In your case it

would certainly rule out Kinning, where I gather you covered the whole range of emotions, from the heights to the depths." Cressida's tone was light. Her eyes, intent on my face, were full of affectionate concern. "Are you sure you want to stir the whole thing up again?"

I felt a sudden loss of appetite. One never really gets used to butterless toast.

"There now! The very mention of the place has brought it back, that haunted look, as if you'd been mysteriously called away. And I must say it's just like you to be haunted. Not an experience I'm ever likely to have, thank goodness. I'm not the type."

"Fate may have other trials in store for you," I suggested. "There must be plenty of different kinds."

"In my case it would have to be something more straightforward: something I could immediately recognize, like a bomb."

"There's not much danger of that now," I said—and could scarcely believe that bombs had at last ceased to fall, on Britain at any rate.

"Whereas," Cressida swept on, "these shadowy states of mind come naturally to you. You always did go about being aware of rather more than there is to be aware of. If there was a ghost available, you'd be the one to see it."

"I swear I've never seen a ghost in my whole life. Wouldn't I have rushed to tell you?"

"Then there must be other ways of being haunted."

She was right. One could for instance have the peculiar sensation of being constantly accompanied, even in solitude. Yet how was it possible in any sense to be in the company of a person whose chief characteristic was that of being absent, forever out of reach?

I drank the rest of my coffee and got up.

"I suppose you wouldn't like me to come with you?"

"Well . . ."

"I can see that you wouldn't. But I'll come with you to

the station and hang about aimlessly while you're gone. You're up to something, that's obvious. And it's going to be another warm day." She pushed open the window. "What are you going to wear—to re-visit the past? A classic simplicity seems called for. Have you brought that green dress? You look lovely in it."

From Cressida's home it was a short journey by train and then bus. On impulse I asked the conductor to let me off at Bank Top so that I could look down on Kinning; but only its roofs and chimneys were visible among the trees and they too sank out of sight as I walked slowly downhill, my view reaching no farther than each curve in the winding road.

Dazzled by shafts of sunlight and shade, I miscalculated the distance and came unexpectedly to a familiar gap in the trees where a narrow lane branched off to the left. With recognition came the first pang of reviving sadness.

It was the last thing I should have done, to leave the road and follow the lane, stepping slowly over sun-baked ruts, meaning all the time to turn back until it was too late. There on my right above its neglected garden rose the grey pile of the Hall. Its iron gates were padlocked. At every window the blind was drawn down. I turned away.

At the foot of the hill the captive air was languorous with the scent of honeysuckle. I had forgotten the seductive beauty of those green vistas and mysterious hollows. The wayside grass felt dry and soft enough to sit on; the milestone, warm to the touch, offered a backrest. Already as I sat dreaming in the sun, the place itself was asserting its influence. Its gentle airs crept about me with all their old power to charm and deceive, giving no hint of how suddenly the sweetness of summer can dissolve into bitterness and loss.

"Remember—it's all over. You're starting again." Cressida had reached up to the carriage window to touch my hand as the train pulled out. Her voice was urgent. "It was finished and done with long ago, the whole affair."

It wasn't true. That was the painful crux of the affair, that it was never finished, never whole. How could it be when one vital factor remained forever unaccounted for? To be haunted, I reminded myself, my eyes on the last curve of the dusty road, means to be troubled by a mystery never resolved, a question never answered.

Here at the foot of the hill there had been little change. In the deep quiet of a mid-day heavy with the scents of summer it was almost possible to slip back in time: to become again the girl I was when I first came here four years ago, knowing nothing of life's power to wound. For it was here on this very spot that I had first—quite literally—descended upon Kinning and set the whole train of events in motion. But for my ill-fated arrival none of it would have happened.

2

I stepped off the bus into total darkness. One is inclined to forget the complete absence of light on moonless winter nights in those blacked-out years: no thinning of the gloom anywhere, only the added denseness here and there of walls or—in this case—trees.

"Are you for Kinning then?" the conductor asked as we nosed our way down a particularly long hill. I was the only passenger. The others had got out ten minutes before. Since then I had been on tenterhooks, craning my neck to look over the painted lower half of the window for some sign of habitation.

"Yes. Kinning House. I've no idea where it is. Could you . . . ?"

His response was an urgent twanging of the bell. I scrambled up in a panic.

"We've passed it, love. You'd best get off at the bottom here. If you'd have said, I'd have let you off at Bank Top."

He handed me my bags from the luggage space under the stairs.

"There's some weight there. You must be stopping for a bit. Is there anyone coming to meet you?"

"Er . . . no."

"It's back up the hill. Keep to the road. Then half-way up there's a sludgy path"—he leaned out from the blue-lit platform and pointed into the night—"if you can find it. Take care now."

I was alone: no sky, no sign of life, but a branch creaked and I could smell moist bark and fallen leaves. My feet slithered in slush. There must have been another fall of wet snow.

The darkness in itself didn't bother me. I was used to groping my way round in the black-out and there were worse hazards than darkness on those war-time nights: moonlight, for instance. In any case I was young and confident enough then to feel equal to most occasions.

I waited until different degrees of blackness emerged. The cold air was refreshing after the frowsty atmosphere of bus and train with their stale smells of tobacco smoke and the various odours of other travellers. I had hoped to reach Kinning in daylight but the railway journey had taken eight hours instead of the scheduled four. The southbound train had been crammed with servicemen and women and their kit. There had been the usual mystifying delays between and in stations, the usual sharing of sandwiches that left everyone hungry. The occasional stampede to find a tea-trolley on an ill-lit platform had been blocked by the bodies of sleeping soldiers who had to be roused and ejected before anyone else could get out. Then an alert had reduced our speed to a slow crawl.

By a stroke of luck I had been able to catch the last bus from Sheffield, which was still licking its wounds from the blitz. Under the soot pall that always hung above the city, the aftermath of explosive and incendiary bombs had been slow to clear. Coming out of the station into pitch-darkness, I was met by the stench of charred timber and doused fires, but there were cheerful voices to give me advice when I asked my way. One man whom I never saw but will always remember, actually carried my suitcase to the bus stop.

The feeble beam of my torch fell dubiously on a grass verge to the right; on the left, an ancient milestone, the name and mileage obliterated by a slash of gray paint. I forced the torch back into my bulging grip. It was a nuisance to have brought so much with me. My trunk had been sent on ahead but it might be days before it arrived. The new term started the next day and I had thought it necessary to bring books as well as clothes.

Grimy, hungry, fagged almost to death, with the grip in one hand and suitcase in the other, I might have shed a few despondent tears but for a circumstance which just at that point relieved my forlorn state: quite an ordinary thing if it had happened anywhere else or at any other time. Ahead of me in the dark someone—a girl—was singing.

The song was what one might have expected. It was heard everywhere, throbbing inescapably on wireless and gramophone, roared lustily at forces concerts.

"We'll meet again,
Don't know where,
Don't know when . . ."

The voice—it was somewhere to the right—was sweet and bodiless like the voice of Ariel, showing me the way, misleading me perhaps. But there was no beguiling mockery in it, nor was she singing to keep up her courage. She too was unafraid of the dark and was exploiting its privacy for her own enjoyment, adapting the song to her own purposes. I could feel her wringing from the overworked phrases a personal meaning, true and fresh. They floated down to me in that dark unknown territory with an effect of light and warmth.

With some notion of catching up to her, I changed the case and grip from one hand to the other and increased my pace. But she was walking much more quickly and was already well up the hill. There had been time for her to hurry through the less poignant lines before launching into the last four:

"But I know we'll meet again some sunny day."

Neither yearning nor merely hopeful but entirely confident, the singer ended on a note of exhilaration. She was gone.

I stopped to rest my aching wrists and shone the torch about more boldly. There couldn't possibly be a warden within miles. And there, on the other side of the road, was a break in the grass verge: this was surely the entrance to the sludgy path. Lucky I hadn't passed it. The conductor had seemed to point to the left, but the curve of the hill would account for that. My doubts were dispelled by a glimmer of light some distance ahead, as if a door had been briefly opened or a blind raised.

Of the sludge there could be no doubt at all; it was impossible to put my bags down. I grieved for my beige fleece-lined boots, my first and only pair, and indeed they were never the same again. It was beginning to snow.

Presently to the right of the lane the hedge yielded to a gate, and beyond, through slanting lines of wet flakes, rose the dense mass of a house. I stumbled up the steps, found a knocker, rapped, waited, rapped again. Had Miss Emmot given me up and gone to bed? Lifting the knocker for the third time, I brought it down with so appalling a crash that I was forced to retreat to the second step in sheer embarrassment.

A curtain was dragged back. The door half-opened. Above me in the narrow aperture stood a man, long-legged and slender. His face, half-turned from the subdued light in the hall, was young; a gaunt face full of shadows.

For a second I was at a loss. Miss Emmot, according to her letter, lived alone. She had made rather a point of it. I was to be welcomed for my company as well as to share expenses. Of course there could be a dozen reasons for this man's presence, but it was sufficiently unexpected to account for the pause before I told him who I was. The pause was long enough for me to realize that he had said nothing—though "Good evening" or "Do come in" might have been appropriate.

"I'm Kate Borrow . . ."

Still he said nothing, but leaned against the door-jamb as if he had been propped there, lifeless. It could be argued—I put the case to myself afterwards—that my own mental state was not quite normal just then. I was keyed up to face a new life full of strangers and physically tired to the point of being—well, light-headed. I must have been. How else could I account for the curious feeling that my shattering knock had brought him from an immense distance; that he too had come a long way to stand on the doorstep looking out as I looked in? Somehow we had arrived there together.

The feeling passed. I must have wakened him from a deep sleep, that was all, though he was fully if untidily dressed.

"I'm sorry to be so late. The train . . ."

Mounting the third step again, I came close to him. His features were indistinct. What light there was fell upon me. I must have looked a pitiful object. I certainly felt it. And yet, the appeal for help that leapt from one stranger to the other came not from me but from him.

"Help me."

Had he actually spoken—or had I picked up the message by means of some other faculty than hearing? His lips had not moved, so far as I could tell.

I pulled myself together.

"Miss Emmot is expecting me."

At last he actually did speak and for the first time. I knew that because his voice, husky and yet resonant, was new to me.

"You've made the usual mistake. Miss Emmot lives at Kinning House. This is Kinning Hall."

I thought that was to be all. He was going to shut the

door on me without so much as a direction to guide me on my way.

"But where . . ."

"Down the lane and across the road. You'll find a path on the other side."

He closed the door and drew the heavy curtain, leaving me once more in the dark. This time I did feel the prick of tears as I picked up my bags and retraced my steps through mud and slush. He had not been friendly. Faced with a genuinely lost and benighted traveller, he had turned away. Not that there was much he could have done; but after the camaraderie of the train journey and the goodwill of the soldiers who had somehow made room for me, this man's indifference had come almost as a shock. So much for the educated and privileged! The conductor had been kinder.

Unless . . . Having trudged at last into the road again, I came to a halt, troubled by an unexpected quirk of conscience. The man must have been ill. His face, so far as I could see in the light from a heavily shaded lamp, had been pallid—and there was that peculiar lifelessness. He had offered no help, but neither had I. Absurd to think there was anything I could have done for him. Yet it was possible, I found, to dismiss the soundless appeal for help as purely fanciful and at the same time to feel that the need for it had been there—a need deeper than mine.

And after all he had helped me, if only by diverting my thoughts from the discomforts of the hour, not least among them my apprehension at the prospect of meeting Miss Emmot. The nervousness was natural enough, since she was to be not only my landlady but also a colleague. Inevitably we would be close companions. But now any misgivings I had harboured left me. However cool the welcome awaiting me at Kinning House, it must be warmer than my reception at Kinning Hall.

And so it proved. Half an hour later I trailed up another

path to another door. It was opened wide in bland disregard of the beam of light cast on the wet path.

"Thank goodness! I thought you were lost. I'm Christabel Emmot. I was waiting at the field gate but the bus went past and when there was no sign of you, I gave you up. Give me your bag. You must be half dead. Take off your things."

I pulled off my ruined boots in a candle-lit hall.

"Come into the kitchen."

It was a low-beamed room with a fire reflected in a red tiled floor. Red-checked curtains flanked two small windows, blacked out by cloth-covered screens; a multi-coloured cat was curled up in a basket; and there were two chairs by the hearth.

"Shepherd's pie? And cocoa?"

I chose the chair without the knitting and put my feet on the warm fender. Miss Emmot handed me a steaming plate, put two mugs on the shelf above the oven, and sat down in the wicker chair. We faced each other across the hooked rug. Fork poised, on the brink of the first of the innumerable meals we were to eat together, I sized her up, taking care not to let her see me doing it.

I didn't yet know—how could I?—that the precaution was unnecessary. She saw everything.

3

The wicker chair creaked comfortably as she leaned back, her person relaxed, her face thoughtful. The small frown between the eyes must be permanent. The crease spoiled her otherwise passable looks, I thought patronisingly. Not that it mattered since she must be in her middle thirties, poor creature: a slightly built woman with fluffy dark hair and light hazel eyes.

". . . That's why this place is always called Bennets, to avoid confusion with Kinning Hall."

"How stupid of me! You put it in brackets at the top of your letter."

"The conductor may never have heard of Kinning House. He would have taken it for granted that you meant the Hall."

But it hadn't been the conductor's fault. He had pointed to the left as he hung out of the bus, holding on with the right hand. No longer hungry, warm at last, I drowsily considered the possibility that some unknown agency had deliberately led me astray. But to what purpose when the result had been so unproductive?

"It would be James Conrad. Strange that he should be so unhelpful! Most people think him a charming person . . ."

At that early stage we could scarcely be on the familiar terms that were to keep us chatting for hours across the hooked mat. I could not tell her of the curious impression

James Conrad had made on me. My tendency to dwell on the few seconds in which the unvoiced appeal was made, to exaggerate and romanticise it into something much more than could be justified by a look of weariness on his part and a tiny spark of insight on mine, marked my first step away from reality. There were to be others. Together they amounted to a persistent straying from the safe world of hard facts into an unfamiliar realm whose delights and perils I had yet to learn.

"I don't suppose we shall meet again," I said rather abruptly.

"You won't be able to avoid it, Kinning being what it is, although he's scarcely ever at home these days. I believe he has rooms in Sheffield. He has some sort of managerial position at the Emberley Steel Works. It's a company now, but his mother's family founded it and it's still very much a family concern. You're sure to meet Mrs Conrad. She'll rope you in to help on one or other of her committees. What's more, she's a school governor. I believe she's away at present convalescing after an operation." She glanced at her watch. "Now about tomorrow. I usually get up at seven. It's about twenty minutes' walk to school."

She went on to initiate me into what was to prove a gruelling way of life but in so quietly reasonable a manner that she might have been explaining one of her favourite geometrical theorems. The effect was soothing. It seemed to set at a safe distance my plunge into a strange and possibly stormy sea. I listened, half asleep, as her pupils perhaps did.

"You're ready for bed."

I apologised. It had been a particularly gaping yawn.

"You've been very kind. The shepherd's pie! Delicious. And I haven't thanked you yet for letting me come here. There was so little time to make enquiries about digs."

"There are no digs in Kinning, not with bathrooms, that aren't already taken. Except Westmain's, of course, and I think he's keeping them on while he's away. In any case they wouldn't be suitable for you. Two rooms in a cottage along Foley Lane. Dubious sanitation and a peculiar landlady. Besides, it's bad enough for you to have to step into his shoes at school without taking on his rooms as well."

"Why?" I asked with renewed alarm.

"You'll soon find out. But now I'll take you upstairs."

The winding stair was uncarpeted. She went ahead with the candle. I clumped after her with my bags into a room lit by an oil-lamp turned low and—

"Oh, Miss Emmot! A fire! I can't believe it."

"Just this once."

She turned up the lamp and left me to gloat over the two half-burned-out logs.

I have never been able to make up my mind about first impressions, whether to trust them or not. The instant revelation they are supposed to give may amount to no more than one facet of a complex personality freshly glimpsed. Besides, the first impression is so swiftly followed by the second and third as to be soon forgotten—that is in the case of people.

But in the case of Bennets there could be no mistake. From the moment I stepped out of the dark into its welcoming firelight, with my first breath of its damp stone and wood-smoke, I loved it and always shall; at least I shall always love the memory of it as it was then, a rambling old wreck of a place which Emmie rented for ten shillings a week and the rates of twenty-six pounds a year.

The owner had not yet seen fit to install electricity. The plumbing was only a little less antiquated, we used to say, than the monogram "C.B." carved in stone over the front door with the date 1688. Draughts moved freely under the heavy oak doors and between the shutters. Gales blew soot down the wide chimneys. In my room four small rugs lay like stepping-stones on the naked floor-boards. I learned to leap barefooted from one to another, and perfected a technique for dressing under the bedclothes. There were days of ten degrees of frost during that bitter winter when we never took off our heavy tweed coats except to spread them over our quilts in a last bid to outlive the icy nights.

But from that first night when I crept under the blankets and felt the ancient darkness of the house steal over my bed and submerge me in its silence, Bennets drew me to itself as no other house has done.

It was only gradually that I got to know Kinning. Throughout January I scarcely saw it. The short days were full, and after nightfall my forays into the unlit main street were concentrated on the post office and the library. Kinning was not a hospitable place: an overgrown village which in those days had not quite become a town, situated in a wooded valley in one of the lower reaches of the southern Pennines. Newcomers were not so much unwelcome as disregarded in the small inbred community whose slow advance into the twentieth century had been halted by the outbreak of war. Petrol rationing and cuts in bus and train services had weakened its links with the industrial cities to north and south. Kinning had turned in on itself again without regret.

But something in the air suited me. It may have been the long walks that drove the cobwebs away and sent me to bed healthily tired, or the placid country atmosphere. After the air raids at home throughout the autumn it felt marvellously peaceful. There were times when it was almost possible to forget the war—and then to feel guilty. It just wasn't good enough. Patriotism demanded more.

"You're going out again?" Emmie looked up from her knitting.

"It's a meeting. They want volunteers for a committee to collect comforts for bombed-out families. It was on the notice-board."

"Ah yes. I suppose you know where it is."

"In the church schoolroom, if I can find it."

"Was to have been. But the roof caved in after the snow last week. The meeting is at Kinning Hall."

"No!"

"There's no doubt about it. You're destined to meet the Conrads."

It was interesting, the way she knew everything without being in the least involved, just as she mastered knitting patterns of incredible complexity without showing the slightest interest in the finished garments. She made these into immaculate parcels and posted them off to relatives she never named. I used to wonder why she spent so much time studying musical scores without ever hearing a note played, in the same way as she worked out complicated walks by poring over ordnance maps which in obedience to the defence regulations she kept locked away in her wardrobe. But at least she went on the walks, alone in studded boots, and never asked me to join her.

There was no snow this time; instead it rained heavily. Otherwise the scenario was much the same. It was just as dark and even more treacherous underfoot. But this time I did at least know the way and this time my knock was answered promptly by Mrs Conrad herself.

"I'm so glad you've come." She had difficulty in placing me. "Oh, one of the teachers. I ought to have recognized the name but I've been a little out of touch. Do come in. Such a wretched night to bring you out."

It had apparently brought no one else.

"Not a soul." She draped my mackintosh over a hall chair. "Of course the Hall is dreadfully out of the way. . . . One can scarcely expect. . . . But they simply don't bother. You can't imagine how difficult it is. The same handful of people do everything."

The complaint was of the gentlest kind. She was a thin, quiet-voiced woman in her fifties, inelegantly dressed in a thick tweed skirt surmounted by layers of woollen garments: jumper, cardigan, waistcoat—and below, knitted stockings and ankle socks. She took me into a sitting-room where a fire burned in a basket grate, giving more light than heat. Above the low mantel a mirror reflected the painted screen which shut off the fireside from the rest of the long room.

"You're the very person. . . . We need new ideas and you're young and intelligent. You'll be invaluable in Kinning, Miss Borrow, if only you can spare the time."

We discussed schemes for fund-raising and the problem of finding volunteers to collect and transport blankets and clothing to the depot in Sheffield. When she went out to make coffee I glanced at the book table, at a print of a Fra Lippo Lippi Madonna on the wall, a pair of bellows on the hearth, yellow spikes of jasmine in a brown jug—until she reappeared, edging round the screen with the tray.

"Let me help."

She had brought three cups but it wasn't until she called over her shoulder, "Coffee, James," that I realised why. He got up from a deep chair at the far and fireless end of the room where he had been reading.

"This is my son, James—and this is Miss Borrow, dear. Miss Borrow has taken Mr Westmain's place at the grammar school. Come and be warm."

The invitation was ambiguous. He responded to both its implications, accommodating his long limbs to the settle at right angles to the hearth as he said without any conventional greeting:

"I'm afraid you got very wet, Miss Borrow. Your hair's steaming."

This time there was no sign of the stress of fatigue or whatever it was I had sensed when we first met; nor, I must say, of the indifference. From the smile that lit his face one would have supposed that nothing could have delighted him more than to see me there. If he was merely exerting himself to welcome a visitor whose unimportance made courtesy all the more essential, it was a tribute to his success that I had no such impression. His remark about my hair had been made with friendly directness.

"Does it look awful?"

"Much less awful than most people's. What do you think?"

He pointed to the mirror above the low mantelshelf. I glanced despairingly at my rat's tails and longed for a moment alone with a comb. My eyes moved to his reflected face. I had not been mistaken about its pallor and gauntness but in the firelight they were less striking. The dark frame enclosed our two faces as we looked at each other in the glass. Behind us the painted screen shut out the rest of the world.

"It's pretty hair." Mrs Conrad settled herself in the chair between us. "Just the colour I would have liked mine to be when I was a girl. Light brown with streaks of gold. But I had to make do with plain brown."

I warmed to their kindness and ease: the ease that comes from genuine interest in others, in this case me. James had his mother's gentleness but more warmth and vivacity. We talked about the drubbing we were giving the Italians in East Africa, local affairs, the school.

"Mr Westmain," Mrs Conrad inevitably said, "was so very highly thought of."

It must have been the one firm impression made by the school of the vaguest of its governors and that may have been why she spoke with uncharacteristic emphasis; but to me it sounded like one more glowing tribute to the man whose shoes I so inadequately filled.

"I'm afraid he is very much missed," I said.

A certain touchiness concerning the person whom I had released for national service might have worn off if only I could have found some fault in him. But he was faultless. It was irksome to see the most sluggish eyes light up at the mention of his name. "Mr Westmain told us. . . . Mr Westmain used to make us laugh. . . . Mr Westmain was ever so good as Falstaff. . . ." He had produced plays with professional competence, captained the Staff and Prefects Cricket XI, founded the photographic society, coached the school's first State Scholar. A keen amateur yachtsman and RNV Reservist, he had already been given a commission and was now Sub-Lieutenant Westmain. I had the details from his friend John Rokeby, the physics master.

I was forever trying to bolster up my confidence by reminding myself that my qualifications were as good (almost) as his, but there could be no question of equality. He could do all that I was doing and much better, according to the evidence available; whereas the idea that I could ever do what he was doing now—minesweeping in the North Sea—was simply laughable.

Mrs Conrad did laugh when I described my trials and Westmain's triumphs.

"You must just be yourself," she said.

But the glance she cast at James was not amused. He had not spoken for some time and was twirling his empty coffee-cup in its saucer with an air of detachment. His mother's glance roused him.

"You'd certainly cut a poor figure as Falstaff," he said, but with only a ghost of the smile I had already learned to expect; and when Mrs Conrad went into the hall to telephone, he relapsed again into silence, gazing into the fire.

I felt some awkwardness and regretted having spoken so freely. Conversation with strangers can be fraught with hazards. Apparently I had stumbled upon one of them, some undercurrent whose nature I couldn't possibly know. His book lay open on the coffee-table. I picked it up desperately and had just opened my lips to speak when James said:

"You find this silence embarrassing."

"No, of course not," I said, relieved. He was smiling

again as kindly as ever. "Well, yes, I did rather, didn't you?"

"I'm sorry. I was treating you as a friend who wouldn't mind my social shortcomings; though to tell you the truth, I don't think one should ever talk just for the sake of talking."

"And that was exactly what I was going to do; make the absolutely unnecessary remark that you must be fond of birds."

He came over and turned the pages, his head close to mine.

"Let me show you my favourite." He pointed to a coloured plate. Our hands touched. "Golden plover."

"I've never seen one."

"They nest on Bardslow Moor. You won't have been there. When the cotton-grass is in bloom, that's the time to go. We'll . . ."

It was disappointing. I was almost certain that he was going to offer to take me; the tone, the look, the touch of boyish enthusiasm, the sudden closeness. . . . But he didn't. He closed the book and moved away.

"Let me give you another cup of coffee."

"No, thank you. I must go."

"James will walk home with you," Mrs Conrad said, finding me on my feet. "It's so very dark."

"There's really no need."

No need either to point out that it wouldn't be the first time I had walked in the dark alone from Kinning Hall to Kinning House. We had neither of us mentioned our first meeting. He couldn't have forgotten it. Would a reference to it come under the heading of unnecessary talk? My first impression—I could see now—had been wildly astray. I must simply have wakened him from a deep sleep. He worked hard and at irregular hours. All the same, however irrational, that first impression of him as a person in need of help and therefore vulnerable never quite left me and may have quickened our friendship.

In the hall he helped me into my waterproof and pulled on a weather-stained Burberry of his own. We went out into the rain, feeling our way at first until we grew used to the dark, and fell into step. I resolved not to be the first to speak. He said nothing, but the rhythm of our walking united us; night closed us in under dripping branches. I felt it then, right at the start, the elation of having floated into a rarer element. There are risks involved in treading on air. Did I feel that wariness too right from the start, as if we were walking not only through a shrouded countryside without moon or stars to light it, but into another kind of darkness altogether?

Dazed by this potent blend of intimacy and strangeness, I found that we had arrived at Bennets.

"I suppose good night is one of the things you don't find it necessary to say."

"I don't want to say it." He was bareheaded, pale and wet; indifferent to the rain. His eyes lingered on my face. "That isn't at all what I want to say."

He opened the gate, closed it quickly like a barrier between us, and in a moment had gone.

Emmie was as usual making cocoa.

"You're all in a glow," she said. "A wet glow."

"There's no such thing."

I hung my coat on the clothes-horse and filled the kettle for our hot-water bottles. We lived almost entirely in the kitchen. Goodness knows, it was big enough, a vast place designed for some ancient Farmer Bennet, his numerous family, and half a dozen servants.

"You've enjoyed your evening?"

"Do you know, I was the only person who turned up."

"Ah, then you felt the full weight of it. The careless Conrad charm."

"You don't like them, Emmie?"

"To be perfectly fair"—she considered the Conrads judiciously with narrowed eyes—"I've had no occasion to like or dislike them. I've had very little to do with them personally. They don't mix—but one hears this and that." In response to my raised eyebrows she went on: "They're the kind of people I tend to avoid. Her forebears were a long line of Quaker folk—the sort who always act on principle and somehow do very well out of it."

"Then isn't that an argument for acting on principle?"

"They're certainly rich."

"They don't look it."

"Oh, that's part of the whole dubious business. Plain living and high thinking. No display. The attitude is admirable."

"Dubious, you said."

"It must be easier to live the simple life when you don't need to; and in a way the Conrads are more exclusive than even the old country families, what's left of them. It must be rather a withdrawn, sheltered existence, just the two of them in that big place, without even a daily help."

She went to rinse out her mug at the sink. We braced ourselves to face the fierce chill of our bedrooms.

"Have they always lived there?"

"It was her family home. She left to be married and came back when James was a small boy. He was away at school when I first came here. That was twelve years ago."

"He brought me home this time. James." I couldn't resist telling her. Then it all came out in a rush. "He's a strange person. Moody, I think, but in a nice way. Unworldly somehow. There's something about him. And the oddest thing—I feel as if I've known him not exactly all my life but somewhere else—before, as if being with him was not—new."

"Oh dear! That is serious." Emmie reached up to the shelf above the sink and placed our stone hot-water bottles on the table. "You know why? You must have heard of the

Platonic theory as to why people fall in love. We are all searching for the other half of our psyche in order to become whole, and when we find it, naturally it feels familiar. We recognise it as part of ourselves." She looked at me speculatively. "I've often wondered if there was anything in it. Your turn for the bath."

Having filled each bottle to precisely two-thirds of its capacity with exactly half the contents of the kettle, she went upstairs. I let in Herbert the cat, bolted the door, and went back to the fire for another luxurious five minutes.

"Your hair's steaming." The husky voice was intimate. I heard it inside my head and found myself smiling.

Then it startled me again: Emmie's chair. It was one of the Victorian basket kind with a wicker base instead of legs and a habit of creaking minutes after its occupant had left it. I should have been used to its delayed action by this time but it never failed to catch me out with its suggestion of a continued presence there. The effect was eerie. It was as if our conversation had not really come to an end; as if there were something more that Emmie had left unsaid.

"One hears this and that. . . ."

It had been scarcely a statement: no more than the hint of an idea, released to float in the mind like thistle-down before settling in my memory.

4

Weeks passed before I saw James Conrad again. When my involvement with blankets, bedding, and warm underwear made it necessary for me to call at the Hall, which had become the HQ of the Comforts Committee, he was never at home.

Once launched, I developed a passion for such war-work as came my way and branched out in all directions: salvaging everything that could be recycled; organising jumble sales; helping with the WVS; and trotting from door to door selling National Savings stamps. The older members of staff had already had their share of such activities and were glad to hand them on to an enthusiastic new recruit. It was a relief to exert myself in an area on which the inimitable Westmain had not set his mark. "Beneath him," I supposed sarcastically as I flattened out knitted blanket squares and counted jam jars.

Something of a friendship developed between Mrs Conrad and the useful young person I was turning out to be. She felt it her duty to take the lead in local good works but she was not a competent woman and was unused to organising. I began to spend a good deal of my spare time at the Hall. The long, haphazardly furnished room became familiar. In daytime, half lit by faint sunshine on its leaded panes, it revealed an unpretentious elegance. The wide view from its windows was always hazy in those winter months. One felt the presence of hills, trees, stone walls and the distant church without ever seeing them clearly.

"It's a change to have young people about the place." Mrs Conrad was watching a group of my sixth-form pupils as they unloaded magazines and newspapers from a hand-cart and stacked them in the stable. "I wish James. . . . He has no young friends in Kinning." She sat down beside me on the window-seat, suddenly confidential. "He works so hard. You know, work has become a fixation with him —to justify his not being in the Services."

"But surely—" I broke off. It had not occurred to me that any such justification was needed. We were all in it together; men of calling-up age were exempted only when their work was of national importance. "The country can't do without steel."

"It does make one feel just a little bitter. It's so easy for young men in the armed forces to be made much of, especially when they look well in uniform—and get decorated."

Men like Westmain, I thought vindictively. It could only be a matter of time before he distinguished himself by some special act of gallantry. I felt a new sympathy for James Conrad. Had that been the reason for his glumness when Westmain was mentioned? A sense of inferiority?

"James is lonely." Mrs Conrad hesitated. "How nice it would be if you could take him under your wing a little, Kate. You make friends so easily."

"I'm not sure he would like it."

It wasn't true. The certainty that he would like it was enough just then to content me. I was in no hurry to see him again, knowing that we would meet; knowing too, instinctively that the sort of relationship she had in mind would not quite do.

One February evening when I was walking slowly home from school, he was waiting in the lane. He leaned against a gatepost in his old raincoat, of the same drab colour as the stone. Taken by surprise, I must have shown the delight that mysteriously recharged my flagging spirits after a nerve-racking day. A moment before I had barely been able to drag myself along. Without a word he took my heavy basket of books, unhooked the bag from my shoulder, and slung it over his own.

"That leaves me free to gather snowdrops." They were growing in thick white clusters all along the lane. "Only it seems a shame."

Indeed I found it impossible to disturb them. A thrush was singing. The air was mild with that indefinable quality more subtle even than scent that promises spring. He had been sleeping at his rooms near the works and eating at a GPO restaurant, he told me, and had come home for a few days of comparative comfort. Had his mother told him to begin putting himself under my wing? It didn't matter. I didn't care how he came to be there.

"Do you have to lug all this stuff about with you?" he asked when we stopped at the gate.

"Yes," I beamed and drifted up the path, remembering not to say goodbye.

"You didn't ask him in," Emmie said.

From behind the curtains we watched him step over a wall and cross the field. It was too soon to ask him in. In any case there was no doubt that he would come again.

The next day I found on the doorstep a bowl of snowdrops planted in soil and not quite in flower.

One day in March Mr Ferrars, the history master, took a party of pupils on a visit to the church of St Michael in the next parish. I was roped rather unwillingly as the statutory extra member of staff to maintain the balance of power and help in an emergency. It seemed an outing more suited to the summer term, but old Ferrars was a fanatic in his chosen field and deemed this to be precisely the time when the Norman windows, piscina, and the Norman-

French inscription on a coffin lid would be most inspiring to his fifth form.

Mercifully the day was fine and dry so that we were able to walk to Hammer as planned. A convenient bus would take us back in time for afternoon school. We ate our sandwiches at the inn, where the landlady brewed the tea we had brought—half a teaspoonful each in a paper bag—and afterwards crowded into the tiny church. A very brief inspection satisfied my thirst for Norman architecture and I escaped into the churchyard.

It was deserted except for a man in a shabby raincoat who stood, hands in pockets, staring at a gravestone.

"How extraordinary—to see you here!" I stepped over a grave or two to join him. "And I'm glad. I've been wanting to thank you for the snowdrops. They lasted a fortnight. But I never thought of meeting you here. It's not the sort of place. . . ."

"Where one meets people? More a place for parting with them, you might say."

To a critical observer my gasp of surprise might have seemed an exaggerated reaction. It was no more than the occasion demanded, so headily had his presence glamorised the humdrum scene.

It was not his way to show surprise, nor in this case was it called for: he had seen us arrive from a window of the house opposite the church where he was visiting his Aunt Harriet.

"So you're not at work today," I said.

"Nor are you by the looks of things."

"Oh, but I am. I'm fulfilling a regulation. You must have noticed that I'm not alone."

"Neither am I. Come and meet the rest of the family."

I glanced innocently at his Aunt Harriet's window; but he was directing my attention to the headstone—and to others ranged alongside it.

"There they are."

"Your relations? But . . ." I tried to decipher the worn inscriptions and could not make them into Conrad. "Oh, I see. They're all Emberleys, your mother's side of the family." John, William, Adam—and with them, also resting in peace, were their wives: Margaret, Elizabeth, and Tamar. "It's cosy for them to be here all together forevermore."

"I wonder if that's what they all wanted."

"It's what married people ought to want—but of course the sisters- and brothers-in-law are here as well."

"Not so cosy perhaps." He pointed to a mossy stone sacred to the memory of Benjamin Emberley, who died in 1851. "That's the fellow who started the whole thing. He was the village blacksmith here and took it into his head to branch out."

"And founded Emberley Steel Works."

"Not immediately—but eventually that was what it came to." He talked about the growth of the firm: about puddling and plating and plant. I didn't listen but watched him, obscurely pleased that he was talking freely albeit on such a deadly subject. "I'm boring you," he said at last, smiling down at me.

"These are your mother's ancestors." I spoke at random. "Where is your father buried?"

The smile faded. He didn't answer; and there was only a second or two in which to feel uncomfortable before the first of Ferrars' flock appeared in the arched doorway and the others began to drift out in twos and threes, yawning.

"It's almost time for our bus. Are you coming back to Kinning?"

"No, I'm sorry. It would have been a pleasure to join the party. My education is far from complete and there's sure to be a good deal of historical information bandied about as you talk over the morning's adventure."

"You're mocking me. You think our goings-on at the grammar school rather quaint, don't you?"

"As a matter of fact"—he still spoke lightly but there

was no doubting his sincerity—"I'm trying to conceal my envy. Yes, I envy those youths, having you to teach them. If I had fallen into your hands at their age, you might have knocked some sense into me, Kate. And who knows, things might have turned out quite well—even if," he added, anticipating my protest, "you were only about ten years old at the time."

"But surely"—I was immoderately pleased that he had called me Kate—"things have turned out quite well, haven't they?"

We were standing with the tombstone between us. He gripped its pediment like a prisoner at the bar, powerless to answer. His expression puzzled me. His eyes, a bluish grey, had darkened with—despair was surely too strong a word.

"If there is anything wrong," I ventured to say, "well, things can usually be put right somehow."

So fatuous a remark could be justified only by the warmth of my impulse to comfort him. I had instinctively touched his sleeve—and drew back my hand casually, hoping he hadn't noticed. But he laid his hand on mine and held it there as if it really was comforting.

"You don't think it can sometimes be too late?"

The question was wistful. I responded without thought as one soothes a child, using the words that come most easily.

"It's never too late." And instantly aware of having failed him by being glib, I repeated them. "It can never be too late."

His expression softened. He patted my hand and let it go.

"I'll remember that. Unfortunately it is too late to join you on the bus. I promised to have lunch with Aunt Harriet. I suppose you wouldn't care to stay and join us."

"Thank you. I don't seem able to convince you that I'm not on holiday."

"I hadn't realised how laborious a life you lead. But

hard work suits you. You don't need holidays to restore your vitality. It's there all the time, a thing to thank God for. I wish you could stay."

The last words were spoken in earnest. When we rumbled off in Miller's bus he was still leaning against the tombstone and seemed to have sunk again into an aimless mood. I thought he looked lonely and wondered what could cause his sudden changes of mood.

I did find one piece of information that shed light on the faintly perceptible tensions in the Conrad household and could well account for James's instability of temperament. It was not from Emmie that I heard it, though she must have known. She, better than anyone else, knew of my interest in the Conrads, and I slightly resented her silence on the subject. It was Miss Butler, the cookery mistress, who told me. Though recognised as a formidable figure in the staff room, Butler was inclined to take me in hand and show me the ropes as she put it, with her usual flair for metaphor.

I had stayed behind one afternoon to help her check her grocery list in the little sitting-room attached to the domestic-science flat, and was enjoying a cup of tea and a slice of the fatless spice cake the fourth-form girls had been making.

"No, it isn't bad, is it?" Butler cut another slice. "Grated carrot would make it more moist and there's sugar in carrots, but of course it's too early for them. It really is a strain trying to make bricks without straw and I've done everything it's possible to do with potato. Things should be easier next term. There'll be tomatoes, eventually. I must say"—she took off her white overall and put on the cardigan of her brown twin set—"I've never been able to stoop to nettle soup. We may have our backs to the wall but we are not peasants or Gipsies, although now that he's after the ports"—news was filtering through to us of the raids on Portsmouth, Merseyside, and Hull—"there's no knowing what we may have to turn to. There's one thing certain: we're not likely ever to see a lemon again."

I glanced out of the window at the drive, where several visitors were making their way to the main entrance.

"Is there something going on?"

"A governors' meeting. If you aren't doing anything in particular, would you like to stay and help serve tea? It would give you an opportunity to meet them." Then, as I waved to a slim woman in tweeds and ankle socks, "But of course you know Mrs Conrad." Together we watched her flutter irresolutely towards the steps. "She's looking better. Poor soul, she does her best. But as a governor . . ." Butler shrugged in despair. "She's no use whatever. She knows nothing about state schools. I don't suppose she ever went to school herself. She probably had a governess, in which case what can you expect?"

We shook our heads over so flimsy a preparation for the battle of life.

But Mrs Conrad, Butler reminded me, had suffered and survived with courage worse trials: not only ill health but an early and tragic widowhood.

"Her husband died when the boy was small, no more than six or seven years old, I believe. They say"—Butler dropped her voice dramatically and mouthed the distressing words—"it was suicide. Shot himself. Such a selfish thing to do. No one here knew him. They lived in Sussex; but after his death she came home to be near her own people."

And she had never quite got over it. I could see that and could dimly comprehend how far beyond the natural grief in bereavement a woman would be taken by such a fearful end to her marriage: how it would destroy her confidence to know that she could not make life even endurable for her husband, much less happy.

As for James, he had been at an impressionable age when it happened. Was it possible ever to outgrow the sudden loss of security, the deliberate and unaccountable departure of a parent, the legacy of horror and disgrace? Such thoughts confirmed my instinct to avoid any subject that might be painful to him, thereby allowing areas of silence to develop between us. Perhaps I was already too much inclined to make allowances for the moodiness and melancholy that sometimes overshadowed his humour and charm.

We met occasionally by chance: at the Hall, at a lecture on poison gases; and once when the Home Guard chose to carry out its manoeuvres in one of the fields between Bennets and the road. Emmie and I had gone out to watch. I was surprised to see James among the handful of spectators. When the troops had taken cover, not altogether successfully, in the surrounding countryside, he walked back to Bennets with us.

It was Emmie who asked him in. The day was cool, the kitchen warm. He gravitated naturally to Emmie's wicker chair. She seemed not to mind but sat at the table with *Time and Tide* spread out before her and open at the crossword page. Considering her slight prejudice against the Conrads, I thought she was behaving well. That is to say, I thought so at first. In her cool way she seemed to find our visitor interesting. There was nothing surprising in that: he interested me enormously. At any rate it was towards James that her casual remarks were chiefly directed.

It was only gradually as I moved about the kitchen making tea, that I began to wonder if those remarks were in fact casual. Something in Emmie's manner made me uncomfortable. Her words in themselves were ordinary enough.

"You don't know Mr Bettle?" She was speaking of one of the officers in the Home Guard. "The Bettles live in Mafeking Terrace, next door to the Monds. I don't suppose you have much time to get to know people in Kinning. . . ."

There could be nothing in such dull little speeches to interest James. Reaching past him to set the teapot to warm, I did just discern a lack of enthusiasm in his look of polite attentiveness—and guessed that he had simply switched his attention to something else; possibly to the cat which had sprung upon his knee the moment he sat down; preferably to me as I demurely cut three slices of fruitless cake. There was no doubt as to the shift in my own attention, and as a result I missed whatever it was that Emmie said next.

There could be no reason at all to suspect her of being devious—of trying to do anything more than to draw James out in a purely social way. Yet she sat with pencil poised as if ready to jot down not only letters in the crossword but any useful piece of information her study of James might produce.

It was a habit she had got into: to sift and speculate and weigh everything, including people, in the balance. But I wished that James of all people could have been spared. Not that he appeared to notice. Only a person who knew Emmie well, as I now did, would sense what she was up to. It occurred to me that, except in the staff room, I had never seen her in company. Nor, for that matter, had I seen James with anyone other than his mother.

"I hadn't realised you were so comfortable here." He had evidently come to terms with the limitations of the wicker chair. "This isn't my first visit. I seem to remember being brought here years ago for eggs. It was still a farmhouse then. Rather a dreary place."

I dislodged the cat, handed James a cup of tea, and sat down in my favourite place on the broad fender.

"Herbert has taken to you," Emmie said as the cat rubbed himself against our visitor's leg and purred ingratiatingly. "He isn't usually so amiable."

"He's probably glad of another masculine presence in a feminine stronghold." James caressed the cat gently with his free hand. "Come to think of it, this place feels like a stronghold. Those windows . . ."

They were mere slits in the thick wall, one on either side of the fireplace.

"Useless," Emmie said. "They don't let in a ray of light."

"No wonder, with that steep garden behind. It's as if you'd dug yourself in with the hill at your back—to face the advancing enemy. No room for retreat, is there?"

"You've been influenced by the warlike display we have just been watching," Emmie said. "Your mind has taken a military turn."

Again I felt uneasy, almost as if she had added "for a change." Was she being playful, in a staid sort of way? She surely had not meant to taunt him for being a civilian in a generation of war. Remembering Mrs Conrad's hints about his sensitivity on that subject, I hastily introduced another.

"Cats are supposed to have a special insight into human nature." James had no sooner put down his cup than Herbert leapt to his knee again. "Just listen to him purring."

Emmie did not comply but pursued her own line of thought.

"But isn't this house situated in exactly the same way as your own? As the crow flies, they're on the same level below the ridge."

"They must have been built like that because of the natural springs."

"So that we must have much the same outlook," Emmie persisted.

"That's about the only resemblance," I said.

"Not quite. Mr Conrad's notion that we have dug ourselves in would apply just as well to the Hall. I was wondering if he spoke from experience when he accused us of keeping out unwelcome visitors."

For a dreadful moment I thought she was going to refer

to my blunder on the night of my arrival, especially as she went on:

"Bennets has one slight advantage over the Hall. At least it could be an advantage to anyone who cared to make use of it."

"I can't imagine what that is," I said nervously.

"It's just that our lane joins the road near the top of the hill so that no one can see our comings and goings; whereas from our field gate we can look down the hill. . . ."

"And see our comings and goings?" James had not moved so far as I could see but Herbert woke suddenly and sat up, his eyes flaring. "And that, you find, is an advantage, Miss Emmot?"

"I merely mentioned it"—pencil poised, she was watching him with interest—"because it is a fact."

"The idea that it could ever be put to use is purely theoretical, I take it." The tone was casual but I detected a coolness in his voice.

"The idea is outrageous." I was suddenly angry. "Let's finish the crossword." I went and looked over Emmie's shoulder. "Three down and six across. 'Sheer folly to exchange this for this.' Nine letters and six."

A combined attack would have made short work of it but James offered little help and presently shook off Herbert and got up to go. The cat followed him to the door, to the gate and beyond. I watched them as they went down the lane between the stone walls: the tall man, the small devoted companion. At last James picked Herbert up, turned him round and gave him a gentle homeward push. Seeing me still at the gate, he waved and smiled.

Herbert took no notice when I called him, but sat down with his back to me, curled his tail round his haunches and settled down to wait until his friend came back. It became a habit with him. He must have spent hours there, gazing in the direction from which James would come. I sometimes wondered whether Emmie ever quite forgave either James or Herbert for the new alliance.

For my part I was less sure than Herbert that Bennets was the right place for James, or for any friend I cared about.

"I'm sure you gave the impression that we make a habit of keeping an eye on the Conrads and their callers," I protested. Emmie had not moved from the table. "It never occurred to me that we could see the entrance to their lane from here."

"Not from here. From the field gate," Emmie said accurately.

"As it happens they don't seem to have any visitors."

"None at all?" She was rapidly filling in the crossword in neat capitals. "Isn't that rather unusual?"

"I don't know. I know very little about them, and of course," I said weightily, "one doesn't pry into other people's affairs."

"Got it." Emmie filled in the last of the empty squares. " 'Sheer folly to exchange this for this.' Ignorance for wisdom."

"Why is it folly? Oh, I see. Where ignorance is bliss, 'tis folly to be wise. I don't believe it actually. How can ignorance be bliss?"

"I suppose it could be a happier state than being wise after the event." She folded the paper neatly and put it away in the rack. "Knowing the worst can't be a particularly blissful experience."

My suspicion that James had not altogether taken to Emmie was confirmed the next afternoon, a Saturday. My call on Mrs Conrad with a list of addresses was no more than an excuse to be out of doors. I had no idea that James was at home.

But having chatted with his mother for a few minutes, I found him waiting in the hall. We went out together. It was a brisk March day with white clouds scudding in the wind, their shadows moving so rapidly over the green hillside that it, too, seemed to move. At a stile half-way down the lane, James stopped.

"I don't know if you'd care to come—but I thought of visiting some friends. They might interest you."

"But won't they mind?"

"They won't mind at all." He laughed, and putting his hand under my elbow, guided me over the stile and into a field.

"Speaking of friends," he said and hesitated.

The path skirted the pasture and ran downhill close to a hedge of gnarled hawthorn; but for a moment we did not take it. He was still holding my arm. Was he going to . . . ? It was hardly a suitable time. The cold wind slapped my face quite hard with the end of my scarf. A strand of my hair entangled itself in a button of his jacket. No, lovemaking was not—at least not then—his purpose.

"We were speaking of friends," I prompted.

"You came to Kinning, knowing no one, I believe. So—you arranged to share the house with Miss Emmot without having met her?"

Our roles had been reversed. He who had roused my protective instinct was now, quite unnecessarily, concerned to protect me. He had spoken tentatively but seriously, like a kind older brother.

"There was nowhere else to go. It all happened rather quickly. But the arrangement does work, you know."

"And you have other friends—the other teachers. Some of them nearer your own age?"

"As a matter of fact the others are all older than Emmie, the other women."

"So that you would have made friends with her in the ordinary way even if she hadn't been your landlady."

"No," I said after a pause in which I realised for the first time that Emmie had no friends at school. "I wouldn't have chosen her any more than she would have chosen me.

But since we've been thrown together . . . And I'm grateful to her for having taken me in."

"The advantages are mostly hers. If the arrangement works, that's your doing. You would charm the heart out of a stone, whereas she . . ."

Naturally I was pleased; thrilled, in fact. But delightful as it was, the compliment was not entirely relevant.

"Heart? Emmie?"

"You're wondering if she has one?"

"She must have, but . . ."

"She is not ruled by it."

We both laughed at the understatement.

"Were you intending to warn me against her?"

In a burst of sunshine so sudden that we looked up, blinking, the hillside swelled like a green cloud. The sky changed and we were plunged into gloom again.

"That's what it's like at Bennets," James said, "with the two of you. Light and shadow. I felt it."

"Emmie does exert some kind of restraining influence, I suppose. It must be rather dreary for her always to be governed by her devastatingly clear intellect."

"Her devastatingly clear intellect may mislead her. Don't let it govern you too. No doubt you talk things over. Her view of things may not always be the right one."

"But she's always so precise."

"Precision isn't the same as truth. It can be incomplete, for one thing; or out of proportion like those mirrors at a fair. All the details are there but the result is untruthful."

"You mean, don't trust Emmie?"

"Don't trust anyone until you know them." He said it so gently as to purge the advice of all cynicism. "That's hard advice for you to take. But you won't take it. You'll go on seeing the best in all of us whether we deserve it or not. And now—I'm going to introduce you to my friends."

"Whom, presumably, you trust."

"Not an inch. Nor do they trust the likes of me. Our

relationship is entirely of the heart. Let's go and find them."

"The trouble is, we can't."

I was making a vain attempt to disentangle my hair from the top button of his jacket.

"Good Lord! Here, let me. No, don't pull."

"We'll have to cut it off. You're a steelworker; you must have a knife."

He produced one, made a swift cut and released me.

"You've cut off the button!"

"What else could I do?"

"I can see that you couldn't go through life with a lock of my hair in your buttonhole. . . ."

"It was too beautiful to cut off. It was almost the first thing I noticed about you. Your hair."

"Do you think it improves it to have a leather button dangling there all the time? Please."

He completed the operation by carefully cutting off a curl and then severing it from the button.

"A memento for you." He handed me the button. "And one for me." He smoothed the curl in the palm of his hand, then put it in his breast pocket. "It isn't at all a fair exchange—but life isn't fair and the sooner you learn that, the better."

A few minutes' walk brought us to the edge of a disused stone quarry. We came on it suddenly and looked down on an unexpected scene. A family of tinkers had taken possession of the sheltered spot. Three piebald ponies were cropping the short grass. Beside one of the hooped caravans five or six children were playing. Two women crouched over a fire.

We had been seen. A boy carrying sticks down the steep track opposite looked across and called out in recognition. All but the smallest of the children came swarming up the stony incline to meet us. James was surrounded. Skinny arms encircled his trouser legs. Dirty fingers found their way into his hands.

"Where's that tooth gone, Ned?" He ruffled the hair of a beaming seven-year-old.

"I'll be getting another one, Mr Conerd, sir."

"And he's an uncle now. Ned's an uncle," one of the girls told us, with a touch of awe.

"An uncle! Ned!" James turned to speak to a stocky man in a cap and muffler who had appeared from nowhere.

"Bring the lady down out of the wind, sir. This way, madam." And as I began to slither down the quarry face he said, "I came up to the Hall last week, Mr Conrad, but you weren't there."

"That's all right. I heard you were here. It's about the usual time. Everything going well?"

"Much as usual. Cassie has something the young lady would like to see."

In the hollow there was no wind. The younger of the two women fetched a piece of sacking from one of the vans, spread it by the fire, and invited me to sit down. The smell not only of the sacking but of the two women nearly turned my stomach. There was nothing for it but to smile gratefully, sit down promptly, and make the best of it.

"You've got a pretty young lady, Mr Conrad." The older woman's sharp look was not altogether welcome.

"Yes, haven't I? This is Miss Borrow." He introduced them as Mrs Merrell and her daughter Rosa. "And what has Cassie got to show us?"

Rosa went to the other caravan and presently came back carrying her sister's baby.

"May I see?" I made it an excuse to get up. "But it's just . . ." The tiny creature seemed to me newly born.

"Yesterday." Rosa adjusted the shawl round the dark little face.

"Here? In the caravan?"

"A son for Ewan," Mrs Merrell said. "Give him to Mr Conrad, Rosa. You hold him, sir. You've had all the others in your arms one time or another. It'll bring him luck."

"But will he bring me any luck?" James took the shabby bundle without awkwardness or fuss. "Is there any luck in store for me?"

Again Mrs Merrell's shrewd dark eyes explored first my face, then his.

"It's not a lucky time for tall young men," she said. "But if you don't have luck, you'll maybe have something better."

"Has Ewan seen his son yet?" James handed the baby back to his aunt. Ewan, I gathered, had been conscripted for regular farm work and was in Nottinghamshire.

"He'll be here tomorrow. He'll get here somehow. Nothing will stop him. Every man wants a son—and every woman too. . . . But what they want and what they get is two different things . . . for most of them."

There was a ruthless severity in Mrs Merrell's pronouncements, as if she saw human life—not surprisingly—as a comfortless affair.

James tucked a coin in the baby's clenched hand. We took our leave and scrambled up the rocky path with a trail of children behind us; and waited until the last of them had been hauled to the top. They stood silent, solemn, their eyes expectant.

"Ready?"

From his trouser pocket James took a handful of half pennies, jingled them in cupped palms, and threw them in the air. They fell into the grass, among stones, down the rock face. We watched the shrieking hunt for a while, then turned into the wind.

"I see now what you meant. But whether you trust each other or not, they love you."

"Love? I doubt it. We let them use our land. Call it cupboard love."

He may have been right; but he himself had called it a relationship of the heart and I thought it more likely that he loved them, especially the children.

His reservations about Emmie didn't stop him from coming to Bennets. He dropped in one morning to bring a message from Mrs Conrad; and came again to rehang the door of a kitchen cupboard which had long been relying on one rusty hinge. This time, I noticed with malicious approval, it was he who took the initiative. He had apparently decided that if any drawing out was to be done, he would be the one to do it: Emmie would be the one to be drawn out. He soon discovered her interest in decimalization. They agreed that it was bound to come after the war.

While they thrashed it out, I watched—and learned to know his face: the strong bones under their spare covering of flesh; the sensitive curves of the mouth; the changing colour of cheeks and eyes as his mood changed—and I wondered if this was the man I would marry. It would take more than a passing attraction, I was careful to remind myself, to tempt such a man as James Conrad into a serious attachment.

Meanwhile I could only marvel that chance had so miraculously brought us together. To think that I had dragged through twenty-two years of existence without knowing him and had actually believed myself to be happy, most of the time—so pitiably low had my standard of happiness been.

Then suddenly there was a softness in the wind. The sky lifted; the earth sprang into life; there were daffodils everywhere. And Celia Mond came home for the Easter holidays.

5

It is hard to believe that I actually saw so little of her apart from that one day in early spring. The weather had unexpectedly turned warm. Somebody, almost certainly Greener, had taken it upon himself to open all the windows. From time to time a breeze crept in from the west and turned a page or two in one or other of our seven copies of *Comus.*

In rather the same way, bringing with her the sensuous sweetness of the April afternoon beyond the classroom window, Celia Mond entered my life; and with the lightness of an ethereal hand drawing attention to the page ahead, directed my thoughts along lines for which I was not quite prepared.

A warm afternoon so near the end of term was not conducive to concentrated study. The story of *Comus* is as simple as a fairy tale. A Virgin Lady, lost in a dark wood, falls into the clutches of the wicked enchanter, Comus. But her unsullied virtue proves stronger than his evil power, and with the help of an attendant spirit, she escapes.

But Milton's poetry was heavy going for this particular group who had found their way into the sixth form and were "taking" literature to what was disparagingly known as Subsidiary Level; worrying away at it with a kind of desperation because there was nothing else they could do better. The desperation had drawn us together. We progressed with painful slowness but with an absence of discord due partly to the knowledge that we were all equally on our mettle.

"Page eighteen," I said with the bright confidence that conceals untold misgivings. " 'But here she comes. . . .' Line one hundred and seventy. We'll go over it again."

Was it merely by chance that we had just reached the point in the masque where the Lady enters? Later on I was to recognise the coincidence as appropriate in a sequence of events bristling with melodrama; so that, looking back or rereading the sparse entries in my diary, I am once again caught up in the mood that gripped me at the time and that I have already mentioned: a sense of submission throughout the whole episode to influences demanding some other faculty than reason to deal with them.

"Read the Lady's speech to yourselves as far as:

> *". . . .Oh, where else*
> *Shall I inform my unacquainted feet*
> *In the blind mazes of this tangled wood?"*

Delphine Mond's small delicate nose pointed anxiously at her book. Above it her thin enquiring eyebrows cleft twin arcs in her unacademic forehead, its skin dragged upward and backward by her tightly tied hair. Each day, as Delphine's difficulties increased, she hauled her hair more resolutely into its white band, as if in that one area at least she had the upper hand.

She sighed. Her doelike eyes strayed and lit up in a smile of recognition. At the window a tall girl was stooping to look in.

"It's Celia, Miss Borrow. My sister."

The stern reply "I'm afraid she must wait" died on my lips. Delphine's flush of pride and pleasure was too much for me. The other five had already abandoned Milton with a relief verging on enthusiasm. In those war years, old pupils were welcome visitors, most of them home on leave;

some, like Celia, on vacation from the university. As a matter of fact I was curious to meet Delphine's wonderful sister.

She hadn't waited for permission but had come quietly in, evidently taking it for granted that her joining us would be seen as the friendly gesture it obviously was.

"Am I intruding, Miss Borrow?"

She smiled down at me: a fair girl with all Delphine's features improved—perfected, one could almost say. She wore her hair rolled up round a blue ribbon into a smooth oval framing her face.

"I know it's *Comus* today."

We all laughed, though heaven knows *Comus* must be the least amusing thing ever penned.

"Why don't you stay and help us through the tangled wood?"

Her eyes, blue as the ribbon, held the clear serenity of a summer sky.

"You might help us to see things in a new light."

"It's all about darkness and light, isn't it? Mr Westmain used to say . . ."

I flinched once more, though I should have been used to it by this time. Greener gallantly brought a chair. I made room for her at the desk.

". . . It's marvellous, though—the poetry." She was entirely without self-consciousness.

" 'The perplexed paths of this drear wood . . .' Whenever we read those lines. I used to think of Foley Wood. Have you been there, Miss Borrow? It's between Kinning and Millford."

There was something about her—some vital quality I recognised at once as rare. It was nothing so superficial as vivacity: she was too calm for that, with a natural assurance and a grace not only of movement but of the whole person.

"Mr Westmain took us there. He wanted us to see how

little the English countryside has changed since Milton's time. Of course we'd all been there before, but . . ."

But it would be different with him! My spite was pitiful. She had sat up, lifting her head with a look of delight. Yes, that was the word: a contained delight like a candle flame, an inward light. She must have been a perfect pupil. The ignoble resentment I harboured against my predecessor gave way to straightforward envy.

Inevitably the lesson degenerated into chat but at least it was lively. Even Mackay left off drawing and contributed a grunt or two. The girls were unusually talkative. Brenda Peel, for instance, had been greatly struck by Celia's reference to Foley Wood, feeling herself for once on familiar ground.

"But do you really believe," she began. I quailed. No vagueness on my part—or Milton's—was proof against Brenda's simple earthiness: ". . . what it says about the Lady being safe in the wood just because she was good. I mean, good people sometimes get murdered. All the people you read about in the paper—and women. There was that girl over at Millford. . . ." She paused. We did not speak openly about rape in those days.

"And soldiers," Greener pointed out, confusing the issue as usual, "get killed however good they are."

"You wouldn't catch me going into Foley Wood"—Brenda made it clear—"not in the dark, especially with a man like Comus about."

"There'd be no stopping you."

"That will do, Greener. Comus is not a man in the ordinary human sense, Brenda. He's an enchanter, an embodiment of evil temptation. When the Elder Brother says that his sister will be safe on her own in the wood, that is Milton's way of saying that perfect virtue is beyond the reach of evil influences. Otherwise, if it couldn't resist temptation, it wouldn't be perfect, would it?" I laboured to a halt, aware of some intellectual hurdle that Westmain would have taken in his stride. "It's a philosophical proposition," I floundered on. "Real people are a different matter."

"Nobody's perfect," Mackay said and seized his pencil again, overcome.

Delphine's eyes, fixed with touching reverence on her sister, suggested a different opinion. She had told me a good deal about Celia. "Now," the innocent eyes seemed to say, "here she is. You can see for yourself."

"Quite true, Mackay," I was nevertheless obliged to say, "no one is perfect. Not all the time. But perhaps at a particular moment a person might rise to such a pitch of goodness that she—or he—could overcome the powers of evil or at least be safe from them."

"The trouble is"—Brenda may have had her own reasons for asking—"how can you know you're good enough to be safe?"

"You can't know without being put to the test." It was Celia who had the last word. Even Brenda was impressed by her quiet authority. "You can only know your own strength when you come face to face with temptation. One can't be truly good by evading evil, not in real life. We must be wholly committed to experience before we can tell good from evil."

I glanced guiltily at my watch. A wasted lesson? Or had we soared into higher realms of thought? A momentary silence had fallen as if some discovery hovered just out of reach, intangible as the scents that floated in at the window, of grass and daffodils and the earth growing warm.

The bell released us. In the rustle of departure Celia stayed to chat while I collected my papers. She was reading English at London University and would take Finals in June.

"One of my friends was at your college," I told her. "Cressida Paget."

She thought she had heard the name.

"We're not in London now, you know. The college has been evacuated to Cambridge."

I asked her if she had ever seen *Comus* performed on the stage.

"No, never. I didn't know that it was still being performed."

"I thought perhaps Mr Westmain . . ." I murmured, enjoying a rare moment of superiority. "We shall be going to see a production by the Adelphi Players on April twenty-fourth at Wantlow. Would you like to join us?"

"Thank you, Miss Borrow. I should have loved to but I'll have gone back by then." She looked down at the book I had not yet closed. "I see you're using his copy. Mr. Westmain's. I know his writing."

It had been a mistake to use his books. I should have hunted out other copies; but on the dark January day of my arrival the set texts had all been there in the cupboard to the right of my knee-hole in the desk—his desk. Their margins were thickly annotated, their flyleaves firmly scored with his name: Edmund Westmain.

"He wouldn't let us write in the margins." It was not a complaint. She was smiling, a tender, indulgent smile. Whatever he did—or said—or thought—was right in her eyes, I could tell: eyes of untroubled blue. He must have seen his own image reflected in them as she looked up at him, on this very spot.

"You enjoyed your lessons with Mr Westmain?" I steeled myself to say.

She closed the tattered book and held it between her palms. The attitude was prayerful; except that again she lifted her head with a little intake of breath. I saw it as nothing less than a thrill at the very mention of his name.

"He has given me so much," she said, adding with just a touch of haste, "of his time, I mean. We used to read together—Eliot and Auden. . . ."

"Mr Westmain was well repaid," I said. "Your State Scholarship . . ."

It flashed through my mind, the possibility that he had been repaid by more than her success, just as he had given her more than his time. It must have been a rewarding relationship. He wasn't there to testify to his share in it, but the raptness in her manner as she remembered him was evidence enough. No one could resist the warmth and brightness, not to mention the beauty of the girl: no man at any rate.

Perhaps on the other hand he had been the one to kindle the warmth. Without his influence she might have remained no more than an intelligent, good-looking girl and surely that would have been enough; but the thrilling happiness, the incandescence would have been lacking; and they were distinctly there. Otherwise how could I have felt them?

Moreover I had divined their source. There could be no doubt of the secret spring from which her bubbling happiness arose. She was in love. How else could one account for the impression of heightened beauty in a girl naturally beautiful? It was love that had brought her here where his presence—I could vouch for it—could so vividly be felt.

In recognising her state, I recognised my own. It was not that she infected me with the power of loving: she simply showed me clearly what I had been content to leave unacknowledged. While I had hesitated at a crossroads, she had chosen her path and was committed (her own word) to whatever it might lead her to. She must be a year younger than I—or more—but she seemed already, in her smiling serenity, to have outstripped me.

Reluctantly, I fancied, she had put down the book.

"I love this room," she said.

"I'm glad you came. We must meet again."

No doubt I would have loved James just as much and just as soon if Celia Mond and I had never met. The enchanted airs of spring had probably as much to do with the soaring of my heart as she had. But I didn't feel that it was so. Our meeting had marked a turning point. It was as if she had gone ahead and was beckoning me along a path she herself already graced. Not that I thought as yet in such positive terms. The image came to me later, together with other images in which the path we shared led us through as dark and tangled a wood as ever Milton's Lady was lost in. But at the time I simply thought of James with a new melting tenderness and longed—as I gathered up my books and made my way purposefully towards Upper IVB —for the evening when I could be with him.

Emmie passed me on her way to the sixth-form room.

"Good afternoon, Miss Emmot."

I turned as Celia spoke. They must have met face to face in the narrow corridor. The odd thing was that Emmie didn't answer but walked on as if the tall smiling girl did not exist.

6

On the following Wednesday I too went home for Easter.

"You mustn't go," James said. "I can't let you."

As recently as a week ago such a speech would have amazed me. Now, having made a number of equally unreasonable speeches myself, having discovered in my dealings with James a whole new style and vocabulary, I accepted it as perfectly suitable.

It was our last evening before the holidays. We were alone in the sitting-room at the Hall. Mrs Conrad was making herself scarce in the kitchen with the clear intention of throwing us together. There was no need. We had forestalled her.

The course of love had been as natural as, seen in retrospect, it was inevitable. From meeting to knowing, from liking to caring, we had progressed with no closer embrace than the touch of hands, without a word of love having been spoken; so that when the time came, there was neither doubt nor surprise: only the delight of being in each other's arms.

I had lingered on my way home from the meeting at the Hall to watch a flock of sheep shambling down the lane. It was a mild evening of blue shadows: a crescent moon, the bleat of lambs, and, miraculously, James. He came over the stile as if from a visit to the stone quarry and saw me. His face, which had seemed tense and drawn between the greening hawthorns, flushed into life.

"Kate!" He came quickly and put his arms round me. "Oh, Kate, you don't know how much I need you."

We clung to each other as if nothing would ever part us. But now, already . . .

"You mustn't go," he said again.

"Two weeks, that's all."

"I wish you wouldn't. Don't you care what happens to me while you're away?"

I was surprised to find that he was serious. We had been light-heartedly making plans for when I came back but his manner had suddenly changed. He had got up to open the door but instead stood spread-eagled against the panels.

"Suppose I won't let you go."

My freedom to do as I liked could never be in question. Yet for all the thrill of knowing how much he wanted me, there remained a nagging doubt. He loved me, he had said so. But after the first rapturous hour in the lane, love was not making him happy. The troubled moment passed. We walked slowly back to Bennets. It took us a delicious three-quarters of an hour to cover three-quarters of a mile.

Despite the pang of leaving him it was good to be at home again with my parents. My arrival on the Wednesday coincided with an alert and we spent the whole of the following night in the shelter.

"At least," my mother pointed out, "they're giving us plenty of time to catch up on each other's news."

In the short time since I had seen them, they seemed already to have grown older. It had been another winter of frozen water pipes and shortages of meat and coal. Then, when the thaw came and the floods had been mopped up, the raids had started again.

Somehow they had contrived to have my room decorated. In fact my first impression was of a sparkling brightness everywhere. I had grown used to the shadowy rooms and dim passages of Bennets.

"Those old houses," my mother said when I remarked

on it, "are so difficult to clean. There's a lot of work in them."

"It isn't only that. Actually we don't do much housework. There isn't time. No, it's the air here. It's so much clearer."

It was thinner, keener, more bracing—with the tang of the sea only a mile away.

"But you're settled? You do like it? You haven't regretted not waiting for the English post at Dame Sedman's?"

"Oh, no."

After our sleepless night we were idling away my first morning in the sunny bay window of my bedroom. Under a sky of aquamarine the lawn was emerald green, the shadow of the chimney velvet black. There was no mistaking anything here: no unlit space in which illusions could grow.

"I had forgotten how different it is—how different it feels."

I tried to tell her. It was as if in the distance figures moved, faceless, voiceless. Their personalities eluded me.

"She seems very nice. Miss Emmot."

"Oh, marvellous. We get on very well."

Far away, indefinite as a shadow, she floated silently up and down the carpetless stairs; thoughtful, unattached, knowledgeable—and into the kitchen where the cat stretched, the wicker chair creaked.

"And James? Is he just a friend?"

"Well, not exactly. I mean . . . You know."

We exchanged smiles.

"I wondered."

"He isn't an easy person to understand, but I know you'd like him."

"You have to get to know people before you make up your mind."

"Oh, I've missed you," I said, suddenly discovering the fact, "and Daddy."

In the field beyond the garden, gulls were landing and taking off, silver and white and gun-metal grey. The level land revealed itself, crystal-clear, plain as a pikestaff, whereas at Kinning one felt so much more than one saw. . . .

". . . So he hardly knew his father."

"They don't talk about Mr Conrad. I don't think it can have been a happy marriage."

"Not to end as it did." My mother looked anxious. "It would be nice to know a little more about them. Still, at least James isn't in the forces."

"He's very conscious of that. It makes him feel out of things. But you know, he was wonderful in the Sheffield blitz. He'd been on night shift and afterwards worked for hours digging people out—where they could be got out. A lot of them are still there under the rubble. He never talks about it."

Was it good to leave the experience unspoken, buried in the mind like the corpses buried in the ruins?

"Perhaps he's still suffering from shock. You say he's a sensitive person."

"And being in a reserved occupation makes him feel guilty, I believe."

I was quoting Mrs Conrad. James had not told me so himself; but as it happened the subject was one of the first to arise when we met again. He was waiting at the station when I returned. He took my bag and hurried me off the platform, barely looking at me as if trying not to show how pleased he was to see me. A fortnight's separation had brought us closer. Our meeting had both the thrill of a new encounter and the intimacy of a reunion.

We had coffee in the run-down café outside the station while we waited for the bus. There were other couples. They sat close together or held hands across the table, making the most of their last few minutes before the London train arrived. Most of the men were in uniform. The corporal at the next table was evidently going to rejoin his unit at the end of his embarkation leave.

"It's sad for them. Such a long parting. Perhaps for ever."

"But don't you see"—James leaned forward, suddenly serious—"the advantage he has. What he has to face is obvious. Everyone understands it—and admires him; well, sympathises at any rate. The sad parting, as you say, is part of it, but it's a straightforward ordeal he has to face openly."

The opposite of that, I thought, must be an inward ordeal endured in secret: a silent gnawing at the mind or heart or conscience. James moved restlessly, his long legs shaking the flimsy table. His face was always difficult to read.

"Why can't you resign yourself," I now asked, "to doing the work you can do best, especially when it happens to be vital to the war effort? Look at Rokeby, our physics master. They won't take him because of his eyesight but he reckons that teaching his subject is pretty important. He says the whole future is bound up with physics."

"For better or worse," Rokeby had added cryptically.

"After all, I'm not in uniform either," I concluded, with a lingering glance at a rather elegant WAAF who was collecting her gear in response to a station announcement.

"But you don't mind. That's because you never think about yourself, Kate. You haven't time," he added lest the remark should be taken as a tribute to my selflessness. I had missed his teasing as I had missed so much else in the two long weeks without him.

"Nor have you. You work much longer hours than I do. How could he manage"—I cocked an eyebrow towards the corporal—"without you? All that equipment he clanks about with . . ."

"He couldn't. But that's not the point. There's no doubt

that a good steelworker is far more use than a half-hearted soldier, which is what I would be."

"Then what is the point?"

"I'll tell you. Being in a reserved occupation has saved me from the ordeal I ought to face. If I had been called up, I would have had to refuse."

"On grounds of conscience?"

"You could call it that. Instead I've been able to dodge the issue, safe at home, but wondering all the time if I'd have had the guts to make a stand. Worse still, I'm supplying the means of destruction so that other people can do the killing."

Privately I thought him in this area a crank but I was sufficiently besotted to see his crankiness as a sign of nobility.

"Remember that you haven't chosen the situation you're in. It's been forced on you. And it takes as much courage to face the truth about yourself as it does to rush off and fire a gun—unquestioningly."

The argument might have been more convincing if I had myself experienced either of these demands.

"Don't try to make a moral hero out of me. It isn't love of mankind that makes me shrink from killing a few of them. It's sheer disgust at the thought of the physical act—and what one would be left with."

"Ugh! When you put it like that . . . ! Still, now that we've got ourselves into this war, somebody has to do it."

"Exactly." He glanced at the next table. The couple there seemed frozen in an agonised silence. The corporal looked at his watch. His companion nodded. Her eyes clung to his face. "While men like me sit on the fence and watch. That's the point." This, then, was the clue to his moodiness: this scruple of conscience. It was a relief to have found it out. "There's no excuse for opting out. Being uncommitted is immoral. I'm sure of that. And I've neither had to refuse point-blank to kill nor have I faced up to actually . . ."

Killing? If he voiced the alternative I didn't hear it. His words had stirred a recollection. Someone else had recently expressed a similar idea and with equal sincerity. But the elusive memory evoked a scene quite different from this seedy smoke-filled room; a mood of radiant happiness.

"It's coming." I sprang to my feet, galvanised not by inspiration but by the shuddering approach of our double-decker bus.

We rattled out into the country. In my absence spring had given to the hills a new shimmering blue, a new fullness to the tree buds. To the west, Foley Wood rose out of a mauve vapour; and everywhere—in clouds, in the air, and in the hollows—hung a luminous softness that stirred the senses and quickened the imagination. There was always in that valley a suggestion of things unseen. The eye was lured to distant objccts and dimmed by gazing until with a change of light . . .

"The shapes change, not just the colours." I turned from the window. "Have you noticed? One minute there's a hill and then you realise it's a cloud. Things dissolve—and disappear."

"I wish to God some of them would."

"Which things in particular?" I asked with interest.

But the driver was making a special stop for me at Bennets' lane end and my question was never answered.

It wasn't until a few days later that I remembered the occasion of the earlier speech about the virtue of commitment. It was in the vestibule between the school hall and the headmaster's study: a sacred place only now and then disturbed by the nervous visitations of those summoned for interviews, dressings-down, and occasionally canings. The headmaster liked to be kept in touch, and I had come to remind him of our expedition that afternoon to see the production of *Comus* by the Adelphi Players.

Thanks to the Council for Education in Music and the Arts and the enthusiasm of actors whom enemy action had banished from the West End, the cultural life of the provinces was being unexpectedly enriched and in the oddest places, in this case the Co-op Hall at Wantlow, eight miles away. The journey would be a complicated affair of interconnecting country buses. We would have to leave at three to be there in time.

I had to wait. From the muffled monologue beyond the closed door I guessed that old Ferrars had come as usual to complain about his timetable. In three separate commemorative brass plaques I could see myself unbecomingly reflected: a sinister apparition in a black gown and green linen dress. No combination, according to Emmie, could be more absurd than that of an academic gown worn over bare legs smeared with stockingless cream. What could one do but go stockingless, I had almost asked, considering the alternatives, then realised just in time that she was wearing them; dense brown lisle stockings with heavily reinforced heels and seams like whipcords.

On the other side of the door Dr Rooke was asserting himself. The voices took on the rhythm of a conversation coming to its close. I cleared my throat and arranged my expression. On the Honours Board to which they had been turned unseeingly for some minutes my eyes picked out a familiar name. Then I remembered that it was Celia Mond who had made the little speech about virtue and commitment.

On the wall to the right of the door stretched one of those long narrow photographs of the entire school, taken, according to the inscription, in 1937. Was there time to look? The dialogue within had given way to the resumed drone of Ferrars' voice. The old windbag! I scanned the rows of faces. Greener's grin had been with him at the age of thirteen and had not changed. And there was Brenda Peel, broad-faced above her collar, her unwavering gaze fixed on the camera, seeing it precisely for what it was; and farther along I discovered the lamblike countenance of Delphine.

After a short search I found her sister, a slim seventeen-year-old, her hair falling in soft waves to frame the perfect oval of her face, the delicate features, the spiritual eyes. To the ranks of unformed faces—anxious, comic, smug—she brought a moment of repose: a fraction of an inch of pure beauty. Lucky girl! It would have been almost impossible to catch her from an unattractive angle even then: and when I had seen her in the flesh, every charm had been heightened by the glow of being in love.

And of course he must be here too, Westmain. Hastily I ran my finger along the short row of teachers, all sitting up nicely, the headmaster in the middle like Job with seven women on one hand and seven men on the other: Archer, Ferrars, Rokeby . . .

The study door opened. Ferrars emerged, older by four years than his likeness, gave me a grim nod and marched off.

"Good morning, Miss Borrow."

"Good morning, Dr Rooke."

Being young, temporary, and of no account, I was out again in less than three minutes, by which time the bell was ringing for prayers. For the time being Westmain had eluded me. But at lunch-time, having bolted my portions of hash and prunes, I gained a few minutes in which to loiter once more in the vestibule.

My worst fears were realised. Westmain, in addition to all his other gifts, was positively handsome, with the looks a foreigner would describe as English: a Beau Ideal, with light hair and blue eyes (so far as I could make out, peering closely and resolving to bring a magnifying glass next time). With everything in the world to be confident about, he looked confident: superbly so, his attitude easy, as if his body sat as comfortably upon him as his well-cut jacket.

How could she fail to fall in love with him, a girl whose nature it was to love? But it had been quick of me to spot the difference, especially on so little evidence, between loving the world and being in love. The second implies a consciousness of some response from the beloved object—if so passive a word could be applied to Westmain, who was, more than most men, active. On the other hand, some very small act of encouragement on his part could have struck the fatal spark in a pupil as responsive as Celia.

Now why should I have thought of the spark as fatal? Was it because (I looked at her again: it was a pleasure to do so) her special blend of youth and fairness made her seem vulnerable? Or had an inward prompting warned me that love must always bear with it the threat of its own decay?

For whatever reason, just for a moment, I felt anxious. Not that there was anything amiss or even unusual in a girl falling in love with her teacher, or vice versa. Far from it. Only in the present circumstances they couldn't be seeing much of each other. Judging by my own feelings, to see each other by any contrivance and however briefly was the constant aim of people in love. So far as I knew, after being called up, Westmain had returned to Kinning only once, near the end of the autumn term, and had been much photographed by adoring pupils. That in itself showed the innate vanity of the man. But at that time Celia would have been in Cambridge, pining for a glimpse of him.

Oh, it was remarkable how accurately I had divined the true state of affairs—how soon, almost at once, came confirmation.

Our expedition to Wantlow was successful. Merely to have arrived in time was a triumph. We all enjoyed the performance ("Better than the pictures," Greener said surprisingly), and as we waited at the Aldernole crossroads for the quarry workers' bus, which would take us the last three miles on our homeward journey, our mood was exalted.

"You could tell what he was," Brenda said, referring to Comus. They had all been taken with his satanic eyebrows, elfin ears, and suave manner. "But I might as well admit that it made him all the more attractive, speaking for myself. Here's the bus."

There was time, as it rattled cautiously towards us along the rough road, for Carole to arrange us symmetrically with me in the centre and take a photograph; and another of me alone with my back against the signpost like Joan of Arc at the stake.

"I do wish Celia could have been with us, Miss Borrow." Delphine sighed.

"She's gone back?"

"Yes. She went yesterday."

Miller's bus was returning empty to the garage in Kinning, having set down the quarry workers at various points farther up the dale. Greener went to sit beside the driver, who was his uncle. Emmie had warned me of the interrelatedness of much of the local population.

"It isn't safe to say anything about anybody—and don't, whatever you do, remark on resemblances. Some of them it's more tactful to ignore."

Delphine and her friend Janet shared the back seat and relapsed into confidential whispers. The rest of us spread ourselves, taking a whole seat each. The windows to the right were filled with green hills that rose eventually to Bardslow Moor. On the left where I sat, the land sloped down to the river through the dense shade of Foley Wood.

We went downhill into thickening twilight. I leaned close to the window looking out and, as we came to the point where a woodland path joined the road, under the trees by the gate I saw—perhaps I was the only one to see

—a pair of lovers standing close together, locked in each other's arms.

In the dimness under the trees they appeared as a single colourless form, its only recognisable features the blonde hair and fair face of Celia Mond half-turned for a few seconds to watch the bus go by. We were quite close. I couldn't be mistaken.

I glanced at the others. Mackay had his back to the window and was making a sketch, since no other subject was available, of Brenda in profile across the aisle. Carole was rapidly memorising the few significant quotations she didn't already know. And Delphine? She and Janet, heads together as they cosily shared a bar of chocolate, were aware of my quick look round.

"Would you like a piece, Miss Borrow?"

I declined, thanked her with the warmth such a sacrifice deserved and turned again to the window. Disappointment was an unreasonable reaction. Nothing could be more natural to a girl in love. What could be more suitable, more poetic in the twilight of an April evening? And who was I, of all people, to feel ever so slightly let down? So long as Celia Mond's emotional state had remained in the realm of theory—an imagined bliss—it had inspired me in a mood both lofty and spiritual. Its descent to a posture so unmistakably physical was a shock—and a warning. The glamour of love-making, I now learned, was strictly limited to the two people involved. With an inward shudder I resolved never, never to be seen by a third person in such a situation.

As for the second person in this case, I had obviously been wrong. It couldn't have been Westmain, who at this very moment was busily sweeping the North Sea clear of mines. Celia's lover must be a local boy: a former school fellow perhaps, someone nearer her own age. Rather reluctantly I revised the story of her wooing in terms of a cottage parlour, a country lad in his best suit, a high tea, a walk in the wood: a perfectly ordinary rustic couple under the trees.

But it didn't work. It just wouldn't do. It was the deception that bothered me. She had bade her family goodbye—and stayed. This gave her a new sophistry and implied the existence of a situation into which the honest local lad simply didn't fit. I could almost see him slouching away, outclassed by a furtive passion he couldn't possibly have aroused. Yet how unfair it was to have idealised her and then to disapprove because she had failed to co-operate.

"Good night, Miss Borrow." Delphine was looking down at me with eyes of the same innocent blue as her sister's.

The next morning—it seemed no time since we had parted—we all met again. A little late, already irritated, I rushed into the classroom, jerked open a drawer in the desk and found a folded paper sticking out of my copy of *Comus.* I opened it and for a minute was speechless.

The message was extravagantly written on a full sheet of foolscap in firm black letters.

"So sorry to have missed you, Miss Borrow."

It was signed "Edmund Westmain."

7

"Just after three. For about an hour, I believe." Emmie was doing something with a slide-rule and didn't look up. "I didn't see him. It was Rokeby who told me."

"No doubt he intends to pop in from time to time to keep an eye on things," I said nastily.

"Oh no, I shouldn't think so." Her frown seemed to have deepened. Probably she needed glasses. "Not unless there's something to be gained by it."

It slipped out, the small disparagement, to confirm my rapidly worsening opinion of Westmain. Was he self-seeking as well as . . . ? What word could one use to describe a man who behaved in such a way with such a girl as Celia Mond? There was not the slightest need for secrecy. Why could he not court her openly? A hasty attempt to substitute Westmain for the local lad in his best suit summoned to tea in the Monds' front room was unsuccessful. Celia wouldn't like it either. Foley Wood with its Miltonic overtones provided a far more suitable setting for their liaison.

It wasn't her fault. Even if her serene innocence was now less striking, the responsibility for the affair must be his. She would be guided by him, her teacher and master. Guided—or misled? Where, after all, had she spent the night—two nights—after refraining from taking the London train? Westmain's lodgings, I recollected, were in Foley Lane.

"What are you doing with that magnifying glass?" Emmie asked.

We were alone in the women's staff room. The others were sunning themselves in the garden for what remained of the dinner hour.

"Oh! It was my grandmother's." I displayed its gold rim and pearl handle.

"Rather heavy, isn't it, to carry about in your handbag?"

"Sometimes they print footnotes very small."

"Perhaps you need glasses," she strangely said.

"Mostly I have it on my writing-table at Bennets. You know I brought a few ornaments and things. If I'm to be here for the duration . . ."

I put the reading glass back casually into my bag. It had been difficult to find a moment of absolute privacy in which to examine Westmain's false visage once more. I had had to kneel on a chair to encircle him in the glass with unavoidable portions of Rokeby and the woodwork master on the outer edges. The close-up had detracted nothing from his good looks. To all the attributes of the man of action was added a poetic dreaminess in the eyes that made me tremble for Celia Mond.

"Who knows, you may be here longer. I doubt if Westmain will want his job back. He's a public-school man himself—and ambitious. Far too ambitious to spend much more time in a small country grammar school. He never intended to stay here long. He'll push off somewhere as soon as hostilities cease, as they say."

The readiness with which I seized on the smallest hint that he was less than perfect sprang no doubt from envy and malice. Come to think of it, there had been no such hints, until now. With interest I realised that Emmie did not share the general admiration of Westmain.

"I was surprised to hear that he had come back at all," she observed and returned to her slide-rule.

She obviously knew nothing of his relationship with Celia Mond. Some of her calculations may have been beyond me, but I could put two and two together. She might be well informed, but it was only to be expected that in knowledge of human nature the student of literature would surpass the mathematician. Observation and intuition had led me to the truth.

The same intuition warned me to keep the discovery to myself. The merest hint that one of the masters was carrying on a clandestine affair with an old pupil could lead to all kinds of scandal-mongering. Celia was too rare a person to besmirch by even the least harmful gossip.

One couldn't blame her if at an impressionable age she had been dazzled by a man who might effortlessly dazzle women of more mature judgement. She had been alone with him for hours at a time. Auden and Eliot scarcely qualified as chaperons; and in a way she and Westmain were alike. Emmie's Platonic theory could well apply to them. I had felt that they were kindred spirits, and now I knew that they were physically of a kind. There was something beautiful, I reminded myself, in so apt a pairing.

Nor was it only the twentieth-century poets who had brought them together. In our English class that afternoon we were inclined to harp on the Adelphi Players if only to avoid coming to grips with the work in hand.

"The Lady had a lovely voice," Delphine recalled.

"No better than your Celia's," Janet said. "You should have heard her in *Twelfth Night,* Miss Borrow, and she really looked the part!"

Naturally she would be Viola, though the wit and sparkle might be beyond her range. She would simply be herself, graceful and composed.

"Who was Orsino?"

Glances were exchanged as at a remembered crisis.

"It should have been Parkinson, but he broke his leg doing the high jump the day before."

"Trust Parkinson."

"There was an understudy?"

"Fenwick. Oh, he was hopeless. He went all to pieces."

"Then who . . . ?"

I might have guessed who had put Fenwick aside and stepped into Parkinson's shoes—splendidly—at the last minute.

"It simply made the play"—Delphine was probably quoting her sister—"having Mr Westmain as the Duke."

Could any situation have been more provocative of tender feelings? The poor girl hadn't stood a chance of emerging heart-whole from Act II, Scene IV. Was it then so long ago that the boundary had been crossed from the friendly comradeship of teacher and pupil to the passionate attachment it had now become? If so, the length of time the affair had lasted made Westmain's part in it all the more deplorable, his intentions all the more plainly dishonourable.

So far I had advanced no farther than to a priggish disapproval, but now more unpleasant thoughts crept into my mind. Perhaps I was tired. Perhaps the nameless anxieties that beset all lovers had begun to cloud my perception of love itself. If Celia Mond's air of unconcealed rapture had influenced me, it was only to be expected that the more worrying aspects of her love affair would influence me too. The furtiveness, the unnatural secrecy, the hazards threatening a young girl in the clutches of an older man . . . Put just a little differently it would almost serve as a description of my own position. The small differences were in fact immense, but our situations were sufficiently alike for comparison.

Before me, six heads were bowed in silent study. No, five. I must speak to Mackay about his ill-mannered habit of constantly drawing. . . .

The idea that virtue alone could protect a girl from evil (I glanced doubtfully at the relevant page) was all very well; but was that the same as to say that nothing could harm her if she was virtuous? The notion suddenly struck me as farfetched.

"Really, Mackay," I snapped, "I do wish you would—just occasionally—stop drawing." And springing from my seat, I snatched the paper and slapped it face-down on my mark book.

Mackay blushed. Delphine raised her startled head. Greener slewed round to peep at the sketch. Carole looked up for a second with her finger on the place she had reached and went on reading. Brenda felt surreptitiously for a nail file. Janet nudged Delphine.

Having broken the blessed silence, I had no choice but to go doggedly on. We girded up our loins. Minutes passed. The bell rang. We dispersed. Absently gathering up my books, I was aware of the blank sheet in front of me and, turning it over, identified it as Mackay's drawing. What I saw brought no relief to my ruffled spirit. It was Comus himself that leered up at me, the "damned wizard" as we had seen him on the stage. The long saturnine face, sharply arched eyebrows, pointed ears, and sensuously full lips were all unsparingly delineated by Mackay's practised hand. A hateful face! The face of Satan himself.

The thing was too much alive to be crumpled and thrown into the waste-paper basket. Taking it gingerly by one corner, I thrust it into the bottom drawer and covered it with old exam papers.

8

Now that I knew his weaknesses, some of them at least, Westmain ceased to be a thorn in my flesh. It was no longer necessary to make a silent request for his permission each time I opened a book or spoke a word in the classroom. Mediocre I might be, but I knew how to care for the moral welfare of my pupils. Brilliance was all very well provided it was underpinned by a sound sense of responsibility. Knowing his inferiority in these respects, I could put him firmly in his place and forget him.

In any case much of my time and most of my thoughts were concentrated on James. Whenever we were both free, we met at Bennets or the Hall, in the lane or in the woods. The long light evenings encouraged us to stay out late. There were nights when it was scarcely dark at all.

The rich soil of that inland county brought forth a luxuriance of foliage and flowers such as I had not seen before. May blossom lay along the hedges in deep swathes of fragrant white and filled the lanes with its disturbing scent. One could have lain unseen all day among the dog daisies and sorrel in meadows where plumed grasses grew waist-high.

At Bennets the sheltered garden became a bower of old-fashioned flowers with deep caverns of shade under its neglected fruit trees. We took our books and ate our meals there and sat talking until dusk; sometimes the three of us; sometimes Emmie and I; or, best of all, James and I alone.

Memory lingers on the idyllic moments—deceptively. It was not a time for lightness of heart. Our personal lives were overshadowed by constant reminders that the war was going badly. Even the ruthless optimism of youth could not be proof against wave after wave of disaster: withdrawals, retreats, fearful losses at sea. Our forces had been swept out of Cyrenaica, Greece, Crete. It seemed as if all the accepted rules were being broken; nothing could be counted on. Not only bombs had taken to dropping from the skies, but men: the solitary Hesse in Lanarkshire, a whole enemy army in Crete. Old friends had become foes; those whom we had regarded with deep suspicion were in that very month to become allies and even saviours.

For all its sweetness the early summer was bitter, too, with the certainty that there were many who would never see another June. Birds sang and flowers bloomed in a climate of death.

Moreover, as the term progressed, the weather became too sultry, the grasses too high, the hedges too close, the trees too dense. All very well for nature to burgeon and blossom, but the process can be carried too far. At school, youthful romances lightly sown in the spring showed signs of ripening too fast. The profusion out of doors induced a laxness within, a general slackening off. Permission was given for ties to be left off. People rolled up their sleeves as far as they would go, not as an incentive to work but to show off their sun-tan. Eyes that should have been purposefully bright were glazed with day-dreams.

"They're simply not working," I moaned, striking out a whole paragraph of Greener's essay. "They don't think. Honestly, Emmie, except for Carole, they're all going to fail."

We were sitting on the stone flags by the front door. It would soon be too dark to see the rubbish Greener had written. Emmie was straining her eyes to count stitches in the white shawl she was knitting to a pattern of extreme complexity. I didn't expect her to answer but presently she reached a point where it was safe to look up.

"You're probably expecting too much. Thinking, as you know, is what most people are very reluctant to do—and especially here."

She had made similar remarks before and I had sometimes wondered why, being a Londoner, she chose to stay at Kinning if it wasn't good enough for her. As a provincial myself, my instinct was to defend it.

"You surely don't mean that people's mental ability depends on where they live."

"The ability is not in question. I was speaking of the habit. Don't forget that ours is a newly established grammar school, less than twenty years old. That means that most of the parents left school at fourteen. Oh, yes, they're anxious for their children to do well, but their own minds are differently attuned. You can't make an academic tradition overnight. Not to mention that there are other influences. . . ."

Behind her chair the wall was draped with red roses. The air was heavy with their scent.

"What influences?"

"You can't expect them to think when the entire countryside is telling them not to. Take warning, Kate. That atmosphere here, in summer, is sensuous. It arouses the primitive impulses."

Deliberately, as if to illustrate the point, the moon was rising over Foley Wood. Among the flower-beds moths fluttered and fell like swooning petals.

"The inherited tendencies of these children are hostile to the intellect. Their environment is still—well, let us not say pagan; there's the chapel, the co-op, and the cinema. But until the last war, nothing can have changed much for centuries. Generations of Kinning folk have gone on living in response to purely natural rhythms. Books haven't influenced them—apart from the Bible. Our girls are closer to their grandmothers than they'll ever be to the likes of us."

"Not all of them."

"Most. In a crisis they'll resort to old wives' tales, not to the stuff we try to push into them."

"Not in exams, I hope," I said, anxiously aware of the sort of thing Brenda might perpetrate.

"That's another thing. To some of them exams really are a crisis, like the ancient trials by ordeal or the ducking of witches. You should make allowance for that, Kate. Don't push them too far."

Sun-tan became her. She looked youthful in her open-necked blouse of cream silk. Had she been pretty once? I wondered if the very influences she was warning against supplied the reason for her staying. The place suited her all the more perhaps because she herself was too reasonable. The seductive airs of Kinning kept her in balance. Those long solitary walks were therapeutic to an over-active mind.

As for me, I seemed to have become the perfect example of a person whose mental balance has been upset by the pagan influences of her environment. The effect of the roses, the garden scents, and the quite magical moon was to make me dream of James to the exclusion not only of intellectual activity but even common sense.

All the same I did grit my teeth and work as hard as adverse conditions allowed; and if the sultry weather was difficult for me, how much worse it must have been for James! I was sometimes shocked by the effect on him of a spell of overtime at the works, which were situated in the low-lying, sulphur-polluted part of the city by the river, where even in summer the daylight was always yellow and thick. Not only the intense heat of the furnaces and the shattering noise but the responsibility of a position he had inherited when still too young for it kept his nerves continually at stretch.

As a rule he recovered quickly in the country air. But now he complained of headaches and sleeplessness. Before the heat wave he had come home whenever possible and had rushed to find me without waiting to change or eat. Now I saw him less often.

"He has so much on his mind," Mrs Conrad lamented. She had always seemed to me over-protective, and had recently taken to watching him anxiously.

"For God's sake, Mother, go away and worry over one of your committees," he burst out once when she brought him an egg-nog and murmured something about not over-doing things.

"It's a breakdown I dread. He pushes himself too far," she confided unhappily when he had gone out abruptly into the garden.

Another time when I dropped in to clinch an arrangement about a concert, she met me in the hall.

"I'll give James your message." She made vague movements with the duster. "When he comes in."

And I had the distinct impression that he was in and not to be disturbed. The next weekend he failed to turn up at Bennets when I was expecting him. Not until Sunday, when he arrived in a silent mood, did I discover that he had been taking a sleeping bag up to Bardslow Moor and sleeping out of doors.

"It was cool and quiet lying under the stars. Only I wished you were with me, Kate."

I forgave him though it was turning into an unsatisfactory day. He was so listless and unenthusiastic about all my suggestions as to what we could do that I gave up. The nut rissoles I had spent the morning making proved uneatable and we spent most of the day drinking weak tea and doing crosswords.

At school we kept all the windows open, and snippets of other people's lessons floated back and forth to confuse our fragile trains of thought. As exams drew near, a nervous depression settled on the Subsidiary English group. Mackay's drawings became increasingly savage as despair seized him. Brenda lost weight. Greener burned the midnight oil and slumbered throughout the day. Delphine grew pale, physically transparent, mentally dense. Her questions became more and more fundamental.

"I don't know *anything,* Miss Borrow. Honestly."

I made reassuring noises. Emmie's warning that for some of them exams might be more than a test of proficiency had impressed me. But the danger didn't really come home to me until the Tuesday of the third week in June. It must have been almost five o'clock. Everyone else had gone home. I had stayed behind to write some lower-school exam questions on a portable blackboard. We avoided duplicating whenever possible in order to save paper.

I had lugged the board into the stock-room and locked it away from prying eyes and was returning through the vestibule when Delphine rose unexpectedly from its one chair: a medieval-looking affair of heavily carved black oak. To my astonishment her appearance was entirely appropriate to this Gothic setting. It might have been Ophelia in one of her mad scenes: bared neck, dismayed blue eyes, and, most startling of all, carelessly flowing locks. They tumbled over her forehead and onto her neck as if they had burst in wild protest from their restraining band.

"Delphine! What on earth are you doing here? The Headmaster has gone home—ages ago."

"Oh, I know. I didn't want to see *him.*"

"Then what's the matter?"

"Oh, Miss Borrow, I don't know . . ."

She was going to tell me yet again that she didn't know anything after all the trouble I had taken to see that she knew something; some small useless piece of information if nothing else. My patience was running out.

"You've had the same opportunity as anyone else to learn your work. It's absurd to make such a fuss."

"It wasn't that." Her eyes filled.

"Then what is it?"

I was beginning to dislike the vestibule, a stuffy little place whose atmosphere combined with the smell of metal polish a hint of nervous agitation left by others who had waited there. And now, as I too waited, unkindly letting the silence develop, my chief impulse was to escape. The clock's callous tick reminded me that I had had no tea.

My sharp tone was having its effect. Delphine pushed back her hair, disposed of the tears with a finger, swallowed.

"I just thought you might . . . I was going to tell you . . . but it doesn't matter." She went to the door, then turned quickly. "It's just that I'm so frightened." She jerked out the words. Her eyes, protruding a little like a hare's, found my face without seeing it. "Terrified. It's so awful. I can't bear to tell you anyway." She groped for the handle. Her steps quickened as she crossed the hall.

"Delphine!"

I heard her running along the corridor. The outer door closed behind her with a desperate slam.

It's the heat, I thought. Her nervousness had infected me. My head ached. What was the point of it all? In a simpler society Delphine would have been happily shaping butter pats in a cool dairy or plating the ribbons of a maypole. I saw her distinctly in a lavender gown, a white kerchief, and a cap.

Unfortunately nothing in the world is simple, as I was distressingly reminded the next day. It was to be our last lesson. Drained of advice, weary of interpreting obscurities, I found relief in reading aloud for the last time some of the simpler and more pleasing passages.

The effect on me at least was healing. Soaring with the Attendant Spirit into the Garden of the Hesperides with its golden tree and its eternal summer, I may have taken too much for granted in assuming that the others were soaring with me. It seems likely that Brenda for one remained earth-bound. Arriving at the foot of a page, I glanced round. Greener reposed like young Adonis in slumber soft. Delphine sat still and pale as wax, her hair once more under control. No need to mention what Mackay would have been doing if he had been there; but he had taken himself off to his married sister's farm at Moor Edge for a few days of solid revision.

Carole was intelligently referring to the notes at the back of her book.

There was not much more.

" 'Love Virtue, she alone is free'," I intoned mellifluously.

That was it in a nutshell. I could do no more. Trivialities sank away. Intent as I was on creating an atmosphere of celestial calm as the best possible preparation for the trials ahead, I was totally unprepared for the gruesome interruption, in mid-sentence, that set my heart pounding.

It came from Delphine. With a peculiar moan she had got to her feet and was leaning forward on her desk for support.

"I hate it." Her voice, unnaturally thickened at first as if she were choking, rose to a wail. "I hate *Comus.* It's not true. None of it's true. Nobody's safe. Not even the very best person in the whole world."

With shaking hands she seized her book, ripped out a handful of pages and hurled them into the aisle; then sank back on her chair, laid her head on her arms and sobbed.

We gaped, exchanging looks of consternation. I went quickly to Delphine, put my arms round her and was coaxing her to tell me what was wrong when I realised that Janet was mouthing some silent clue, impossible to understand.

"What's the matter with her? I had no idea the exam was worrying her so much," I whispered anxiously.

Janet shook her head, leaned closer and murmured between her teeth:

"Nothing to do with the exam. It's her sister. Celia. She's disappeared."

9

"Do the others know?" I whispered after a dumbfounded silence.

"No. Nobody knows except me. She's kept it bottled up, but she had to tell someone."

I judged it best to pack the other three off to the library. They departed swiftly. Only Carole paused to pick up the mutilated *Comus* and collect the scattered pages before closing the door quietly behind her.

"Have a good cry, Delphine," I said needlessly when Janet had gone to fetch the obligatory cup of tea. "It'll do you good. I'm sorry about yesterday. You should have made me listen."

Having groped for and failed to find a clean handkerchief, I could only stroke her stricken head until her grief became more manageable.

"I'm not supposed to talk about it."

"You can tell me. I won't breathe a word. Friends can always help," I added, knowing no better at the time.

There was not much to tell. Nobody knew where Celia was. She had vanished—it was this that shook me to my depths—in the middle of finals; had taken four papers and had been seen no more. The exact time of her disappearance was not known. Since she had handed in her Middle English paper at twelve-thirty last Friday, June 13, no one remembered seeing her.

The news had not reached the Monds until Sunday evening. Since they were not on the telephone, Celia's tutor had wired, asking them to ring her. She had apparently expected to hear that Celia had gone home for the weekend without permission and been prevented from returning, presumably by illness.

"But she hasn't been home." Delphine heaved a last sob and became rational. "Dad was furious about her not finishing her exams, but that was just at first. He knew straightaway that something was wrong. It's getting us down, Miss Borrow. We've none of us slept since we heard."

Celia had now been missing for five days. I tried not to show my alarm, which was still strongly tinged with disapproval.

"Your parents have told the police?"

Mr Mond had done so at once and had left for Cambridge first thing on Monday morning. The usual enquiries were being made, but so far they had been discreet, partly in the interests of the college but also because the Monds, having been born and bred in Kinning, knew only too well the wisdom of keeping the matter to themselves for as long as possible.

The immediate task was to comfort Delphine.

"People do sometimes lose their heads in the middle of exams. And then, if she missed one paper, she would feel awkward about turning up, wouldn't she? So that it may be a little time before she can face . . ."

"Celia isn't like that."

There lay the problem. What was Celia like? She had seemed a person of rare serenity as she stood in this very room looking down at me from eyes as clear and blue as a summer sky. Her poise had seemed too natural a grace ever to leave her. But there had been that other glimpse of her in Foley Wood when the impression she gave was of a less sedate kind. And now? This time she hadn't even bothered to lie but had simply taken herself off . . .

"I brought one for you, too, Miss Borrow."

Janet had come in bearing a tray of tea.

"You can ask permission to go home if you like, Delphine. But it would be better if you could pull yourself together. Your parents would worry even more if they thought this was getting you down."

"I know. And I've made up my mind"—the sniff was childlike, the decision heroic—"to sit all my exams. They can't have two of us going to pieces."

Janet hovered maternally while we sipped our tea.

"In my heart," Delphine said, "I feel that whatever's happened, Celia will be home for my birthday. That's what keeps me going. Nearly the last thing she said to me was, 'I'll be home on your birthday, Delphie.' "

We were interrupted by the bell and the entrance of Carole. Without a word she laid on the desk Delphine's copy of *Comus,* the torn-out pages neatly replaced with sticky tape. On this inspiriting note I left them.

If it proved even harder than usual to interest Upper IVB in noun clauses, the fault was not theirs. Celia Mond had intrigued me from the moment we met, and now even more intriguing than her presence was her absence. Her appeal had such a positive quality that it was difficult to think of her in negative terms: as not being like this or that, not being here or there. But it was more difficult still to put her out of my mind.

A school is not the place in which to breathe a secret, as I discovered on my return to the staff room forty minutes later.

"Of course you've heard . . ."

Miss Butler, alerted by Janet's request for tea, had wormed the story out of her and had taken a proprietary interest in it. There were seven of us in the women's staff room. By the time we were all assembled for our mid-morning break, Butler had told her tale six times.

"I could tell from Janet Pethrick's face that there was

something up. 'Come on,' I said, 'What's happened? Who's put the cat among the pigeons this time?' "

The recent sensational theft of biscuits from one of the air-raid shelters was forgotten. Regrettable it may be but there is a stimulus in hearing bad news. We are reminded of the razor edge on which security rests. Conversation had never been livelier.

". . . wouldn't have expected her to crock up . . ."

". . . lost her head . . . a pity . . . she should have done well . . ."

"It's the heat and they don't feed them properly in those places. . . ."

"You can say what you like, but if people can stand up to the blitz, there's no excuse for a girl like her getting into a panic over exams."

"Standards of personal behaviour have gone into the melting-pot, if you ask me," Butler declared.

I spent most of the evening alone. Emmie was in Manchester for an examiners' conference. She had left on Friday. The meeting would last the whole of Saturday and if necessary continue on the Monday. On Tuesday morning she had telephoned the school secretary to say that trains were being delayed and she would therefore not be back until today, Wednesday.

I ate my supper in the kitchen, then went out into the garden and looked across the valley. It was warm and oppressively still. A heaviness in the air thickened the texture of walls and shrouded the hills. An inscrutable landscape that always hinted at more than it disclosed. . . .

I had intended to walk down the lane to meet Emmie. On those windless nights one could hear the bus half a mile away. But I was still sitting on the wall when the click of the gate startled me.

"How was it?"

"Tedious."

"Your supper's all ready."

I was interested to hear about the conference, which was to have been presided over by Cressida's father, Professor Roger Paget, the distinguished mathematician. But I was also dying to talk, being for once in a position to tell Emmie something she didn't know. However, I restrained myself and hung about usefully until she drank her soup and revived a little.

Then just as I opened my lips . . .

"What's all this about Celia Mond?" she asked, tackling her salad. "Everybody on the bus was talking about it."

I told what I knew.

"She must have had some sort of breakdown," I concluded. "Couldn't cope with things. Isn't it a pity?"

"When you say things, you mean Finals?"

"What else?"

My surprise sounded unconvincing. It was hard work to be so discreet. Almost everyone (Butler had her own theory) had assumed that because Celia had vanished in the middle of Finals, the exams must be the cause. Even with my exclusive knowledge of her secret life, I, too, had connected the two things. Her clandestine goings-on had wrecked her studies: she was astute enough to realise after the first four papers how ill-equipped she was to take the rest; a sudden fit of despair and she had bolted. Recalling her graceful self-confidence, I rejected that word as unsuitable; she would never bolt.

Emmie was munching lettuce like a thoughtful rabbit. Had she implied that other factors might be involved? Perhaps Finals had nothing to do with Celia's departure. "It's nothing to do with exams," Janet said, speaking of Delphine's distress. She had swept aside examinations as being of small account compared with the human drama of a missing sister. Celia could have behaved in the same instinctive way. She could have ignored the obligation to take Finals in response to some other demand: some crisis of a more personal kind.

"The usual reason" had, needless to say, been touched on in the staff room; but if she had found herself in that kind of trouble, a few days would have made little difference. There would be all the more reason for taking her degree before melting away discreetly in the vacation.

"In every situation," Emmie observed, "there are at least two possibilities. Either she went off of her own accord or she was forced to."

"She could have gone somewhere and been prevented from getting back—by illness, as her tutor thought—or by something else."

"Ah! Don't tell me. Let me guess. Butler has been talking about the White-Slave Trade. It's one of her favourite topics."

"She did rather go on about it."

"It has an old-fashioned ring these days. That's one thing the war seems to have rescued us from. It must be difficult to get the white slaves out of the country, though they could of course be enslaved here. There must be plenty of demand for them."

"Well, you said yourself she might have been forced to leave. What had you in mind?"

"There are so many kinds of compulsion. Physical, mental, moral . . ." She considered them but when she spoke again it was to revert to my other suggestion.

"You were thinking of an accident?"

A car crash, amnesia, a stroll by the river too close to a weir . . . None of these would have left so mystifying a lack of all trace. By this time she would have been seen, found, washed up. So far as we knew, enemy action in Cambridge on Friday could be ruled out. Yet any of these possibilities seemed more likely than that Celia had been forcibly plucked from the walled garden of her college at noon on a summer day.

We aired our theories, Emmie cool and detached, I growing warm and intense. The warmth and intensity may have been responsible for my over-reaction to something that happened earlier that evening: a harmless little incident which to a person in a normal state of mind might have been rather pleasing.

I was getting into bed when it occurred to me that Emmie had not mentioned Professor Paget. She had promised to give him my best wishes and to ask for news of Cressida. I went out onto the landing. On those warm nights we both slept with our doors open. Her candle was still burning. She hadn't gone to bed. I heard quiet movements and had actually opened my lips to speak when something unusual in those movements warned me not to intrude. Instead I stood stock-still, astonished to the tops of my bare toes.

Her room, like all the rooms at Bennets, was large. My view was limited to about a third of its area, which included one long window, still pale against the late twilight; and I could see Emmie only when she appeared in that comparatively narrow strip. But there was ample room in it for her to move freely and there was light enough for me to see her, though not distinctly.

She had taken off her dress but was still in her white slip. Except for the occasional creak on a floor-board, her stockinged feet made very little sound. I watched open-mouthed. People can do as they like in their own bedrooms, of course—but this was so unlike her.

She was—incredibly—dancing.

Waltz? Slow foxtrot? Or even, absurdly, a solitary tango? It was, so far as I could make out, none of these; more an affair of glissades and rapid twists, arms extended at shoulder level or flung high above her head. In response to a sudden air-displacing swoop the candle went out, leaving the pungent smell of hot wax.

Standing disorientated in the dusk at that half-way point between her room and mine, I felt a distinct tingling of the scalp. Was this something she did, unknown to me, every night, or did the impulse seize her only now and then—and if so, why tonight?

Pondering these alternatives as I crept back to the safety of my bed, I found that neither of them appealed to me.

10

By the next day the news of Celia's disappearance had spread throughout Kinning and the neighbouring villages. It produced a rich crop of horror stories, tales of crime and vice, dark references to the Ministry of Information, touching accounts of reunions in rest centres. Listening furtively, I heard not so much as a hint that anyone knew of Celia's attachment to Westmain or of her propensity for being where she was not supposed to be. As the only person in possession of the secret, I felt a peculiar responsibility—without having the least idea of how to act on it.

I never asked whether or not my message to Professor Paget had been delivered. Marvelling over the spectacle of a strangely liberated Emmie gliding inexplicably about her bedroom, I forgot how it was that I had been there on the landing to see it. Moreover, quite by chance the next morning brought a letter from Cressida. She would be spending a few days in Richmond on leave from her WRNS station somewhere in the West Country. Was there any hope of my joining her on June 26?

Unfortunately that would be Alexandra Rose Day and also the day of the school fête, to each of which, in my capacity as general busybody, as James put it, I was heavily committed.

But there was something Cressida could do for me. I wrote her a long letter. She was interested enough to act promptly. I was in the garden just after breakfast on the following Tuesday when the postman brought her reply.

> I'm glad you pushed me into going, though it was a fag getting to Cambridge. I enjoyed the visit for sentimental reasons as well as acting as private investigator on your behalf, and the Principal put up a convincing show of being pleased to see me. I gathered they're pretty upset about your Celia. All the same—and this may shake you—they weren't entirely surprised! Apparently she had taken herself off twice before, and been warned. Twice that they knew of. Her tutor was well aware that there could have been other times. "Unfortunate," she went so far as to mutter. "An intelligent girl but oddly aloof. Not altogether of our world." Typical, according to old Kitty, of the kind of promising girl pushed into the University by a highly successful teacher rather than drawn there by personal inclination. All the same they had expected her to take an averagely good degree—and obviously now regard her as doomed. Must say I agree. How can she go back there—or anywhere else?
>
> Any chance of seeing you at the end of July? All being well, I'll be home for a week's leave . . .

I put the letter in my pocket, with the now familiar feeling of disappointment. How could a girl be so intelligent and behave so irresponsibly?

The air was still fresh, every vista shimmering with veiled sunlight. The world was stirring. Farther down the steep hill a miniature woman was scattering meal for pin-sized hens.

"Good morrow, my love."

It was a greeting to give the final touch of perfection to a summer morning.

"James! How on earth . . . ?"

"Isn't it time you went to school?" He sat on the wall. "I'll wait while you collect your baggage if you're quick."

He had come out on an early bus after a night at the works and was haggard and unshaven. I rushed indoors and flung books into my bag.

"You didn't need to come this way."

"I thought there might just be a chance of seeing you and picking up some wholesome and edifying thought for the day. I came out on the bus with one of your men friends. Physics master. Nice chap but rather down in the mouth. In fact, very gloomy. His summer holiday has been messed up somehow."

"He was going climbing in the Lake District. What can have happened?"

"The man he was going with has had to back out."

"What a shame! He's rather a lonely sort of person. It can't be much fun being the only youngish man left on the staff."

We parted at the lane end, lingeringly. I had to run to be at school on time. As it happened everyone was unpunctual that morning. The staff room was still full of people who should have been with their forms. Heads were turned as I went in. Had I heard? Mr Mond had come home the night before bringing ominous news. On the Friday afternoon of her disappearance, Celia had been seen boarding a London train: a development which did nothing to solve the mystery but added a new dimension.

Since the fearful bombardment of May 10, heavy raids on London had ceased. On that moonlit night the Abbey, Mansion House, Mint, Law Courts, British Museum, and the Tower had all been hit. But the Germans had lost thirty-three bombers, and that was to be the last major attack for three years. Nevertheless, the lightness of the raids that followed was only comparative and they were to continue on and off for the next few weeks until the Luftwaffe was more urgently needed on the Russian front.

On the nights of Friday and Saturday, June 13 and 14, there had been several fires, including one at the entrance to an underground station. A bomb had demolished half a street in the St Pancras area and a derelict building in Kensington had collapsed and buried a small queue of people waiting for a bus. Some of the bodies had not yet been recovered.

The buzz of talk was subdued. We stood about in mournful groups telling each other that the odds must be in favour of Celia's survival. Only by sheer chance could she have been burned to death, blown to pieces, or buried alive. But statistics were against us. People were being burned, blown up, and buried every day.

"She asked for it," Butler said, "going to London. What are people evacuated for? But don't any of you try to tell me that there's nothing in Friday thirteenth, if you don't mind."

She must be dead. There could be no other explanation of her silence. It was the silence of death, whether from enemy action or some other cause. No other possibility could resolve the inconsistencies of her behaviour, which would otherwise be quite out of character, whatever that character might be (I reflected dubiously). It was like her to slip away but not to stay away when so much was to be gained by going back. However urgently a young woman might wish to disappear, the decision could surely be postponed when a few more days would have brought the culmination of years of hard work and safeguarded her future.

The uncertainty was not so much a source of hope as an added affliction to the Monds. Neighbours lamented that they couldn't even send wreaths. Prayers were offered in both church and chapel.

Otherwise it is sad to recall how quickly the affair died down. The German invasion of Russia on June 22 by dramatically extending the theatre of war diminished the local tragedy. Besides, in those abnormal times, disaster was growing familiar. During the last few weeks of term we prayed in assembly for the relatives of Livingstone, lost at sea, and Bailey, killed in Crete, and others, until Miss Wetherby, who played the hymns, said that she was beginning to hate "Eternal Father" and "For All the Brave."

Not only the school but the whole population of Kinning turned out to give a hero's welcome to Pilot Officer Enderby, DFC, a former head boy, by which time Celia Mond had almost ceased to be talked about.

"Oh, yes," someone might murmur if her name was mentioned, "wasn't that awful? Nothing's been heard? Have you finished with those reports?"

Instead we talked of clothes rationing and how to circumvent it without being unpatriotic. Butler forgot about the White Slave Trade in rehearsing her solo for the Red Cross concert at the end of term. The fête had been washed out by a thunderstorm. I organised a raffle of those contributions to the stalls that could be salvaged and dried out, and made eleven pounds four shillings and twopence for the Comforts Committee.

But Kinning—as I found out when I went round selling Savings Certificates—in its own mysterious way was absorbing Celia into itself and making her an enduring part of its long experience. One way and another the few facts became, not falsified, but poetically draped in flights of fancy, as a coffin is made less stark by a covering of flowers.

A girl had been seen on the mill path—in the woods—in the fields behind Mafeking Terrace: always in the evening or early morning or too far away to be recognised. A man had likewise been seen—in Foley Wood—on the moors—a deserter or an absconding internee by the look of him.

. . . These rumours later effected a merger: Celia had been seen on Bardslow Moor with an escaped German prisoner.

There were more sinister tales. Mrs Mond's sister May had never once set out the cards without seeing a blonde woman with nothing but spades around her. Somebody dug up a story, Greek-like in its theme of maiden sacrifice, that every ten years a fair-haired girl was doomed to die in Kinning. Examples were given. There was some difference of opinion as to whether the interval was one of ten or seven years.

Celia was rapidly slipping into folklore.

There was one sad little footnote to the tragedy: a piece of information significant to no one but me. I alone was in a position to see the irony in it.

Having dropped into a deck chair to watch the last stages of the School versus Staff and Prefects cricket match, I was conscientiously noting the familiar features of so traditionally English a scene: the subdued thud of leather on willow beneath the immemorial elms, the slow ritual movements of white-clad figures, when I discovered my immediate neighbour to be Rokeby. I told him how sorry I was to hear that his holiday plans had been upset.

"You've heard?" He was a friendly person in a subdued sort of way. Even in the most cheerful circumstances his pebble-thick glasses gave him a despondent look. "I'll still go, but it won't be the same on my own. It had got to be a regular thing, August in Langdale. We always stay at the Old Dungeon Ghyll. Of course we didn't hope for more than a week this year. That was as much as Edmund thought he might wrangle."

"Edmund?"

"Westmain. He's a superb climber. We were hoping to break some records. But he had a sudden posting. I'm wondering if it could be to Suez. We've certainly got problems there. It's all very much hush-hush and needless to say Edmund didn't let on, if he knew; but I got it from a friend in bomb disposal. Apparently the Germans have been dropping mines in the Canal. Nothing can get through until it's dredged. We've set up a mine-watching organisation with the Egyptians. Oh, well played, Archer."

My applause for whatever Archer had done was absent-minded. With Westmain on the spot, I reflected, we need not fear for the Suez Canal. His mere presence would ensure the safety of the entire Middle East.

". . . not a healthy place to be," Rokeby was saying. "It's going to be a bit too easy for the Germans to bomb our shipping there now that they've got bases in Crete."

"When did he go?"

"He was reporting for duty the morning after he telephoned me. He'd been spending a few days in London."

My interest quickened. It was on the second Tuesday after Celia's disappearance that Rokeby had told James about the change in his holiday plans but he could have known of it for some time. I wondered just when Westmain had telephoned him and whether his stay in London had been before or after Friday, June 13.

"I suppose he was upset when you told him about Celia Mond." The indirect approach seemed to me well contrived. "After all, he did teach her."

"Er . . ." Rokeby was nonplussed. "As a matter of fact, I didn't mention it. Oh well, I couldn't have, could I? It hadn't cropped up, her going missing, I mean, when he rang. It wasn't until the next week that I heard about it myself. The day he rang up was a Friday, in the evening. It must have been the same day that she disappeared. Didn't somebody say it was the thirteenth? Unlucky all round."

Without warning, for no reason that I could see, the match had ended. It had lasted just long enough for me to discover why Celia had been in London on that particular day—and night? He must have left the next morning and gone off to Suez, never to see her again.

So far as I was concerned, the case against Westmain was complete. There was no more harm that even he could do. He had been her evil genius from the start, had ruined her career, and in the end had lured her to her death.

From the corner of my eye I saw Delphine drifting in my direction. We had got into the habit of walking home together, though it meant going out of my way. It did her good to talk, and I had not forgiven myself for having discouraged her once before.

I felt in no mood to talk to her just then and basely hurried off to the library. But a day or two later she was waiting for me at the end of the afternoon and we set off together. Even without the black armband she would have seemed a creature set apart as she walked sadly between the scented spikes of meadowsweet that fringed the lane. She had become withdrawn: skin whiter, voice fainter, as if she might dissolve into thin air as her sister had done.

"If only she hadn't gone to London!" It was Delphine who introduced the subject. "I haven't told anyone, Miss Borrow, but I think I know why she went."

So she knew. I glanced at her quickly. Her face was in profile, only a little less beautiful than Celia's: more sensitive perhaps. The long upcurling lashes, the thin eyebrows, the fairness—all were very like her sister's. But Delphine's innocence was genuine, I told myself, and was instantly ashamed of that slur on poor dead Celia.

"Why did she?" I asked after a pause.

"I can hardly bring myself to say it because it makes me feel so guilty, but I'm sure she went for my sake."

Her eyes, turned to me, swam with tears.

"I told you, didn't I, that nearly the last thing she said to me was 'I'll be home for your birthday, Delphie'? Every year since we were little, she gave me a china ornament for my birthday, an animal."

The birthday, alas, had come and gone.

"You must have quite a collection."

"Twelve, going back to when I was five. A big rabbit was the first, then they got nicer. Celia grew more fussy about finding something tasteful. She'd seen one she liked in a shop in Kensington but hadn't enough money at the time. Dad sent her two pounds just before the exams . . . and you know Kensington was one of the places . . ."

"Yes, I know."

"It would have to be something special to make her go up to London when she couldn't really spare the time—and in the raids and everything."

"Yes. Something very important to her."

"She died for me," Delphine said. Tears ran down her cheeks, pure clear drops, and dripped upon her spotless blouse.

One could certainly say that she had died for love. A farewell meeting with her lover before he rejoined his ship, neither of them knowing that it would be the last! Very likely he still didn't know: he couldn't have heard.

I almost found it in my heart to pity the man. How terribly sad the whole thing was, I mused, half-drugged by the fumes of meadowsweet! How haunting a tale of doomed love, of lost innocence and trust misplaced! There was only one word for it—a word sometimes misused and more often than not better avoided—but in this case perfectly apt. Romantic.

11

I must have slept a little. At first there was nothing but sky, nothing left of the world but the nest of heather where we lay. Raising my head, I saw the warm air shimmer above the moor and through its translucent waves. . . .

"Look! A pool—or a tarn."

"Not in this part of the world, love," James said. "It's an illusion. You're looking at cotton grass in bloom."

The sparse white tufts seemed insubstantial, as if they had alighted on the coarse bents while I slept. One might blink and find them gone. I lay down again, pillowed on James's folded jacket, and breathed the mingled scents of bog myrtle and tweed. The long walk had been uphill all the way. James never used his car for pleasure and only occasionally for work. We had come by Miller's bus as far as the solitary Drovers' Inn, crossed a stile into uncultivated land, and tramped the rest of the way. By the time we came out on the moor we had forgotten all about the golden plover. In any case the nesting season was long over. We simply threw down our packs and subsided into the heather.

"You're glad you came after all?"

He didn't answer. I had felt from the start that he was in low spirits and I wished we hadn't chosen this particular Sunday for our long-delayed outing to Bardslow Edge. But it was chiefly on his account that I had suggested it, knowing how he loved the moors and needed the upland air.

"You're frowning, Miss Borrow. Your professional look."

"Just thinking."

"About me, I modestly hope."

"I think of you almost all the time. I have from the very beginning."

The confession seemed to touch him more deeply than I had intended. He took my hand and kissed it with—was it humility?

"It's all a matter of fate," I went on, "whom one meets and loves. You were the first person I met in Kinning." We had never discussed that first meeting. He too may have been conscious of its imperfections. In any case it had soon been outdated by more satisfactory encounters. "I'm afraid I woke you that night. You seemed so remote. Do you know—I had a strange feeling . . ."

"Feeling about what?" He had drawn away, unsmiling.

"Nothing. You know my strange feelings." The evasion was a mistake, but his changes of mood could be upsetting. Only a minute ago he had seemed to be recovering from the gloom that had rather spoiled the morning. "It must have been maddening for you to be disturbed by that thunderous knocking. Like Macbeth. Especially when it must have been one of the few times you had the house to yourself. Your mother was still in the nursing home, wasn't she?"

His face relaxed into the teasing smile I loved.

"I could scarcely take you in."

"I didn't expect you to."

"That's not what I meant. I couldn't take it in, that you were there. You appeared out of the dark like a vision, as if you'd been sent. Afterwards I wished . . ."

It was his turn to leave a sentence unfinished. Instead he put his lips gently to my hand again.

"You were half asleep," I said.

From the high empty moor, through the diffused brightness of summer heat, it seemed far away, my arrival on that January night. The cold smell of wet bark, the treacherous slush, a light briefly shone farther up the hill . . . and there had been something else, some detail just beyond the grasp of memory, something that had given me courage. Tired though I was, as I picked up my bags and plodded on, my mood had been buoyant.

"And you are half asleep now." James laid his cheek against mine. "Altogether too far away for my liking."

There should have been no shadow on the blissful afternoon. If the bliss was less than perfect, the place was not to blame: the great shoulder of a hill sloping southward to a deep dale and rowan-fringed stream, to the north backed by bluer, higher hills. And we did almost regain the lighthearted mood we were used to sharing. How could it be otherwise when, as I reminded him, this was one of his favourite haunts?

"I suppose it is." His eyes clouded. "One of them."

He turned to me quickly. I recognised like a tug at my heart his need of me—and waited. But "It's usually worth the climb" was all he said.

We rambled about, admiring the views and exploring the territory. The Edges are a dramatic feature of that region: cliff-like outcroppings of dark millstone grit, like natural fortifications. Bardslow was one of the lowest and no more than a foretaste of the heights farther north, but high and bare enough to seem like another, wilder world, far remote from the sheltered woods of Kinning.

One quick look down its sheer side into the tumble of broken rocks below was enough for me. Besides, though it was still warm, the light was changing. The best of the day was gone. We finished off the sandwiches and drank from a stone spout under a crag.

"You knew it was here?" And when he nodded. "Of course I should have known. There'd be sure to be water. Otherwise they wouldn't have built a house here." I had only just caught sight of its grey turrets, almost indistinguishable from the boulders below the eastern brow of the hill. "I was wondering why there should be azaleas in the middle of all this moor."

They had strayed beyond the garden and were growing wherever a patch of smooth turf would let them, each bush encircled by a confetti of fallen petals. Their faded pink and flame gave a touching effect of civilised life struggling to survive in a wilderness.

"An odd place to build a house. Would you call it a folly? I've never seen one."

"That would be a good name for it but actually it was intended as a shooting lodge."

"I'd love to explore it. Presumably it's empty. Can we get in, do you think?"

"Another time perhaps." He looked at his watch. "I'm afraid we must go, Kate. Night shift."

I wasn't sorry to leave. In that exposed place one could almost feel the awesome tilt of the earth as it turned from the sun. The few things that could cast shadows—a single tree, a chimney, a mock battlement—flaunted them abruptly. The dragon-headed boulder in whose shade we had lain reared its dark bulk and became unfriendly.

It was easier walking downhill, at first over rough ground, then on stony tracks. We were within sight of the grey roof of the Drovers' Inn but still a quarter of a mile from the stile when we saw Miller's bus creeping along the road towards Kinning.

"That's torn it! Unless we can hitch a lift," James said in quiet desperation.

Not a vehicle in sight! Nor had one appeared five minutes later.

"You should have gone straight into town from Bardslow."

"And leave you to walk all this way alone?"

"I wouldn't have come to any harm. We haven't seen a soul all day."

"Wouldn't risk it all the same. You never know."

There was nothing for it but to take a short cut over the stile on the other side of the road, through farmland and eventually into the sudden twilight of Foley Wood.

"I'm going to be late." James broke a long silence.

"Honestly, I can't go any faster. Why don't you go on?" It would be a relief. I had felt his impatience as he tried to adjust his stride to my much shorter one. "We must be near the gate."

Beyond it the wood thinned into pasture and one would see the chimneys of Kinning.

"You don't mind? As a matter of fact this path on the left is a quick way to the main road. I'll get the bus straight into town instead of going home. I'm sorry, Kate. I should have managed things better. We stayed up there too long. But it's your own fault. You bewitched me as usual."

His smile had the same bewitching effect on me—always.

He turned once to wave and was gone, walking without a sound on the deep leaf mould. Alone, I could take my time. In retrospect the small frustrations of the day were more than outweighed by its various delights. Between them they had drained my powers of response and left me in a vacant mood, physically spent, mentally inert.

It was farther to the gate than I had thought. After a while, from being restfully alone, I became aware of silent company: the trees were with me, ancient beech and oak with huge sinewy roots and vast poles. Scabrous markings on the bark here and there gave an impression of puckered faces, unimaginably old.

There grew on me the feeling of having strayed into an inhuman world of ageless presences, possessed of their own knowledge and keeping quiet about it. But they were not indifferent. I was being noticed. Branches reached out like arms. A wrinkled face watched me with the gravity of an ancient elephant. The farther I went, the more of them there were to close in noiselessly behind me. By this time the glades should have widened. There should have been glimpses of open fields. I had taken a wrong turning. I began to run, not caring where.

"Now then, what've you been up to?"

And suddenly there was a woman between the trees on my left. She had made no movement but had simply materialised out of the green dusk: a woman with a thick mop of curling dark hair above a floral summer dress. She had spoken without removing the cigarette from her heavily reddened lips, so that I saw her thin face through a cloud of smoke.

"Oh, you startled me. I didn't hear you coming."

Her husky chain-smoker's laugh was for some reason derisive. I was struck by the fact that she didn't seem to be going anywhere, certainly not for a walk. Her bare toes were doing their painful best to accommodate themselves to her high-heeled once-white sandals.

"So you've had enough, eh?"

"What do you mean?"

She laughed again.

"He's gone a bit too far, has he? And you've left him to cool off?"

"He?"

"There's always a man in the case, isn't there? It's always the way. I could tell you a few things about what goes on under these trees. You're not the first and you won't be the last." She turned her head to flick ash from her cigarette and lapsed into a wheezing cough so that I missed the next few words. "That's what I said. My very words. You come running through the wood with your dress ripped and your skin scratched till the blood runs. What's your mother going to say to that—and your eyes starting out of your head like hat-pins?"

Involuntarily I glanced down at my aertex blouse, intact with every button in place, and at the unblemished brown of my arms and legs. She must be crazy. She had bared her teeth in an unappealing leer. Her leisurely manner puzzled me. It was as if she were taking the air in her own garden.

"I want to get back to Kinning. . . ."

"You should have kept to the path along the river. You've come too far this way, but if you go up there"—she pointed—"you'll come out in a lane and then you'll see Kinning."

"Up here?" I could just make out the faintly defined track leading uphill. "Thank you very much."

"I'll come with you."

"No, it's quite all right."

"You don't want to get into any more mischief, do you?"

"You're quite mistaken."

My lofty manner was wasted on her. She cackled again and tottered to the path, her high heels sinking into the sandy soil, her ankles bending excruciatingly outward.

The few minutes we spent together were uncomfortable. Some vestige of politeness made me reluctant to go ahead when she was supposed to be showing me the way. Her innuendoes disgusted me. I kept a frosty silence while she went on insisting, with relish, on the absurd notion that I had been running away from some kind of indecent assault. . . .

"What'll your mother say? That's what I said. My very words."

We came out at last into a narrow lane between high hedges intertwined with wild roses and honeysuckle.

"I've never been here before. Is this Foley Lane?"

"Lovers' Lane, you mean," she inevitably said. The woman had a distressingly one-track mind. Now that we were out of the shade I saw with a slight shock that she was old. The slim figure, stylish shoes and smart make-up had misled me. Her sagging neck and sallow face were lined with wrinkles. The hair must have been dyed. Its lustrous black had unconvincing glints of red, and there were white hairs close to her scalp.

"I see them, night after night, year in, year out."

"Who?"

"The couples. Who do you think?"

An endless procession of lovers, centuries long! Somehow the thought depressed me. Unexpectedly she opened a gate. The bushes grew so high that I hadn't seen it; or the disorderly garden plot; or the house, a low thatched dwelling of immense age and thickly shaded with lilac bushes.

"You live here?"

"I've lived here all my life off and on."

A lifetime, I thought, of peeping out from her uncleaned windows through the lilacs at the unsuspecting couples.

"Do you live here alone?"

It was not a question she would fail to exploit if only by another suggestive chuckle as she lit another cigarette.

"You'd like to know, wouldn't you?" Then, in a brief rational interval: "There's a gentleman lives here, when he *is* here; but he's in the Navy now."

It was amazing how through sheer curiosity all my faculties revived. So this was where he chose to live, with this slatternly hag of a landlady, in this picturesque slum, infested with rakish cats. There were two of them on the ridge of the wash-house roof. Not for him the seedy respectability of Jubilee Terrace where poor old Ferrars was content to lay his blameless head. *Our hero* would require a more colourful setting.

". . . I've nothing against your Victorian terraces and semi-detached red brick," I could imagine him saying as he lit his pipe, an old briar cherished from undergraduate days, "nothing whatever—except the neighbours. In a place like this one can do as one likes. . . ."

One could do anything, unobserved, within the murky

walls, under the thatch, behind the lilacs, between the deep hedgerows: anything at all.

"It's very secluded," I said.

"Five minutes' walk and you come to the road."

"Your lodger has kept on his rooms?"

I said it simply for something to say and was surprised by the change in her manner. Behind its smoke screen her face grew watchful, as if for the first time she recognised the presence of an interloper. When she spoke again it was more loudly and defensively, as though I had accused her of some irregularity.

"He wouldn't leave me in the lurch, nor wouldn't I let him down. He's a really considerate gentleman. 'You keep an eye on my things, Mrs Buckle,' he says. 'I'll be back from time to time. So long as the rooms is ready when I want them.' Ten shillings he pays me for when he's away and the usual when he's here. So long as the rooms is ready . . ." She repeated this more than once as if, excellent teacher that he was, he had nailed the instruction into her thick head and hammered it down. "If you're suggesting that I would let those rooms to another when I've promised . . ."

I assured her that the idea had not entered my head and she simmered down.

"As long as it's understood that those rooms belong to the gentleman that's always had them. I'm not the sort to take ten shillings a week from one and then let the rooms to another. Oh, no. Some might do it when he's far away and won't be back except now and then—if he isn't blown to pieces with one of them mines. . . . I've been in good service and know what's right. . . ."

Through the tangled hedge which separated her front garden from the back, a slight movement caught my eye: a white shape: a sheet hanging on a line. Stepping to the left, I saw that there were others: a row of sheets and pillowcases stretching out of sight. So many, and on a Sunday!

"You've been busy, I see."

She had been leaning on the gate in the attitude of a woman who had spent a long Sunday on her own and was disposed to chat. Now she too glanced at the clothes-line and stood upright. The cigarette between her lips stiffened and pointed at me suspiciously. It was time for me to leave.

"Your lodger must be Mr Westmain." I backed into the lane. "I know of him. I teach at the grammar school. My name is Borrow."

There was no doubt as to the change in her. Was she conscious of having talked too freely? She was suddenly on edge, eager to be rid of me. By remarking on the washing and establishing my connection with her boarder, I must have brought her too abruptly out of her private world of trees and cats and passing lovers.

"You won't have seen him lately." I stooped to disentangle my shoe-lace from a clinging briar. "I was told . . ."

She didn't wait to hear what I had been told and must have moved quickly. I looked up to see her closing the door from the inside with a distinct slam. An odd creature —and no wonder, living alone in such a place. One of the cats, prone on the wash-house tiles, eyed me steadily. With the door closed, the house had relapsed into its tangle of green. Beyond it there was nothing to be seen but trees. Their attitude was threatening, as if they had stopped just short of the garden and might change their minds.

Deep in the lane, I could see no more than a strip of sky. A morbid sort of place! A disgusting old woman! No better than a female Peeping Tom. All that rigmarole about ripped dresses and eyes starting out like hat-pins! Emmie had been right when she warned me that Kinning had not yet emerged from the Dark Ages—or even from the primeval slime, I mentally added with a superiority that seemed justified; but only for a moment. It would be only too easy to sink back into it. The threat of those pagan influences Emmie had mentioned was certainly there. Well, here, at any rate, in this God-forsaken lane. I felt it strongly.

Stepping into the open road was like coming up for air.

12

The prospect of making an introductory speech before the curtain went up at the Red Cross concert was keeping me awake at night.

"Keep it short," Emmie advised. "They'll want to get on with the concert. Nobody in Kinning listens to speeches anyway."

"It's got to be something worth listening to. I'd like to work in that quotation about a great people moving towards an unfeared future."

"Aren't you pitching it rather high?"

"I don't know where to pitch it. In any case I can't find the poem. It's by John Freeman, I think."

Emmie left me to struggle with yet another rough draft and went upstairs. A few minutes later she came back with a little green book in her hand.

"You'll find it in here."

"Emmie! That's wonderful. What a dear little book!"

It was a pocket-size edition of First World War poems, suede-bound. She must have bought it second-hand. The flyleaf had been torn out rather carelessly. "Is it one of a series?"

She shrugged.

"That's the only one I have."

" 'What-e'er was dear before is dearer now.' That's it. Marvellous!"

"Marvellous!" Emmie's echo was of the word but not of my tone.

"I'll finish this and then I must go to the station in case they've heard anything."

The non-arrival of my bicycle had become a minor scandal. My father had sent it off by rail in May, since when it had been seen no more. Letters and telephone enquiries had produced no information. It was now the second week in July. Hopes for its survival had almost faded. In the context of a world war, the loss of a civilian bicycle, even a practically new Hercules, must be seen as negligible; but everything not utterly demolished must be somewhere and —as I observed to Emmie—it would be typical of the way things turn out if it were to arrive after I had gone home for the holidays.

"This idea of a universal plan working against us," she said, "doesn't really hold water."

"Do you mean that it sometimes works in our favour?"

"I mean that there's no such plan."

"Just a lot of things happening at random?"

I hadn't expected her to take a religious view. As a matter of fact I was less easily impressed by Emmie's views than I would once have been. James's warning that she was not altogether to be trusted had been too mild to impress me deeply. It had not affected our day-to-day relationship, in which no issue involving trust seemed likely to arise. Besides, I rather prided myself on my insight into human behaviour and could confidently claim by this time to have got Emmie pretty well summed up as a frustrated and slightly embittered spinster well on the way to becoming an oddity.

Since that startling glimpse of her in her room, my respect for her intellectual powers had faltered. A deep thinker would not have behaved like that, I felt, recalling the day-long meditation of Socrates, upright and motionless in the market-place of Athens.

"Not entirely at random."

She was a trifle flushed after a long spell of writing letters. It was only recently that she had taken to spending so much time on her correspondence. Not having paid much attention to her during the past few weeks, I sensed vaguely that she had changed and eyed her covertly as she lay back in the wicker chair with the false Herbert in her lap. It was not unusual for Herbert to purr, but for Emmie to do so (there was no other way of describing the luxurious air with which she gave herself up to the very moderate comfort of that particular chair) was a new development.

"We are not the slaves of circumstance," she said. "One can make things happen."

"No one so far has been able to make my bicycle arrive."

Resolving to adopt a firmer approach, I doggedly made my way once more to the branch-line station, which in the inconvenient manner of its kind was situated half a mile from the last row of houses in Kinning: Mafeking Terrace. A face at an upstairs window of the Monds' house warned me that I had been seen. Knowing how jealously they were keeping themselves to themselves, I tactfully gave no sign.

"Miss Borrow." It was Delphine calling from the door. She came down the path. "I just happened to see you."

She was wearing a cotton dirndl skirt with her school blouse and had resumed the Ophelia style of hairdressing. It was obvious that she wanted to talk and could find nothing to say.

"Would you like to walk with me to the station? It's such a nice evening."

"Well, I would, really, but we might meet somebody—and it's so awful. They don't know whether to ask questions or pretend nothing's the matter."

"Are you on your own?"

"Dad's in London. Mother's gone to Millford. Aunt

May's going to look at the cards again." She had lowered her voice in a manner appropriate to the occult. "Celia and I never really believed in it but Aunt May swears by the cards."

"If it's a comfort to your mother . . ."

"It's a funny thing—how you go on hoping. It's not as if we knew definitely that she's dead. It's only that if she isn't —then where is she? So she must be." There was nothing I could say. "Would you like to come in for a bit, Miss Borrow, if you're not in a hurry?"

We went up to the girls' room where Delphine had been spending her solitary evening. *Anne's House of Dreams* lay open on her bed, the one behind the door. Celia's was to the right along the wall. It was strewn with scarves, gloves, papers and notebooks evidently taken from the open drawer of a chest.

"She liked looking at the sky."

There was plenty of it. The window framed a view of cattle browsing in level fields by the river: a secure and changeless scene, under the wide, changing sky.

"These are the things I told you about." Delphine fingered china ornaments on the mantelpiece. "The presents Celia gave me."

Cats, dogs, a rabbit bigger than the neighbouring camel, a horse smaller than the nearest dog.

"She was looking for a tiger."

I looked sympathetically at the gap where the tiger should have been.

"I felt awful turning out all her things." She smoothed the creases from a blue night-dress. "But I've been looking for her prefect's badge."

To satisfy some sentimental urge, I supposed, marvelling that it should centre on an object so impersonal.

"She used it sometimes as a brooch, and so far as I can make out she must have lost it and that would be why she took mine. Anyway, they've both gone."

"I thought the badges had to be given in at the end of the summer term. Why didn't Celia give hers in when she left school?"

"Oh, she did."

Delphine explained. The run-of-the-mill prefect's badge was a rectangular brooch of beaten pewter inscribed with the motto: "Semper Veritas." It was the property of the school. But those upright souls who wanted to carry a more lasting talisman into the world could buy a silver replica.

"Twelve and six, including the person's initials. It's mostly the girls. The boys don't bother. Celia wore hers quite a lot to fasten her scarf. Just before she went the last time, my badge was lying on the chest. There. I'm sure it was there. And when I came up after she left, it was gone. They look about the same, the silver and the ordinary ones. In a hurry she could easily think it was hers."

Our thoughts diverged. Mine found their way back to my glimpse of Celia clinging to her lover under the trees. Had she been wearing the badge then? Its stern reminder always to speak the truth had not prevented her from deceiving her family.

"Miss Butler collects them," Delphine told me woefully. "She'll be in a state if I don't hand mine in. I did write to Celia but she must have forgotten. There's no chance now of getting it back, so I thought if I could show Miss Butler Celia's badge and explain that it wasn't just carelessness . . ."

"Under the circumstances she'll understand."

We eyed each other dubiously. In the hot-bed atmosphere of school, emotions can rise to fever pitch over a missing scrap of paper. I could imagine the furore if one of the prefects' badges failed to find its way into Miss Butler's hands at the end of term.

"You don't know what Miss Butler can be like. The way she goes on when her temper gets up. Nearly as bad as

Miss Emmot." Misinterpreting my surprise, she added, "Well, no. Not so deadly as Miss Emmot. Everybody's scared stiff of *her.*"

"I didn't know."

"She's so calm, you see, when she's angry. At least you think so. Then, if you look into her eyes, there's a cruel little flame that withers you with fright." Delphine's shudder was her own, but not the phrase, apparently. "That's what Celia said."

"I shouldn't have thought Celia would ever be in trouble with Miss Emmot. They can't have seen a great deal of each other."

"Not in lessons."

"Out of school?"

"No. It was something about a book. I don't know what it was all about and neither did Celia. She was flabbergasted. It wasn't even a school-book, never mind a maths one."

"What happened?"

"Celia was working in the library—with some books in front of her—and Miss Emmot came in. She was walking past—and then she stopped and snatched up the top book. Celia nearly jumped out of her skin. When she looked up, Miss Emmot was shaking. She was pale to the lips, Celia said, but she never said a word. Perhaps with it being in the library, and the 'Silence' notice," Delphine suggested in enviable good faith. "But hatred and fury boiled out of her. She took the book away and never from that day on did she speak to Celia or even look at her."

She was obviously quoting again, having heard the history of this oddly silent exchange many times.

"What was the book?"

"Some book Mr Westmain had lent her."

I could only think that the book had been offensive in some way: so blatantly offensive that Emmie had recognised it at a glance and confiscated it in puritanical wrath.

It was not an aspect of her character I had seen or even suspected; and the book must have been pretty awful to justify the rage. Celia had probably exaggerated the incident. (Highly discreditable to Westmain, as might be expected.) On the other hand, I had seen how Emmie reacted to Celia's smiling "Good afternoon" when they met in the corridor. Four years—or more—seemed a long time in which to leave the hatchet unburied.

"There's one thing. Now that people think Celia must be dead, it's put a stop to some of the gossip. You know what they've been saying."

"People do talk at such times. They don't always mean it or believe what they say."

"I know Celia. My own sister. If anything like that had happened—" We were sitting on Delphine's bed. She lifted her head with a movement that might have been Celia's as with an effort she put the thing into words: the dread which in Mond circles would more often be conveyed by a hint or a nod. "If Celia was expecting a baby, she would have come home. She would have wanted us, especially Mother. And she wouldn't have been afraid. She was hardly ever afraid of anything."

I believed her. Whatever Celia's imperfections, she was not a girl to skulk. That was the strongest reason for supposing her to be dead. Suppose she were, after all, alive. I tried to picture her in a seedy London room: popping out to a dairy or tea-room, wandering in a dusty park, losing her looks. If she had got herself into trouble (to me too the vague phrase came more easily than the clear biological statement) or been got into it, would she not return to this cool wide-windowed room to lie on her bed, merge her spirit with the consoling influence of field and sky, and sink back into the simple world of Mother and Aunt May?

Especially if Naval Command had abruptly snatched away her natural protector at the very moment when she had discovered her state! In that case, how silly of her not to take her exams. Even if she had done badly, she would have gained a degree of some sort. He would come back, the unspeakable Westmain, and marry her. . . .

"We talked about that sort of thing when Mavis Dalkeith threw herself under a train. I said I wouldn't have dared do that even to escape the disgrace."

"And what did Celia say?"

"She said Mavis had no right to cause her parents so much suffering, worse even than the disgrace of having a baby."

It would be easy, head on pillow, eyes on the sky, to make high-minded pronouncements on the plight of another. One's own downfall might tend to cloud the issue. Faced with Mavis's dilemma, even Celia might have wavered between calm acceptance and panic-stricken flight. A sudden surprisingly vivid image crossed my mind as of a figure waiting in the wings to appear at a given cue: the figure of a terrified girl, dress torn, skin scratched, eyes starting out like hat-pins.

"Did Celia . . . ? Was there anyone . . . ? She wasn't engaged or anything?"

Between delicacy and subterfuge I almost blushed.

"Oh, no. Celia didn't care about boys. She always had so many. From being a little girl, all the boys liked her best. It was just an ordinary thing to her, to have them hanging round. She hardly noticed them. But I knew she'd be interested"—Delphine hesitated—"I hope you don't mind, Miss Borrow, but I told her, the very last time I wrote, about you and Mr Conrad."

"What did you tell her?"

"Well, I didn't know for sure because you're not wearing a ring, but everybody says you're engaged and we all think you make a lovely couple. I don't know whether Celia ever got the letter."

"It would have been returned to you if she hadn't."

Delphine opened another drawer and began anxiously lifting out Celia's winter pyjamas.

"Mother can't bear to look at her things, and at first I couldn't either, but in a way it's like having her here again."

To me it was a case of intruding on the privacy of a person I had barely known. A sudden revulsion at finding myself in this charnel-house of personal remains brought me to my feet.

"I must go, Delphine."

"It's been lovely to see you. And I hope your bicycle has turned up."

The station master had withdrawn to the house for his supper by the time I arrived, treading softly along the platform for fear of disturbing the profound silence peculiar to country stations between trains. But his son Denis was smoking a cigarette on the seat among the lupins and hollyhocks.

"You're feeling better?"

He was home on sick leave, having been wounded in the leg. Moreover, this was the unfortunate Parkinson, sandy-haired and blue-eyed, who had broken his other leg in the high jump and been obliged to hand over the Dukedom of Illyria to Westmain.

"Doing fine—and there's good news for you too, Miss Borrow."

"It's come?"

"It's in the parcels office. Dad's straightened the mudguard and tightened a few screws."

"Where on earth has it been?"

"Having a nice long rest at York as far as we can make out. Lord knows why. It's labelled clearly enough."

"I'll go and look. No, don't get up."

But by the time I triumphantly wheeled the bicycle onto the platform he had limped after me and was leaning against the weighing machine.

"Wish I could join you in a ride, Miss Borrow."

"You'll soon be able to."

"It's a date?"

"Yes, of course. Just you get well."

He had on the whole been lucky. The leg wound had probably saved him from a worse fate. He had been in action with an armoured brigade in Cyrenaica and from there had been sent to Greece: a mistake, according to Parkinson. He had taken some pains, on my last visit in pursuit of the bicycle, to extend my knowledge of military strategy. It would have been better if we had consolidated our gains and made an all-out effort to capture Tripoli before the Afrika Corps could land there.

"But they didn't ask me," he pointed out. In Greece he had been at once involved in a rearguard action as the Allies fell back before the advance of the Second and Twelfth German armies. It was near Mount Olympus of all places that he got his wound, serious enough for him to be sent home before the disaster in Crete, "where we really copped it."

His gratitude for having escaped was half-hearted. It grieved him to be out of things. There was very little going on at Kinning station.

"I feel trapped here. You don't see anybody. All the old crowd are scattered anyway. Bailey's gone—and Evans went down with the *Lancastria* at Saint-Nazaire. But what about Enderby, eh? DFC. Not bad."

He stepped on the scale and felt in his pocket for a penny.

"You've lost a lot of weight."

"It's the malaria. But I'm piling it on again." The coin clanged; the pointer moved. "If this leg would loosen up a bit, I'd soon be back with the lads. By the way, your lamp's gone."

"I never had one."

"Just as well. You don't want to go riding around at

night on your own." As if struck by some association of ideas he became serious. "What do you make of this business of Celia Mond? They say she's been killed in a raid."

"No one knows."

"It shook me when I heard, I can tell you. I mean—Celia!" His eyes were troubled. "As a matter of fact it was only a few days ago that I did hear. My temperature's been high for a bit and I didn't know what was going on."

"She was last seen on her way to London—from Cambridge."

"Then she must have gone back after I saw her."

"You've seen her—recently? Since you came back?"

"The night I came home. It was Friday—the thirteenth of June."

I gazed at him in disbelief.

"But that was the day. No one has seen her since then."

"Good Lord! I didn't realise. I must have been one of the last people to see her."

"Where was it—that you saw her?"

"Why, here." To my astonishment he indicated the spot where we were standing. "We must have travelled on the last train that night. They had brought me as far as Chesterfield by ambulance. I suppose she must have changed there from the main-line train. Sometimes it's just a bit quicker than going on to Sheffield and coming out by bus."

"You spoke to her?"

"Not a chance. I had no idea she was on the train until I got off and what with the crutches and Mum and Dad fussing about, I nearly missed her altogether. She didn't wait."

"She can't have seen you."

"Well, I don't know. It was half past ten but still light enough to see. There was nobody else there but us Parkinsons and we were making plenty of row. I wish she'd waited and had a word. Still, Celia never would look at me." He grinned ruefully. "I just saw her pass the ticket office and then she was gone. You all right, Miss Borrow? You look a bit pale."

The eeriness of this unexpected sight of Celia, as if she had reappeared only to vanish again, had caught me unawares. It was illogical—to be upset by the news that she had been seen alive.

"Life's a funny thing." Parkinson too was moved. "You never know these days when you're seeing someone for the last time."

"You couldn't have been mistaken?"

"It was Celia all right—and it wasn't her ghost, Miss Borrow, although I've heard of some peculiar things happening since I've been in the army. The next morning Dad found a half-ticket from London on the windowsill of the office. People do that if he's not here to take the tickets. We don't get many passengers here. It's mostly goods."

A half-ticket. Then she must have bought a return and intended to go back.

"She must have gone back on the main line," Parkinson said. "Pity she didn't stay in Kinning. She'd have been safer here as things turned out. A girl like Celia! It hits you, Miss Borrow, to think she's gone."

"Have you told the police, about seeing her?"

"No." He looked surprised. "I mean, her family would have told them that she'd been home, wouldn't they?"

"Yes, of course."

Only she hadn't gone home. As for her being safer here than in London . . . I left Parkinson rather abruptly, pushed my bicycle up the path and mounted. If the girl he had seen was indeed Celia, this was the way she would have taken. This quiet road should have led her directly to her home and the bosom of her family. Surely that must have been her intention. If so, then something unforeseen must have happened to her between the station and Mafeking Terrace.

It was getting late. In the failing light the wayside flowers had faded to a colourless blur. Ahead stretched a dull green vista of arching boughs. At any moment I would pass, if I had not already passed it, the exact spot where she had vanished. Once again it seemed to be my destiny to follow her.

It was then, absorbed as I was in anxious thoughts of her, that I experienced a curious little revelation. Metaphor became fact as I recognised the truth of what had begun as no more than a flight of fancy. The notion that she had gone ahead and was pointing out the way must have come to me unconsciously as we talked in the classroom, because that was exactly what she had already done. On the night of my arrival in January the girl I had heard singing in the dark farther up the hill could have been—must have been—Celia. "A lovely voice," Janet had said, comparing it favourably with the voice of the actress in the masque. It was typical of Celia to be elated by her private happiness in such unpromising circumstances. What other girl in Kinning would have been capable of imprinting her own brightness on the dark?

And then I saw her—about a hundred yards away—a white shape in the half-light like a cameo in an oval frame of leaves. I lurched to a halt and almost fell. This time she wasn't walking about but coming towards me: a light figure in a white blouse. Her fair hair hung in long waves about her pale face. She held out her hand.

"I was waiting for you, Miss Borrow. I've found it. It was under some handkerchiefs in her drawer."

It was a silver brooch.

"You startled me, Delphine."

"Thank goodness, I can show it to Miss Butler. Then she'll have to believe that Celia took mine by mistake."

"Of course she will. You mustn't give it another thought. It isn't important."

"I know. I can't think why I'm worrying. Nothing's important now. Sometimes I think they've heard definitely that she's dead." Her voice was laden with sorrow. "And they're not telling me."

"If they knew, they wouldn't keep it from you. Why should they?"

"I suppose they want me to go on hoping. But at times like this, when it's getting dark, I can't hope any longer. I know Celia is dead."

How can one know when someone out of sight ceases to be? A moth moved in the downward-flowing dusk: a creature so fragile as to be scarcely embodied at all, yet entirely alive. I felt the slightness of the margin between living and not living, and turning to Delphine remembered how vast the distance was.

Whatever had happened to Celia had happened here or hereabouts. There was a kind of consolation—at first—in the thought that she had come back, if not to her home, still to the country of her roots. The poise I had so admired was not sophistication but an inheritance from the long line of grandmothers Emmie had spoken of: deep-breasted, low-voiced women who knew the earth that sustained them; who would have ignored, if they had noticed them at all, the studious utterances of Emmie and Old Kitty, as they would have ignored the clucking of hens in the poultry yard. And if one had to die, would it not be better to be snuffed out among the poppies and moon daisies in the hidden corner of a field than to be blasted into oblivion in London?

To die! To come to an unnatural end in Kinning? How could such a thing happen? It was beyond belief.

When Celia had left home in April, she had gone to her lover. I had seen them on the fringe of Foley Wood. And before that, in January? Where could she have been going at that time of night a mile or more from her home and walking away from it? A left turn at the top of Kinning Bank would have led her into Foley Lane and the dark mysteries presided over by Mrs Buckle. And the third and last time, her destination must have been the same. Where else could she have been going?

"Listen!"

A dreadful sound had broken upon the quiet evening: a wild undulating call that curdled the blood.

"It's next-door's dog. It started doing it the night before we heard about Celia. It never used to."

A university education is no defence against the elemental. The mournful cry broke out again, and again my scalp lifted. It took a howling dog to teach me the folly of trying to reason oneself into comfort. The worst things could actually happen; they were happening all the time, at sea, in the air, in the desert, even at the foot of Mount Olympus, home of the gods. No one was safe, as Delphine had truly said, hurling her book from her in a frenzy of lost faith: not even the best person in the whole world.

I was not so demented as to rate Celia in quite that way. All the same, in the mood of superstitious fear that gripped me I was sufficiently unbalanced to feel my own safety threatened. If the girl who had seemed to show me the way had taken her chosen path and gone to her death, was it a warning that I must choose a different direction—or disaster would befall me, too?

13

At the end of term I stayed on at Bennets. There were sound reasons for doing so as well as others more dubious.

For one thing, there was the faint hope of a lightning visit from Cressida at the end of July. On the other hand, there would be no one at home in Chardon: my parents would be spending the next two weeks in Teesdale. Meanwhile someone would have to stay at Bennets to let in the plumber, who had at last nerved himself to look at the drains. Emmie usually spent the first half of her holiday in London.

I also planned to do six nights of fire-watching before I went home. Our statutory spell of duty was forty-eight hours a month, but during the holidays a special rota operated whereby we took several nights en bloc. A good deal of swopping went on. There was nothing magnanimous in my offering to take on three nights for Emmie. She would reciprocate by doing three for me in September.

We broke up on Thursday, July 25. The next day she left for London without saying how long she would be away.

"You'll be back before I leave?"

"It's hard to say when you haven't decided when that will be."

With this characteristically rational remark she placed her packet of sandwiches in her bag and departed in Miller's taxi.

But even without such perfectly good reasons for staying

on I would still have stayed, being quite unable to tear myself away: from Bennets; from Kinning's haunted woods; from James.

It might have been easier to leave him if all had been well between us. But we rarely met without differing as to where to go or drifting into depressed silences: a state of affairs common enough between lovers, had I but known it. Since there was nothing personal to quarrel about, we wrangled about the war, the correct thickness for pancakes, the existence of God, and even about Celia Mond, whom I couldn't help occasionally mentioning.

"For God's sake," James said at last, "if you can't talk about something more cheerful, don't talk at all." I had grown so used to his tenderness that its absence from his voice was as painful as if he had been deliberately unkind. Seeing my distress, he was instantly remorseful, kissed me and begged to be forgiven.

"What he needs is a change—and a rest from so much responsibility" was Mrs Conrad's constant refrain. Her eyes, which followed him anxiously, were turned more coldly on me. Nothing was said but I was aware of having failed in my allotted role, which had been to rescue James from the occasional bouts of depression he had suffered from childhood and which I privately diagnosed as the trauma left by his father's death. She had hoped that I would divert and keep him happy: like a geisha, I furiously thought, and vowed never to set foot in the Hall again. The next day found me having tea with Mrs Conrad much as usual. All the same I went less often and took to roving about on my own, by bicycle or on foot.

I was learning what it feels like to be haunted. One of its effects is to isolate the sufferer in the exclusive pursuit of one idea. In a way, James was justified in resenting my deep interest in Celia Mond, though he couldn't possibly know the extent to which she intruded on our privacy: that she made a third, as it were, in our embraces. From the start it was as a girl in love that I had seen her, a girl in an even more exalted state than my own. "And look"—it was impossible not to think—"where it's got her." (Where had it got her?) Naturally on these occasions James must have felt my absence of mind. It would scarcely have been surprising if he had also felt the presence that came between us. It is not only the spirits of the known dead that walk. Even more active are the spirits of those who from one day to the next may be thought of as either dead or not dead. In this state of mind I was best left alone.

My actual involvement in the mystery had at first been that of an interested observer. The discovery that Celia had last been seen not in London but here in Kinning made all the difference. What had seemed an unhappy accident now took on the colouring of a crime. I was well versed in detective fiction. So far in its total lack of evidence it had been not so much a case for Maigret or Lord Peter Wimsey as for Father Brown. Nothing but sheer concentration of a positively mystical kind could solve the conundrum. Concentrating on the matter was what I seemed to be good at and indeed could not help doing.

Somewhere within reach must lie some trace, some clue. I had time on my hands—and other advantages. They included a certain aptitude for finding things out. It was remarkable how I had sniffed out the love affair with Westmain. Then there had been the coincidence of Cressida's turning up to confirm that Celia's last disappearance had not been her first. I had even been in close touch with Milton, whose specialty it was to show how subtly evil practices can corrupt the good.

In deliberately poking my nose into the affair I was asking for trouble, and trouble on the whole was what I got. Only with acute discomfort can I look back on my activities as an amateur sleuth.

I began my investigation with confidence and had no difficulty in finding a path that skirted the meadow to the left of Station Road, by-passed the back of Mafeking Terrace, and wound its way eventually to Foley Wood, where the tracks—and the problem—became more intricate.

Which of the winding paths had she taken, assuming she had got this far—and why? Reluctantly, because it would have made things easier, I had ruled out an assignation with Westmain. He had telephoned Rokeby from London on that same Friday. Even for one last passionate reunion before sailing for Suez, he could not have risked coming so far. It would have been impossible to get back from Kinning and report for duty on the Saturday morning: unnecessary, too, for the two of them to travel north when they could have spent more time together in London.

It was equally imperative for Celia to be back in College on the Sunday, a day of infinite delays on the railway. For what conceivable reason other than love would she undertake the tedious journey to Kinning—and in secret? It occurred to me that they might simply have made a hash of their arrangements: had planned to meet and she had thought it was to be in Kinning. In that case she would go to the usual rendezvous, wherever that might be.

There wasn't much doubt as to where it was. Westmain's crazy landlady had obviously been concealing something. She couldn't have used all those sheets and pillowcases herself. Someone had been sleeping in Westmain's bed.

The Three Bears had always struck me as a horribly sinister tale, and Mrs Buckle's house, when I called there early one morning, had the air of having survived unchanged since Goldilock's last visit. The lover-frequented lane lay as still and quiet as the woodland glades beyond. Dew drenched my cotton skirt as I threaded my way to the front door between riotous beds of love-in-the-mist. Lushness, in these surroundings, was to be expected.

My knock roused Mrs Buckle from her bed. The door opened a chink. From under a tousle of hair she peered through it, clutching a skimpy pink dressing-gown that failed to cover her skeleton-thin figure.

"I wondered, Mrs Buckle, if you would care to buy some National Savings stamps. They're sixpence each."

Roused from luxurious dreams, she gaped uncomprehendingly at the contents of my open attaché case. My plan had been that while she went to look for her purse I would step inside and—well—just look round. I had chosen this early hour deliberately. If anyone did happen to be staying there, that person would still be indoors. In the evenings Mrs Buckle was always at the pictures.

It was, unfortunately, too early. Mrs Buckle needed time, on rising, to collect her wits.

"Stamps?" she croaked after a longish pause. "What do I want with writing letters? And if I did, the stamps at the Post Office would be cheaper than that."

"But these are savings stamps. You stick them on your card until you have fifteen shillingsworth and then you exchange them for a certificate."

So far as I could make out, though it was difficult to penetrate the interior darkness beyond Mrs Buckle's uncombed curls, the front door opened directly into a living room.

"It's for the War Effort. You see what it says." I produced a pamphlet. " 'Lend to Defend the Right to Be Free.' "

The slogan was altogether too rousing and at the same time too abstract for Mrs Buckle, especially in her present state. Yet the more romantic and sensual approach that might have appealed to her was not easily adapted to the sale of savings stamps.

"No," she said—and shut the door.

Next time I made an evening visit, late enough to catch her on her return from the cinema in a mellower mood (I calculated) and before she went to bed. I would step boldly inside and deduce from her manner whether or not there was anyone else in the house.

The smell of fried onions and a long delay before she answered my knock suggested that she was having her supper.

"Concert?" She looked suspiciously at the bundle of tickets I produced. "When is it? Friday?" She shook her head. "That's my night for the first house at Millford." With her tongue she pursued an unswallowed morsel of food. "You go about a lot on your own, don't you? You want to find yourself a nice young fellow to take you for a walk, eh?"

This should have been my opportunity to step inside with a suggestive leer to match her own, to humour her by chatting a while on her favourite topic and so draw her out a little. I hesitated. She closed the door once more and returned to her onions.

I put the tickets away. The likelihood of selling one had been small but it was exasperating to stand face to face with the person who might—just—be a source of information, without knowing how to worm my way into her confidence. The heavy make-up, I now realised, having seen her without it on my previous visit, was an improvement. At that hour of the evening the light had fallen more kindly on her face. She had looked deceptively youthful, as when she had first materialised under the trees when I was walking back from Bardslow Edge.

The details of that first encounter came back to me. There had been something odd about her from the start: a disillusioned mockery, as if the sight of a girl lost in the wood and running to get out of it was no more than she had come to expect.

Among the love-in-the-mist a cat moved. The evening was humid. In the lane a bramble sucker caught at my bare leg. I stopped to dab at drops of blood with my handkerchief and remembered the whole rigmarole about scratched skin, a torn dress, and starting eyes. There was a bit that I had missed. It had been lost in a series of wheezing coughs. The rest had floated from her lips in a cloud of smoke. I had dismissed it as some kind of fantasy or half-witted rambling but—could it have been a description? Had I reminded her of someone else she had seen; another girl in real distress? She had called out to her: "What's your mother going to say?" as if it was a girl she knew.

But when? I must find out at once. With my hand on the gate I hesitated. It could have been any girl in Kinning. It could have happened years ago: an ancient memory lodged for decades amid the lumber of Mrs Buckle's disorderly mind. It would not be easy to winkle it out from all the other unseemly scenes she had witnessed from behind her curtains as the long procession of lovers sauntered by. For all I knew girls by the score might have run out of Foley Wood in a state of disarray during Mrs Buckle's longish lifetime.

In any case the matter was altogether too vague and fanciful to be treated as evidence. It could have nothing to do with Celia. It didn't sound like her; and it didn't fit in with my theory that this had been a regular meeting place and that Mrs Buckle was keeping it dark.

A few penetrating questions could certainly do no harm. But not now. I turned away, defeated by the smell of cooking, the closed door, and by the place itself—overgrown, languidly still, profoundly secretive. It was getting late. I must come back and try again.

And yet the notion of panic-stricken flight stayed with me. Had not I myself been close to panic during my solitary walk through the wood? What exactly had I been running away from when I ran into Mrs Buckle?

With my back to the lane I could see nothing but trees. It was the trees that had frightened me with their size, their inhumanity, their suggestion of latent power. But the dim glades might harbour a worse threat than the elephant faces and leopard's haunches sculptured in bark: evil in a human shape to be fled from until breath failed and one sank helpless on the deep leaf mould.

A horrible sensation came over me, of being cut off from the sky; of being not only shut in but forever imprisoned by unmoving boughs. I could close my eyes and feel myself lying six feet deep under soil and fallen petals. I could almost imagine what it must feel like to be buried.

The sensation passed. I was myself again, alive and safe —and more than ever dedicated to my chosen task. Simply because I was alive and safe, I felt it was my duty to go on trying to find out what had happened to Celia Mond.

14

"Can't get into it. It's far too tight." Cressida struggled out of my pink Horrocks dress in despair. "You're thinner than ever. I saw that straightaway."

"Try this yellow thing. It's one of Aunt Susan's. I haven't had time to alter it."

"That's better." Cressida fastened the buckle, shook out her hair. "It's sheer heaven to be out of uniform!"

I tried on her WRNS jacket and hat and imagined myself in an operations room, coolly saving the odd minesweeper by a well-placed point on a graph.

"It's not quite you." Cressida gave me the benefit of her whole attention. "Too clear-cut and obvious. You don't fit into the mould. I'll tell you what: something in this place has changed you. No, not changed. Made you more so. You're more other-worldly than ever. Don't tell me. I know. It's James."

"Wish you could have seen him."

We went down to the front terrace and laid ourselves out sacrificially in the sun.

"He's to be the one, Kate?"

"He *is* the one. Absolutely the only possible one."

"But you're not engaged?"

Far *too* clear-cut and obvious: that was Cressida's one fault. It was no good trying to explain how irrelevant the formality of an engagement would be to James: how bourgeois. I hit upon the word with some relief. As for the greater formality of a wedding . . . With a faintly worrying glance at the future I struggled to answer truthfully without losing face and came up with nothing better than:

"Not exactly."

"Ah well, there's no point in tying yourself down. I rather envy you living here in this ghastly old place."

From time to time throughout the day we ate ravenously: eggs, tiny raw peas, morsels of cheese, porridge, vegetable stew—and talked unceasingly: about Life, about the extraordinary habits of all our friends, and, needless to say . . .

"No sign of her? Sinister, isn't it?"

I spared Cressida nothing, not even the howling dog, and when the recital was over closed my eyes, fagged out with the drama of it.

"I'm afraid Delphine is right," Cressida said. "If she was alive, she'd have been in touch with them by now. But how can it ever be known—without a body?"

"Don't!"

"You need to clarify your thinking, Kate. Not easy, I admit, when there are so many irrationalities to sort out." After a little silent sorting she went on: "There's one thing you don't seem to have thought of."

"Believe me, there can't be."

"I suppose you're quite sure about Westmain: that he really is the most unspeakable cad alive."

"Well, surely."

"Inconsistent too to add to his other sins. Granted he was in London while she was taking Finals—she can't have been with him unless she also sneaked away earlier in the week. Besides, having taken so much trouble to get her to that point (slaving away for hours in a classroom), can you imagine him letting her throw it all away at the last minute? Scratch the RNVR officer and you'll find the teacher underneath. Teachers never change."

"Those plums aren't a bit ripe," I warned her.

"I don't care." She took another from the basket. "I'm on leave, aren't I? If she was completely under his thumb, as you suggest, wouldn't all his influence, stronger even than his depravity and lust, have been in the other direction: to make her take the exams at any cost? If he truly cared for her, wouldn't he want to safeguard her future in case he gets killed? It's more than likely you know. The losses at sea are truly frightful. If he doesn't intend ever to marry her, then surely he'd be all the more insistent on her finishing the course, unless he really is the most awful hound. . . ."

I too bit into an unripe plum, chiefly to postpone the recommended clarification in my thinking.

"I think she'd be the sort of person to go her own way," I said.

"Perhaps. But you haven't exactly depicted her as a solitary soul dwelling like a star apart. Everything points to an absolutely sizzling love affair. You must be right there. But I can't imagine a girl like her being smitten by a randy, deceitful, self-centred, underhand—"

"And glamorous," I interposed guardedly.

"Goodness, I suppose so. He must be oozing with it to be so popular. It really is hard luck that you've never seen him."

It certainly was a weakness in my case against him that I had never so much as laid eyes on the man. My picture of him was pure collage. But then it was not unusual to form impressions and to pass judgement on people one had never seen. At that very moment the destiny of the entire world lay in the hands of men whom we knew only by the effects of their actions: and that was how I knew Westmain.

All the same a faint misgiving troubled me, such as an architect might feel on suspecting a structural flaw in the building he had designed.

"I believe you're right." Cressida spoke with sudden conviction. "About these plums."

"Oh, I thought you meant . . ."

"About him? No, I can't quite fit him in. Supposing the poor girl is dead. Accident, suicide, murder. None of them can be ruled out, but if any of them could be, I personally would rule out murder. Wouldn't you?" She gave me a shrewd look. "Admit it. You've wondered."

"Only theoretically. It's out of the question, isn't it?"

"Oh, I don't know. Passionate love affairs do lead people into extraordinary situations. Still, no one in his senses would murder Celia Mond—but of course there is another possibility. Do you think, with all his other attributes, Westmain may be insane?"

"Not a chance. He's far too efficient to be insane."

"They say it's very difficult to tell when a person is mentally unbalanced, until it breaks out in the form of some uncharacteristic behaviour."

"Such as . . . ?

"Well, anything. Something you would have sworn that person would never do. Or it might be something totally unacceptable that the rest of us, sane balanced folk like us, recognise as being right off the rails. There's no knowing who might suddenly . . ."

"Me, for instance."

"Or even me! Except that I genuinely have been elsewhere while all this has been going on. But apparently it's the obvious suspects that can be relied on to stay sane. It's never the eccentrics: absent-minded professors like my father or a lewd old witch like Mrs Buckle don't qualify as possible lunatics. Whereas your friend Westmain, looking like an advertisement for *mens sana in corpore sano,* might in fact be just the type to. . . . Only . . ."

"Only in this case, sane or raving, he was a hundred miles away at least."

"That's what I've been feeling all along, that she didn't

come here on his account. Isn't it more likely that she was the one to go off her head and put an end to it all?"

The awesome thought silenced us for a while. Such things were not unknown in Kinning: there had been Mavis Dalkeith, for one.

"It's odd that she took a long and awkward journey before doing it," Cressida resumed. "On the other hand, a primitive homing instinct might account for that. See Kinning once more—and die. That sort of thing. And in the circumstances her entire behaviour would be strange. I mean—this business of her running amok in the wood. When was that, by the way?"

"We don't even know that it was Celia." I regretted having included this particular red herring in my summary of events. "And according to Mrs B, it wasn't so much running amok as running away."

"From something or someone that had distressed her. Do you know, there is a factor we haven't even considered. We've ruled out Westmain though he was probably indirectly involved; we've ruled out enemy action though she could have gone back to London on the Saturday or Sunday; but what about some other sort of enemy? In short, another person altogether."

"The lunatic you were describing."

"Well, yes. A beautiful girl could have enemies. She affected you in an uncanny sort of way. In other souls less pure she may have roused an insane envy—or base desire, as she did in Westmain."

"I never want to hear the man's name mentioned again. He can be a homicidal maniac for all I care; and if he is, you can be sure that he'll outshine all the others. He'll be outstanding at it."

Cressida wasn't listening. She seemed lost in speculation.

"Another person altogether," she mused. "With a motive for destroying Celia—the ability to carry it out—the opportunity. That's what you must look for. The unknown human factor."

We wandered down to the old mill and bathed in the stream under the alders; came back for a tea of bread and treacle and went to the pictures to see Charles Boyer in *All This and Heaven Too.* Owing to the warm weather there was an unusual number of empty seats but three rows ahead of us in a dense cloud of smoke sat Mrs Buckle, taking her fill of the fictitious lovers before tottering home to observe without charge from behind her curtains those of flesh and blood who came her way. Glancing behind me, I caught sight of Greener in the back row with his arm round Brenda, who stared sceptically at the screen in unsuspended disbelief.

"A pastoral interlude!" Cressida summed up her visit. "I've enjoyed every minute of it."

Professor Paget came for her the next morning. We chatted in the garden while Cressida threw her things together. He had been lecturing the day before at an Officers' Training Course in Nottinghamshire and had not needed to come far out of his way. All the same he was apologetic about seeming to use his car for a private journey. The basic petrol ration had not yet been abolished. It allowed 150 miles a month; but in view of the risks involved to tankers and the havoc being inflicted by U-boats, it was not to be used lightly.

I hoped to make him feel better by telling him how much Cressida's visit had meant to us both.

"We're all so far apart these days. It makes us desperate to meet when we can."

"And you must keep in touch. The Russians are giving us a respite but it could still be a very long time before you young people can get back on course again. Meanwhile"—he glanced up at the house—"you've found a picturesque old place. You're not alone here?"

"Oh, no. I share the house with Christabel Emmot. She's a mathematician, too, by the way."

"The name's familiar! Ah, I know! Would she be at an examiners' conference in Manchester in June?"

"That's right."

"I saw the list of names but I don't remember seeing her. A gruelling time! Far too much to pack into one day, but nobody would have wanted the thing to go on over the weekend. Here comes Cressida."

He took her bag to the open car.

"Let me take a last look at you." She drew back from the affectionate hug. "Yes, certainly thinner. But lovelier than ever. Did I tell you that? Only you won't get too mystical and insubstantial, will you, Kate darling? Promise."

I actually shed a few tears as I waved them off. Ridiculous! But it had been touching, the reminder that Cressida really did love me. I had forgotten that talk could be perfectly open, confidences equally shared. But then I had known Cressida since the days when we stared at—or past—each other from our prams. There was no one in the world to whom I could chatter so freely, not even James. For the first time I realised how restrained I sometimes was in his company, how over-tactful.

As for Emmie, my confidential talks with her were entirely one-sided. She was almost too good a listener: brilliant, one might say, at snapping up trifles of information to add to the accumulation of knowledge she silently contained. She had imbibed with her cocoa a stream of revelations from my side of the hearth without offering so much as a drop or trickle in return. Strange to have lived with a person for six months and to know so little about her! Why, for instance . . . ?

At the end of the lane Cressida stood up to wave; then

they turned into the road and were gone, leaving me alone in my rural backwater; unsettled; at a loose end; with nothing much to do except to wonder why, if the conference had lasted only one day, Emmie had stayed away for five.

15

It must be evident by this time that a sober grasp of reality was not, at that period of my life and in that place, the keynote of my character. But in the affair of Celia Mond I did once try to give practical help.

At the end of term I had been paid two months' salary, for July and August. So large a sum of money (£38.5s.10d) rather went to my head; but acting on Emmie's advice, I prudently opened an account at one of the banks in Chesterfield and received my first cheque-book.

Without this additional incentive for making the trip, I might never have screwed up sufficient courage to present myself at the County Police Station.

"It's about Celia Mond," I told the sergeant in charge, "the girl from Kinning who is missing." And when he had written down my statement, my name and address and date of birth, together with Parkinson's address, "I thought it might help," I said.

He seemed less startled than I had expected: more interested in me than in the vital evidence I had come all the way from Kinning to impart. His searching look alarmed me. Had I in some way incriminated myself or, worse still, Parkinson?

"I just thought you ought to know." I fixed my eyes earnestly upon him even though I knew full well that the most innocent-looking people are always thought to be guilty, and was thankful to find myself back in the street without having been detained.

No, I was much more at home in the realm of imaginative surmise. I was convinced—and never lost sight of the fact—that some terrible thing had happened; but again and again reality lost its keen edge, blurred by the magical beauty of its setting. Catastrophes of whatever kind could not but seem less dire, for instance, among the butterflies and clover where I crouched one afternoon to gaze through a gap in the thorns at the back of Mrs Buckle's house.

Mrs Buckle was constant in her movements. On Mondays and Thursdays she went to the pictures in Kinning and on Tuesdays and Fridays to the rival cinema at Millford, which meant catching the five-o'clock bus from Kinning Post Office. This was Tuesday.

The back window slid open. Mrs Buckle was hastening the exit of one of the rakish cats. The time was four-twenty. At four twenty-nine came the distant thud of her front door. I gave her five minutes in case she had forgotten anything, then slipped between the thorns and let myself into the back garden by a much but imperfectly repaired gate.

Until a quarter of an hour ago I had not known that the window opened horizontally. Mrs Buckle had left it ajar, after ejecting the cat. The aperture was narrow, but so was I, and motivated by a compulsion strong enough to get me through a needle's eye.

The house was bigger than it appeared from the front, where its dilapidation was so remarkable that one could scarcely believe there was anything at all behind its tumbledown façade. But a new wing had been thrust out into the back garden no more than a hundred years ago; and to that, on the south side, had been added—within living memory by the look of them—another two rooms. The window through which I squeezed admitted me to a stone-floored wash-house with a copper boiler, a portable zinc bath-tub, and an open gully into which to empty it.

The latched door led to a scullery. Beyond that was a lobby where a door stood open to reveal the room within: brown carpet, folk-weave curtains, a leather-upholstered chair, and another of the reclining kind with brown velvet cushions and an adjustable back supported by a rod. A man's room.

I could be arrested for this, I thought, and without the least feeling of guilt, walked in. In the circumstances a small act of trespass—or was it housebreaking?—could surely be justified, especially if no one found out about it.

My first discovery was that I had underestimated Mrs Buckle. The room was spotlessly clean. Two silver cups for rowing, a brass coal-scuttle and pewter tea service, each according to its lights paid glowing tribute to the care she gave them. The door to the adjoining room stood open: a bedroom with a double bed; and here I did hesitate. It really was the most awful cheek. Besides, the shameful thrill of having come at last to the crux of the matter was not a feeling to be indulged.

Nevertheless I did take a few steps onto the blue carpet and surveyed two dressing-gowns hanging on the door, one tartan, the other grey Shetland; slippers under the wash-stand; a tobacco tin on the mantelshelf. (I had been right about the pipe.) Walking boots and a rucksack under a table reminded me of poor Rokeby. With the swift movement of a sleuth I threw back the honeycomb bedspread. The bed was made up; the sheets were clean but had, I thought, been slept in.

It may have been the thought of harmless, upright Rokeby that served to strengthen a mental process which the inoffensive contents of the room had already set in motion: a recognition of the absolute normality of everything I saw. What on earth had I hoped to find? Too much wandering about on my own in the heat was beginning to turn my brain. The sooner I got out, the better. If anyone did find out, it would be difficult, very difficult indeed, to explain what had possessed me to behave in this lawless way, especially as I was already known to the police.

His table stood in the sitting-room window; on it a lamp, a clean blotter, and a tray of pencils. I had expected him to be orderly in his ways. There were bills on a spike, receipted, judging from the topmost, which was for photographic materials. Specimens of his work framed in passe-partout covered most of the wall to the left of the window. Except for a ploughman with his team in a steep field, they were all views: light falling on a stream, moorland scenes, the turrets of a fortresslike building similar to the shooting lodge on Bardslow Moore. In fact I recognised the dragon-headed boulder where James and I had picnicked. So Westmain went there too.

And that was all. Nothing more ominous than the razors on the wash-stand, an unusual number considering they were in short supply. Just like him to be so well provided that he could leave behind enough for two men: two safety razors, a packet of precious blades, and a cut-throat such as my father used! But of the amorous deceiver I knew him to be there was no trace: nothing that could be recognised as characteristic of a lair or Blue Beard's chamber into which young females might be lured—other than myself. But then what traces of his indulgences would a philanderer leave when he went off to serve his country on the mine-infested seas? To my dismay I was conscious of something like a weakening: a disposition to melt. It must have been the sight of his slippers. It is difficult to look at a man's slippers and hate him.

I sat down on the edge of his chair and was confronted by the massed ranks of trees in Foley Wood: layer upon layer of living green spread above caverns and labyrinths of dusky shade. And I knew that things were not as they seemed. Beneath the reassuring normality of appearances some distressing abnormality lay concealed. The instinct which had brought me here was not to be ridiculed. If I was behaving strangely, it was in response to strange circumstances. In fact, taken as a whole, my view of the situation was to prove, with one or two glaring exceptions, more remarkable for its accuracy than its folly.

Every vestige of my civilised upbringing told me that it was time to go; yet I lingered, still unaware of the emotional minefield (the metaphor seems suitable) into which I had strayed. A certain closeness to the tenant of the room was to be felt, however unwillingly. We had, after all, a good deal in common. Being some years my senior, he had been luckier in one respect. His three long shelves of well-bound books were far superior to my paltry collection of poorly printed war-time editions. Alas, it would be a long time before the five million books destroyed in the blitz could be replaced. I ran my hand enviously along the uniform Oxford classics and was rather taken with a set of elegant little poetry books bound in green suede and evidently designed for the pockct.

Carefully, without a sound, as though through the pounding of the seas he might be listening, I took out the first in the row and opened it, as our devout elders used to open the Bible at random in search of a guiding text. The pages slipped back to show me instead the inscription on the flyleaf.

"To my dearest Edmund from your own Christabel with all my grateful love."

Christabel! Emmie! Emmie in love with Westmain! Impossible! She had never breathed a word of it. The date was six years ago. When had it ended? For of course it had ended. Hot with embarrassment, as if I had seen Emmie stripped naked, I replaced the book, resolving to intrude no further. But the resolution was beyond the capacity of flesh and blood to keep. Half a dozen flyleaves confirmed the message of the first; except—I writhed for her—the endearments grew more tender, more private. How foolish, how tasteless, to lay bare her passion in *books,* even if he never took them outside these four walls!

Considering my reckless habit of jumping to conclusions, I was slow to grasp all the implications of this astounding discovery. They came to me later. What I did notice was something about the books. They formed a chronological series of anthologies covering the whole of English poetry and were numbered from one to twelve in Roman numerals. Conscientiously restoring them to the shelf in the right order, I found a gap. Number eleven was missing.

Of course he could have it with him, close to his heart as he faced death on the perilous seas. My impression that the infatuation had been on her side was based only on the limited nature of the evidence: there was not a word from him. How could there be? But it didn't take me long to trace the adventures of Volume XI after it became separated from the rest. *Poets of the 1914–18 War* was safely back in Emmie's keeping, with the flyleaf torn out. Very likely Westmain had forgotten the inscription when he snatched up the book among others to thrust into the hands of his favourite pupil. "Here, you'll find what you want in these," he would say. What diabolical luck that Emmie should actually have found Celia using it in the library! Whether or not she knew by then that Westmain's eyes had strayed in another direction, the humiliation was enough to account for her silent fury, her ripping out of the page and . . . No. Much as the idea appealed to me, I couldn't quite see her hurling the book at his treacherous head. Besides, it was too small. A pity!

The smallness, the intimacy of the messages, their insistence on the privacy of the relationship, affected me like claustrophobia. I couldn't leave too quickly. There was no need to suffer the ordeal of the window. Mrs Buckle had left her back door unlocked. I walked out into the air, my cheeks burning. How Emmie would hate it if she knew I knew!

As for Westmain . . . Oddly enough, in view of this fresh tribute to his personal magnetism, he had ceased to interest me. Quietly closing Mrs Buckle's door, I forgot him, so completely had the focus of my attention been shifted—and to a point much nearer home. Unconsciously I had begun to think of her as Christabel, influenced no doubt by having seen the name eleven times in her handwriting; and as Christabel she was assuming a much more exotic character.

It was a relief on the whole to remember that when I got back to Bennets, she would not be there. When next we faced each other across the hooked mat, things wouldn't be quite the same.

16

Not that I had yet realised just how different they would be. For the time being I remained lost in the kind of confused thinking Cressida had warned me against. Indeed, from the muddle of impressions that absorbed me as I trudged unseeingly along Foley Lane, there emerged two or three of Cressida's own phrases: "Passionate love affairs do lead people into extraordinary situations. . . . A beautiful girl could have enemies. . . ." They were only generalisations: she hadn't meant to apply them to an actual individual. "Insane envy" Cressida had confidently said, was one of the undesirable reactions beauty might arouse.

Insane! The thought was unnerving. Madness could lurk, unidentified, unrecognisable, until it broke forth in some uncharacteristic act: something you could have sworn that person would never do—something much worse, obviously, than dancing alone in one's bedroom. Though that was unusual on the part of the person in question, in others it would be quite a natural thing to do, I told myself, remembering not only the incident but the curious repugnance it had roused in me at the time: the sense of something not just out of tune but worryingly discordant.

As a deliberately sane and practical gesture I thrust my hands into my skirt pockets, found a dusty cube of barley sugar and, sucking it, regained my own mental balance.

Bennets was in an inhospitable mood. The day was too

warm for a fire, the house too cool without one. The kitchen seemed to have slipped farther down the steep garden and smelt of soil, its small window green-shaded by inward-leaning ferns. In the hall, as usual, it was neither light nor dark. The uncarpeted stairs stained with permanganate wound up and out of sight in a half-spiral. Looking up, I saw between the oak balusters of the back landing a murky greyness emanating from the cob-webbed window of the low room containing nothing but the water tank; heard an unfamiliar drip and went up to peer ignorantly at the ballcock. Something else to tell the plumber about?

For all I knew the drip might always have been there and had become audible only in the unusual silence of the house after decades of tapping out its hopeless message—that Bennets was crumbling away. Not that it cared. Halfway down the stairs I paused to feel what I had more than once seemed almost to catch, the spirit of the house. But all I felt was its coolness. Taking the hint, I went out.

The postman, trudging up the lane with a parcel, was pleased to see me and no wonder: this was his second attempt to deliver it and his round was a long one.

"It's for Miss Emmot. You'll take it?" He handed it over. "Thanks, love. You're younger than what I am. It's nothing to a spry young lady like you to slip back to the house. I brought it this afternoon, but there was no one in."

"You should have left it, Mr. Boothroyd."

"Well, I would've done, but it's been on the way a middlin' time. It's from London—and I wanted to make sure there was somebody to take it in."

The package had a shabby look. It bore a Harrods label and felt like a dress. Emmie was evidently lashing out. Her wardrobe was pretty drab on the whole, with one or two surprising exceptions—not that I had penetrated to its depths the huge cupboard built into the wall of her room. Like mine, it reeked of damp, so that we had to hang out our clothes to air from time to time. The one attractive outfit I knew her to possess she had never worn in Kinning since I came: a soft green suit with matching chiffon blouse. It had dangled from the clothes-line outside the kitchen door one evening a few weeks ago.

"That's nice," I had called; but Emmie had been upstairs packing for her trip to Manchester.

And now she had evidently been spending part of her holiday and eight clothing coupons on a spending spree. I wondered why she had had the dress—if it was a dress—sent to Bennets, and glanced at the smudged postmark—July 2. The parcel had been posted well before the end of the term, yet Emmie had not been in London between Easter and July 25, not officially; not so far as I knew. In fact she had not left Kinning throughout the whole of the summer term except to attend the mysteriously protracted and increasingly intriguing conference. Could she have made the order by post?

I left the parcel on the hall chest and resumed my interrupted ramble. After all, other people's affairs were of only remote interest in view of the pressing nature of my own problems. A dull worry about James niggled constantly at the back of my mind; and almost at once came fresh cause for anxiety.

Turning into the road, I saw Mrs Conrad walking down the hill and went to meet her. There was no need for her to urge her thin legs to a quicker pace, as if there wasn't a moment to be lost. I recognised the hasty, erratic walk as one more sign of the fussiness that had grown on her in recent weeks; and the same nervousness drove her to burst into speech when she was still some distance away.

"I've been taking some table napkins to Sarah but she was out. I had to leave them on her doorstep."

"Sarah?"

"An old servant of ours. She does them beautifully and likes to feel that we still need her. But we entertain so little these days . . ."—she was flushed and breathless—"that there isn't much starching. When Sarah was with us we had two maids and a girl in the kitchen."

She had never before alluded to her servantless state, though she obviously hated domestic work and the Hall's eighteen rooms were more than she could be expected to keep clean single-handed.

"But there are advantages. We like being on our own. They do talk so much."

Did she mean that they chattered in the Hall or gossiped when they left it? It was unusual for a woman in her position to be without regular help even in wartime. There were plenty of local women who would be glad, one would have thought, to work for the Conrads. Before I could reply, she went on quickly:

"I saw you take a parcel from Boothroyd."

"It was for Emmie."

"You're expecting her back?"

"Not for another week at least."

"Not more, I hope. It isn't suitable for you to be there on your own."

I reminded her that I had been spending several nights at school with my fire-watching partner, Miss Butler, and that Sadie Peller, a young woman from one of the farm cottages who did charring for us, was sleeping at Bennets while Emmie was away.

"Very wise, although it isn't the same as having an older person like Miss Emmot, just to see that things go on in a suitable way."

She was inclined to harp on this theme, to my annoyance. In the eyes of the school governors Miss Emmot might be the soul of propriety, a staid and restraining influence on the giddy likes of me. But what about Christabel and her sultry endearments, not to mention her three days' truancy or the withering rages that paralysed her pupils with fright? Delphine's description had been graphic. I had been sceptical then about the cruel little flame in Miss Emmot's eyes and the hatred and fury that boiled out of her, but now I knew better. A woman capable of one kind of passion could be equally capable of another.

It seemed a long time since I had seen Delphine. After the ponds were dragged, she and her mother had gone to relatives in Devonshire for a change and rest before taking up normal life again.

". . . alone with a young man," Mrs Conrad was saying. "Girls don't always realise . . ."

"I hope you don't imagine, Mrs Conrad, that I don't know how to behave—with James, I suppose you mean."

Her concern for my moral welfare or for the social proprieties seemed to be belated—and out of character. The Conrads were unconventional compared with my own parents. Having quite unnecessarily thrown James and me together, she had apparently decided to reverse the plan. Was this conversation part of the cool process of rejection I had already noticed?

But she was not cool. She had stopped, so that I stopped too. Her thin neck was painfully agitated as if she were swallowing a series of unmanageable lumps.

"Are you feeling ill, Mrs Conrad?" I had already taken her basket and now looked round vainly for a possible seat. "You shouldn't have hurried. Here—take my arm."

"Oh, Kate!" At the sight of her tears all resentment left me. "If only . . . What a comfort it would be to have you for a daughter! The loneliness one can feel with no one to talk to!"

I drew her arm through mine, and since there was nowhere for her to rest, guided her gently down the hill. Did she mean a daughter or daughter-in-law? Had it been a hopeless longing or a wish easily fulfilled? A hint of resignation in her manner depressed me and so did the reminder that she could not talk to James. His embargo on pointless chat was altogether too lofty and pompous. Talking for the sake of it is not an indulgence but a necessity.

"You're too much alone up there. Couldn't you have someone to stay for a while?" The words were no sooner spoken than I regretted them. She might think I was offering myself. "A relative," I went on quickly, "or an old friend. My mother often has friends to stay."

The endless reminiscences, the little spurts of argument, the exchange of household lore which had annihilated me with their tedium, I now recognised as vital messages from one solitude to another.

"Your mother is a lucky woman. I envy her. From the beginning I took to you, Kate."

"Yes, we've always been friends, haven't we?"

"That's why . . ." The swallowing was resumed, as if things demanding to be expressed were being painfully restrained. "You and James . . ." She patted my hand.

"You mustn't worry. We're quite capable of sorting things out for ourselves."

"I wouldn't for the world have you hurt, nor would James, only . . ."

"Of course not. Now, I'll take you home—and I do want to tell you about Cressida's visit."

I prattled on until we reached the Hall, where I settled her on a sofa and made her a cup of tea. She had been sleeping badly. I left her for half an hour while I tidied the kitchen and came back to find her asleep. In repose she should have looked relaxed, but the anxious lines remained. It was a refined face with narrow cheek-bones and thin lips: not much like her son's. He must take after the Conrads.

Suddenly I couldn't remember what he looked like; could remember him only as a feeling, or rather as a series of rapidly changing emotions: and I longed for him to be there for one definitive moment so that I could find out once and for all what he was really like, what he felt for me and I for him. But all I could be sure of was the longing.

There was something exhausting—it was long past the time for my evening meal as I made my way back to Bennets—in this business of finding out about people. I seemed to be doing it all the time, as if I had no being of my own, only a pair of eyes (startled or even incredulous) and ears (pricked or even strained) to detect the amazing signals other people gave off. And yet there had been one such signal less than an hour ago which I had failed to pick up and which I remembered only a long time after.

But how interesting it all was! And how despite all my worries I loved the soft vistas of grass and trees, of pasture melting into wood, the green below, the fading blue above, the mist of hedge parsley, the ivy on Bennets' wall, the cool dim hall. I stood rapt in the centre of the house gazing at the hall chest as if even that humdrum piece of furniture had something to communicate.

The kitchen had continued to sink into the earth; had become a vault smelling of damp and ancient bones. Green shade had stolen the colour from the floor tiles. What was there to eat? I thought of steaks, of liver and kidneys, oxtail soup—and of how delicious cream crackers used to be when plastered with butter. I thought of millions of hens slaughtered to save foodstuffs, who if they had lived would have laid billions of eggs. I thought soberly of yet another omelette made from dried egg powder, which was all that Cressida's visit had left me.

Then unexpectedly my thoughts took a different turn. Into the silence came another of those signals, not from a person this time but from an object: the wicker chair. It creaked—and creaked again as if to recover its equilibrium after being released from the weight of whoever had been sitting there a few minutes before. Presently from above came the sound of a drawer being closed.

It caught me unprepared. Anyone might feel nervous on

finding a supposedly empty house occupied—by an intruder?—a burglar perhaps. No such thought occurred to me. There was nothing alarming in the discovery that Emmie had come back unexpectedly; and yet the slight quickening of my heartbeat and the faint tremor down my spine were uncomfortably like the symptoms of fear.

17

The sheer impossibility of behaving in anything but a normal, conventional way came to my rescue. Even so it was after an instinctive pause that I called out, "Emmie! Is that you?" and went slowly up, giving her ample time to desist from anything abnormal or unconventional that she might be doing. It was clearly a sign that I was going to pieces, this nervous feeling that she must not be come upon suddenly.

She was standing in front of her dressing-table, one of those with a sunken portion between two sets of trinket drawers and a long central mirror. It reflected a slim woman, still young, with thick brown hair, her arms and neck softly tanned. She wore a sleeveless dress of Wedgwood blue finely checked with grey.

"Oh, it's lovely!" I realised what had been missing from the hall chest. The wrappings lay on the bed. "You found the parcel." Her raised eyebrows reminded me that I had come in uninvited. "Sorry. The door was open."

"You like it?" She pulled out the full skirt.

"Mm. A marvellous fit."

"I had to leave it to be altered."

"They've been quick," I remarked falsely, "with the alteration. It must only have been a few days since you bought it."

Her movements were casual as she crumpled the brown paper with its tell-tale postmark and dropped it into the waste-paper basket. She thought me not worth trying to deceive while at the same time deceiving me as if I were. That nettled me. The separate flaws in her conduct fused to form a planned duplicity: the secrecy, the absence without leave, the endless letter-writing, the new frivolity. Good heavens! Could the affair still be going on, on her side at any rate? Supposing she never went to Manchester—Professor Paget hadn't seen her at the conference—but had gone to London instead. There would just have been time for her to see Westmain in that fateful weekend—and then to console herself after the parting by buying clothes far too young for her. It was pathetic. The difference in age between her and Westmain must be much the same as that between him and Celia.

"I've never seen you looking so—elegant."

"You've never seen me on holiday. In term time *I* have other things to think about."

Her emphasis on the pronoun was slight but it warned me not to go too far or even, just then, any farther. Where I found myself a minute later without knowing how I got there was on the landing outside her closed door.

A few minutes had served to establish the change in our relationship. The alteration was in me. It had begun in Westmain's room and had had time in which to fester; but it was as if she had known of it at once. Her reaction was to be characteristic; to remain as she had always been. The warmth of our comradeship had come from me. She had merely done nothing to spoil it: and now she had not changed any more than one changes when an intrusive fly, having circled aimlessly, begins to buzz. The creature can be disposed of.

The idea must have been there already waiting in my increasingly murky subconscious, the notion of a creature being disposed of. Possibilities, all of them unpleasant, had loomed as yet mistily like distant peaks in cloud, barely visible though known to be there. I think it was then, as I glared in concentrated thought at Christabel Emmot's worm-eaten door, that the possibilities grew startlingly less vague.

Once before I had stood here on the landing while she was in her room; but then the door had been open. I knew now why that extraordinary capering had been so distasteful: one of the reasons at least. The weekend break from which she had just returned was the weekend in which Celia Mond disappeared. Fears for her safety had distressed us all that day—except Emmie. Whether, as she claimed, she had first heard the news on the bus, or whether, as was beginning to seem likely, she had good reason to know of it already, she had certainly not been distressed. The trippings, as Milton would have called them, the outstretched arms, the swoop that put out the candle had not expressed regret.

More likely it was triumph—over some project satisfactorily carried out. Perhaps she had achieved more than her illicit trip to London. I considered the possibility that Celia had been decoyed into coming to Kinning. Fantastic as it seemed, it was the only explanation to have occurred to me so far as to why she had come.

"Someone with a motive for destroying Celia," Cressida had said. "The ability to carry it out—the opportunity. That's what you must look for. The unknown human factor."

I went thoughtfully downstairs. Whichever way you looked at it, the only person who had anything to gain from Celia's disappearance was not far to seek.

"And how is James?"

We had fallen back as usual on bread and cheese and tea. I was devouring mine, famished yet preoccupied, as she had certainly noticed.

"Er, fine, when I last saw him. He hasn't been home for a week."

"He's home now, or was an hour ago. We came out on the same bus. No, we didn't talk. He didn't see me until I got off."

Leaping from the table, I rushed upstairs to wash my hair, remembered that there was no hot water, and came down again to boil kettles.

"I was wondering why you came back. I didn't expect you so soon."

She didn't look up from her magazine.

"I wanted to make the most of the country while the fine weather lasts."

Making the most of it involved her in the long walks she so much enjoyed. Sometimes she vanished for an hour or two in a summer dress and sandals; sometimes in a sensible skirt, a jumper, and studded boots for the best part of a day. While James was at home I too was out a good deal. Emmie and I met occasionally at mealtimes, which became increasingly haphazard. The long talks had ceased. The keeping at arm's length was now mutual, my watchfulness as unflagging as hers and probably much more noticeable. After all she had had more practice. But we remained on polite terms and gradually my state of mind became more normal. Common sense prevailed. One had only to look at Emmie to see that she was incapable of the kind of behaviour I had almost begun to think her guilty of. All the same . . .

"It's time I thought of going home," I told James, hoping he would object. "I've only two more nights' fire-watching to do—and I'm not enjoying Bennets so much since Emmie came back."

I hadn't been able to resist telling him of her love affair with Westmain, though without mentioning the unorthodox way in which I had ferreted it out—or the suspicions I had been tempted to entertain. My nervous tone had certainly improved; I could see now how bizarre those suspicions had been.

"You mustn't fall out with her, Kate. The arrangement will only work so long as you stay on good terms."

This piece of advice worried me. He apparently saw no alternative to my staying at Bennets. Was it not time, I asked myself yet again, that marriage should be at least mentioned?

"I won't quarrel—and she never would. But I don't feel the same now that I know more about her. Oh, I don't mean because she's in love with Westmain . . ."

"Being in love is not a thing one can mind in other people."

". . . or even because she has never confided in me."

"As you presumably have confided in her."

"Only in a general way. There are things one never tells: things not to be put into words."

My mind was full of them. In every direction uncertainties hovered, defying speech.

"Doesn't that explain why she has never tried to?"

His willingness to gossip cheered me a little. His mood, for a long time sombre, had seemed more steadily cheerful during the past few days.

"Not altogether. She's deep, you see, and I dislike deepness—not depth—in a person."

"Shallowness is more to your taste?"

"Openness. When you don't know what's going on, you assume the worst."

We had come down through the pasture, crossed the stream by stepping-stones, and were sitting on the bank in the sunshine. On our left lay the southern fringe of Foley Wood; from the opposite bank green slopes mounted to Foley Lane. The murmur of water, the shimmer of dragonflies, the scent of thyme together evoked one of those moods one remembers when more important events have long been forgotten.

"You can be open, my darling, because you have nothing to conceal."

It wasn't true but I didn't deny it. James lay prone, his binoculars trained on a row of young trees where a sparrow-hawk had been hunting. We had watched it skim the tops of elder, hazel, and thorn—then dash into the woods to thread its terrible way between the trees. The small birds were in a state of continual unrest.

"People shouldn't do things that have to be concealed," I said sententiously, ignoring my illegal entry into Mrs Buckle's house.

"Has she—Emmie—done anything of the sort? A deed, as it were?"

"I don't know."

"Do you want to ask her? She's over there."

"Where?"

"Just inside the gate—under the oak."

"Good heavens!" It was involuntarily a whisper, though she could no more have heard our voices than we had heard her sandalled feet on the fallen leaves. She could have been there for some time, motionless. Her grey dress made excellent camouflage. "Watching us! Well, really!"

"Not us." James was looking through the binoculars. "She's arrived in time for the kill."

A scatter of birds had risen from the hedge as the enemy tore out of the wood, selected its victim and . . .

"He's got it."

We had only the river between us and the patch of turf where the sparrow-hawk made its meal, both feet on its prey, a hedge-sparrow imprisoned between the strong lowered wings. The creature's helpless fluttering was soon over as the ferocious bill ripped off feathers and plunged deeper to rend its living flesh.

"Let me see."

James handed me the binoculars. I adjusted the lens; looked first at the hawk; saw with dismay its raised head and pitiless orange eyes before they were bent again and the fierce tearing was resumed. Then I turned the glasses towards Emmie; found her face. . . .

It should have been familiar, too familiar to be of any interest; a face too thin, too thoughtful to do more than suggest the beauty it had somehow just missed or the charm a different range of expression would have given it. Having lived with it for more than half a year, I had stopped noticing it.

But now through the new medium of the binoculars, which detached it from her body like a severed head, I saw a different face: intent, Medusa-like under its snaky brown locks, lips parted, light hazel eyes blazing with more than interest in the bloody carnage on the grass.

She was enjoying it.

"Here." After a sickening moment I lowered the glasses. "I don't want them."

Turning on my back, I looked up into the gentle sky. The slaughter had been only natural in the sparrow-hawk; and evidently it was natural for human beings too to uncover in private their darker side. One must not assume that because a person relished the spectacle of bloodshed that same person would ever *act* in such a way. He—or she —might want to perhaps, and the enjoyment in such a case would come from a desire successfully repressed.

The psychology lectures I had scornfully attended were proving useful after all; but how pallid their content seemed in comparison with the scene we had just watched. And one could never be sure, especially about quiet people in whom suppressed impulses might simmer away harmlessly for years before erupting into strange and violent acts.

"No sane person would behave like that bird."

The remark was ill-considered or rather not considered at all; a clear example of wishful thinking that had found its way to my lips as the unconscious outcome of a series of unpleasant ideas. It coincided with an extraordinary piece of behaviour on the part of James. For a few minutes I had forgotten him, though conscious of his rigid attentiveness as he sat, palms pressed to the ground. All at once a stifled exclamation, little more than a quick intake of breath, made me turn to look at him. The rigidity had turned to trembling. His face was dewed with perspiration.

"James!"

I had barely time to be alarmed by his sickly greenish pallor before he sprang up—literally came to his feet in a single movement—and, impelled by the same abnormal release of energy, leapt to the water's edge, seized a heavy stone and hurled it at the hawk.

Startled by the flurry, the bird was already gone, leaving a gory mess of feathers and tiny bones. The other witness, I saw with relief, had also disappeared. The stone had fallen far short of its target. Even so it had travelled much farther than might have been expected, as if James's frenzy of revulsion had given him superhuman strength.

He stood with his back to me, staring down at the water. I went and put my arm through his and was close enough to feel the painful thumping of his heart.

"Horrible!" I said. "Wasn't it? One needs to see it at close quarters to understand the beastliness of it."

And it was happening all the time. Beyond the horizon, above the clouds, on and under the sea the carnage was going on, all the more terrible because so much of the killing was at long range, organised, rationalised, as the hawk's ferocious commitment to necessity could never be. The friends I had danced and played tennis with, talked and laughed and argued with had mysteriously been transformed into the killers and the killed. My limited vision could not encompass the vastness of the destruction we were all involved in; but some notion of immeasurable ruin overwhelmed me with a feeling of darkness as if a dense cloud had blotted out the sun.

Then I saw the innocent stream still flowing clear and

bright between the cresses: the sunlight through a dragonfly's gauze wings; the trees serenely still and heavy with the foliage of high summer; and I felt James dearer to me than ever after his useless protest. Self-revelation was a weakness he contrived as a rule to avoid. This lapse had been like the brief lowering of a mask. It taught me how little I still knew of him, though I had always sensed that his poise was not the outcome of a natural balance of temperament but the product of a strict control: unnecessarily strict, I thought.

"But you didn't need to be reminded," I said. "You've always seen the obscenity of it—the impossibility of ever doing it."

"Doing what?" The mask was in place again but a faint pressure of his arm drew mine closer to his side in the ghost of a caress.

"Killing. You said you never could. That's one of the things I love you for—just one of the things."

"Oh, Kate." He drew away as if shaking himself free, not altogether playfully. "Why do you think so well of me? It makes me feel ashamed. Don't you know—you love me because it's your nature to love, not because there's anything in me worth loving. Don't make me out to be better than I am." He seemed to speak out of a deep sadness. "The impulse to tear each other apart could be in any of us."

"I honestly don't think it's in me, nasty as I am, or in you."

"Speak for yourself."

We shared the unspoken decision to leave, but without recrossing the stream. Instead we scrambled up the steep bank and took one of the paths that twisted with many intersections through fields and copses.

We walked slowly, hand in hand, still without speaking, until the silence became significant as if the first of us to break it would set in motion some momentous change.

Having closed a gate behind us, we turned with one accord to lean over it and look back. It was a secret place, a hidden hollow among lush fields that leaned to enclose us in their unbroken quiet. Moon daisies shimmered in the long grasses and there were poppies and wild scabious in the deep tangle of growth at the field's edge.

James had laid his hand on mine as I gripped the gate. Never in all the time we had spent together, not even in the closest embrace, had we been closer. He felt it too.

"Kate." He took me in his arms and looked down at me with a new kind of gentleness: whole-hearted, with no teasing in it. "My dearest Kate." Had I not been perfectly sure that he was going to ask me to marry him, I would have thought his voice and manner sad again, sadder than ever. "What incredible chance brought you into my life, out of the dark? If I had never met you . . ."

He stooped and kissed me. It was an undemanding kiss of tenderest love. Many a time I have thought of it and the meaning of it. It certainly didn't mean that he was going to say what I had hoped—not yet—if ever. The moment held no promise of wonderful things to come. How could it, when the very air was heavy with the threat of things coming to an end? Even then, with no more than a foreshadowing to warn me, my heart ached with the sense that the flowers, now in their fullest bloom, could only fade: the leaves had no richer green in store; the river would murmur on, heedless of who came and went. The highest point of happiness was now, was already passing, had passed.

When every nerve, every impulse told me that we belonged together and that he knew it too, the kiss had in it something of the heartbreak of farewell.

18

"So you've decided to stay."

Across the kitchen table she observed me, weighing up the possible reasons for my change of plan; so that there was no need for more than the dispirited nod which was all I could manage. She returned to the letter she had been reading. Leaning on my elbows, I made an awning of my joined hands and watched her from under it as I had watched her through the binoculars. The contrast between the pensive calm of the face by the teapot and the fierce interest of the face under the oak tree made me wonder if I had been mistaken or if James, too, had noticed her expression.

At the thought of him my spirits sank again into the misery that had kept me awake most of the night; needlessly, I reminded myself. James loved me more than ever, as I loved him. The deepening of our love was mutual. We had passed through a period of discord and emerged into a new certainty. What earthly reason was there for being miserable?

"You haven't eaten anything," Emmie remarked as though making a note of some less than interesting statistic.

It was not that I pined for marriage itself. Indeed I was happier to envisage domestic life as a future rather than an immediate blessing. But it was time—more than time—for the future to be talked of. The longer the subject remained undiscussed, the more heavily it weighed on my mind; the more impossible it became to mention it. Obviously then to leave James for a whole month at this critical stage was out of the question, even though a painful restlessness was turning the long hours without him into meaningless tracts of time and all my busy little activities had ceased to interest me.

Slumped over the breakfast table, I contemplated with distaste the day ahead, gulped another cup of tea, and forced myself into action. It was my turn as housekeeper. We took alternate weeks.

"You'll be in for lunch?"

"I think not. I'll take a picnic. Don't bother. I'll do it."

Half an hour later she left, pausing at the door to call out: "I haven't put my pound in the tin. If you're short, there's my handbag upstairs."

Since this was the soft-fruit season, we had taken our jam ration in the form of extra sugar. I spent the morning making jam, ran out of jars, and was faced with the problem of what to do with the four inches of sticky substance cooling wastefully in the pan. Hastily covering it to keep out the wasps, I went up the garden to the Pellers' cottage, where Sadie produced three jars. I sat on the step while she obligingly washed them for me.

"Saw Miss Emmot go off again in her boots. She's a regular hiker, isn't she? All on her own as well. You should have gone with her. It looks like being another nice day and I could turn out the downstairs if you were both out."

She brought the jars, stepping from the dark kitchen where she spent most of her time and looking round as if surprised to find daylight. Yet she was a fresh-coloured girl with the luxuriant brown hair and soft slow speech typical of the women of Kinning.

"She's a rum 'un, Miss Emmot. I thought you'd done her a bit of good, brought her out of her shell a bit; but I don't know. . . .There's more there than meets the eye.

That's what father said when she walked past this morning. 'What's she up to,' he says, 'wearing out good shoe leather?' 'If you want to know that you'd best ask her,' I says, 'it's more than I durst do.' There's half a dozen eggs for you, Miss Borrow."

"Sadie! Are you sure?"

"I'll bring them over this afternoon."

"No, I'll take them now and fetch some money. I wanted to settle with you for this week anyway and I may not be in this afternoon."

With the jars poised on three fingers and the bowl of eggs in the other hand I went back to Bennets. There was only half a crown in the cash box in the dresser cupboard and in my enthusiasm for my new bank account I had left myself short of cash and was down to my last ten shillings. In any case we tried to keep the housekeeping money separate from our private purses. But before I could run upstairs to collect Emmie's contribution, the darkening syrup in the jam pan demanded attention. Recklessly I added water, moved the pan back to the stove and stirred vigorously until its contents began to rise and fall sullenly like molten lava seeking a mountain slope down which to ooze.

There were two handbags. The one on the dressing-table was Emmie's best: a stiff, wide-bottomed snakeskin with a fastening of twisted knobs. Even with her permission I felt uncomfortable about opening it, but its contents were impersonal: a slim black engagement book, her identity card, a gold pencil, a compact in a black velvet case—but no wallet. Her everyday brown leather bag was equally uncluttered by the kind of debris I lugged about in my own; and in it I found a single pound note between the sides of the wallet, as if she had intended to bring it downstairs and had forgotten.

Had she also forgotten, in giving me the freedom of her handbag, something else it contained: a rectangular metal object shining dimly in the loose folds of a handkerchief? "Semper veritas," it said.

It could be anybody's. People were forever losing things; other people were continually finding them. There were twelve prefects, any one of them more than likely to shed a badge; but not since the end of term, when all the badges but one had been given in.

"Oh well," Miss Butler had sniffed, "in the circumstances I couldn't very well say anything. Those badges are school property and I have been put in charge of them, but what can I do if the prefects will not co-operate? Delphine's story was that her sister had taken her badge by mistake. She showed me the silver one. 'Take it away,' I said. 'It doesn't alter the fact that yours is missing. That one belongs to your sister, wherever she may be. She's paid for it.' But I must say it was careless of Celia Mond to pick up the wrong one. Nobody could confuse silver and pewter. You can see the difference at a glance."

Actually you couldn't. The metal down there in the depths of Emmie's handbag could have been either. I pulled it out warily, as if it had been a grenade. The pin was missing. On the back had been pasted a Cash's name tape with the name in red letters: D. Mond. The badge was made of pewter. It was the one Celia had been wearing when she left home.

Hard and cool, it lay in my hand, the one material link with Celia Mond since she disappeared. So far there had been only guesswork, much of it fantasy. This was real. She had handled it, worn it.

It was only a moment before she withdrew into the shadows where she now belonged; before I told myself that the reappearance of the badge proved nothing except that she had parted company with it sometime after she left home at Easter: either at the end of the vacation, before she went back to her college, or after she came back to Kinning on June 13.

But how on earth had Emmie got hold of it—and when? Since the end of term she had been absent from Kinning until her unexpected return. To have found the badge within the last four days and not to have mentioned it was unforgivable: she knew my interest in the Monds. If, on the other hand, she had found it before the end of term, she would surely have said so and put Butler's mind and Delphine's at rest;—depending, of course, on the circumstances in which she found it.

Suppose, for instance, it had been not only the badge that had fallen into Emmie's hand, but with it, Celia. I sank down on the window-seat with a sudden weakening of the knees. I must not be so foolish as to suppose anything sensational. Impossible to imagine Emmie clawing the badge from Celia's bosom with impassioned hands before strangling her with the loosely hanging scarf! All the same I did imagine it. Few things are unimaginable.

I leaned back in the deep recess, overcome by a fit of homesickness—for the flash of gulls' wings in sunlight, for the freshness of a cool day by the sea and stretches of damp sand with every footprint as clear as the foot that made it. Here one looked out on fields falling to the valley bottom in a warm haze and saw nothing clearly. Earth melted into sky and tree into tree. Alone in the wood, one became aware of company, a woman watching from the green shade. People emanated from the landscape and disappeared into it, beckoned by mysterious shadows.

Yes, it was tempting to think of Emmie as a beckoning shadow. Her methods would always be subtle, her movements meticulously planned and quiet. What, at her worst, inspired by insane jealousy, would she be capable of? Violence would not be her way. It would involve her too closely, be too soon over. Horrible thought! Her style, supposing her in this mood of limitless conjecture to be a criminal, would be to submit her victim to prolonged mental distress: to shut her away from normal life.

Involuntarily I glanced at the cavernous wardrobe where in accordance with the defence regulations Emmie kept her maps locked away, and got up, preparatory to edging past it. The movement cleared my head and rescued me from unwholesome mental adventures. But there was no escaping facts. Emmie had been inexplicably absent from home when Celia disappeared. She had a strong motive, jealousy; the necessary streak of cruelty; and—with a shudder I remembered the wild movements of her limbs as she danced—perhaps the touch of insanity that alone could turn motive into action. And now, here in my hand, was tangible evidence that she had been in direct contact with Celia. . . .

All at once mystification seemed to have taken on a physical shape—out there on the landing. A tall blue column of vapour rose from the curving staircase like a genie from a bottle. Bennets was disintegrating at last in a pungent stench of caramel.

It took nerve to edge the red-hot jam pan from the hotplate. When it was cool enough to handle I dumped it at the top of the garden. What did a ruined jam pan matter, I mused, as it sizzled quietly among the nettles, or even the loss of two sugar rations, when thousands of people in London alone had lost their entire homes: when libraries, churches, cloud-capped towers and gorgeous palaces were everywhere being reduced to dust and blown away?

At the soft sound of a footfall behind me my flesh crept. I turned.

"I see you've been making jam," Emmie said.

"Some of it's all right." Then, cutting at last through the miasma of suspicion and concealment, I blurted out:

"You've been keeping things from me, haven't you? All the time. But I've found out." She drew back, startled. "You said I could take a pound from your bag. I couldn't help seeing what you had in it, hidden in a handkerchief. And I must say"—between indignation, excitement, and a dismal attempt at sarcasm, my voice must have been shrill —"it seems rather odd to hide something that could be a clue—the only one so far—as to what happened to Celia Mond."

19

"Oh, that! I thought at first . . . You mean Delphine Mond's prefect's badge."

The quietness of the question was effective. It implied that a return to reason was desirable and must not be postponed.

"Why didn't you tell me? You don't say anything. Why do you keep everything to yourself? Can't you see it makes me wonder . . . ?" So swiftly had her tone and manner restored a rational atmosphere that I floundered, unable to find my bearings; crushed, too, by a calmness of authority in her presence which in her absence I had forgotten. The sinister personality I had fabricated vanished as in a puff of smoke. What remained was a civilised human being, not so much incapable of the dark deeds I had suspected her of as not needing or wanting ever to act in such a way. Nevertheless, if only to save face, I persisted. "The badge? How long have you had it?"

"Since yesterday."

Deflated, I clapped my hands to my temples and looked round distractedly, avoiding her face yet inwardly thankful that, knowledgeable though she was, she would never know the awful thing I had suspected her to be concealing.

"I believe you think I murdered Celia Mond," she said. "Shall we sit down?"

She took me by the elbow and guided me to the seat

under the apple tree, where to my further shame I burst into tears.

"You'll feel better in a minute."

"I forgot to have any lunch—and the beastly jam . . . The stove's in the most awful mess."

"You've been working yourself up into some sort of state for a long time."

"It's this wretched mystery," I said quickly in case she should think my emotional state had anything to do with James. "I keep on thinking about her."

"So do I."

She undid the knot in her left bootlace, unhooked it, and eased off the boot. Her answer had taken me aback, but now that my criminal investigation was collapsing in ruins it was hard to recognise amid the rubble a single item that might be significant. How could that be when a few minutes earlier there had been so many?

"I didn't know. I mean, I formed the impression that you didn't like her."

"The impression was correct. I detested her. But that doesn't stop me from wondering, or caring, what has become of her."

She began on her right boot while I strove to put my thoughts in order and as usual seized on the least rational element in her last remark.

"Detested? She didn't seem a person to detest."

"How well did you know her?"

My self-respect had already suffered more than one blow. Emmie's simple question came near to annihilating it altogether. For the life of me I could not have given the truthful answer: "Hardly at all." The shock of discovery kept me silent. The character I had created was based on one short meeting, a glimpse of her clinging to her lover, a visit to her room, a few facts culled from Delphine about the sister she idolised. The rest was pure speculation.

Humiliated, I studied the dust on Emmie's boots and a

thin place in her right sock which would soon become a hole. All the same . . .

"You must have had some reason for detesting her," I felt entitled to say, recalling the tell-tale inscription in the book, which Celia must presumably have seen.

"Not necessarily. Dislike can be instinctive, can't it?"

"And so can liking. That was the effect she had on me."

"Which shows what different people you and I are."

"And tells us nothing about her."

" 'Detest' was too strong a word." The thoughtful crease between her brows had deepened. Otherwise, I perceived for the first time, her looks seemed to have improved. "Celia Mond always irritated me, even when she was in the first form, and as she grew, the irritation grew—and made me angry."

Because it intruded on her detachment, I supposed. She would have preferred to ignore a pupil she could not like, and Celia must always have been impossible to ignore.

"Irritation is the last thing I would have expected," I said. "She was so . . ." But I was neither in the mood nor in the right company to enlarge upon the limpid loveliness of Celia Mond. "So full of light," I might have said, however inadequately, to anyone but Emmie; so that I was surprised when she said:

"Smugly enclosed in her own bright self. There was a kind of obtuseness at the heart of all that beaming and glowing—a hard little core one guessed at but could never reach. I suppose it was the inevitable by-product of her unbroken personal success. Everything had always been in her favour and that must cause a thickening of the sympathetic arteries—a coarsening of the sensibilities. No one ever found fault with her. She just didn't know what life is like for ordinary people. How could she? Most of us spend our lives struggling against one setback after another. For her nothing ever went wrong."

"But now something has. She's made up for being so

detestably successful," I said bitterly, wondering yet again how and where and why she had at last come to grief. "You're right. I never knew her, although funnily enough, she was the first person I was aware of in Kinning, the night I came. She was walking up the hill ahead of me, singing. At least I'm pretty sure . . ." Emmie nodded. "You knew?"

"When I heard the bus go past the lane end without stopping, I walked along to the road thinking you might have got off at either the top or the bottom of the hill. I heard her and recognised the voice. Just like her."

"I've often wondered where she was going."

Emmie hesitated. I turned and she looked quickly away.

"There was only one place she could be going to," she said—and seemed to feel an awkwardness. Out of respect for her feelings I forbore to ask what place that could be. She had been more informative than usual, but in speaking of Celia she had given no hint of any rivalry between them. My conclusion that there remained a good deal she had not told me was to be justified, but I was still very far at that time from grasping its painful irony.

"So you've been . . ." I mopped my eyes, smoothed my hair and sat up.

"Prowling round? Yes. You see, it intrigued me. A puzzle must have a solution. I thought all along that the answer must be here"—she indicated the drowsy countryside—"somewhere."

Had it become for her some sort of holiday task, like a superior kind of crossword puzzle or a mind-defying mathematical calculation: a cerebral process, nothing to do with the feelings that could on occasion seethe within her sedate person? I couldn't be sure. She had used the past tense too, as we had done throughout our discussion of the missing girl, as if the incident was over, the conundrum solved.

"Have you found the answer?"

She seemed uncertain how to reply. Her shrug was negative. Heaven knows I should have learned by this time that my powers of intuition were faulty instruments with which to probe into other people's minds. All the same I felt some change in her—or, as she gave me a sideways look, a change in her attitude to me.

"I don't suppose you thought of Mrs Buckle," I said, treading carefully.

"I've thought of everything."

Her capacity for thought, its energy and thoroughness were so much greater than mine that the words impressed me as somehow ominous, especially as they were accompanied by another barely detectable rift in her detachment, as if she might be sorry about something.

"I had a feeling she was concealing someone," I said.

Emmie shrugged again. "If she was, there's no getting it out of her."

"You tried?"

"I knew it would be a waste of time. No, I just walked in when she was at the pictures and took a look round. She leaves the back door unlocked."

"Really?" I said disingenuously, and ventured to add: "Why did you think of Mrs Buckle?"

"Because of certain associations I'm not going to talk about."

"It isn't right, though, is it, if she knows something that may be helpful to the Monds . . . ?"

"The Monds," Emmie said, "would not be the people she would be interested in helping."

"And was that where you found the badge? At Mrs Buckle's?"

Her investigation had almost certainly been more systematic than mine and must have included a careful search of drawers and cupboards, the turning up of rugs . . . or so I supposed. I was still far astray, as her next words made clear.

"The badge? I didn't find it. It was given to me."

"Someone else found it? But who?"

"A pupil of yours. Mackay."

This unexpected change of direction brought me to the edge of my seat.

"How on earth does he come into it?"

"I happened to see him yesterday when I was walking up to Bardslow Moor. He's staying on his married sister's farm, where you strike off from the bridle-path onto the moor. The path skirts the farmyard and goes up the hill. He asked me to return the badge as he won't be coming back to school."

"Did he tell you where he found it?"

"On the hillside behind the farm. It was lying near the path by a gorse bush."

"Recently?"

"He wasn't sure when. He'd put it somewhere and forgotten all about it."

"Typical!"

"He had other things on his mind, I suppose, and he evidently saw nothing remarkable in a lost prefect's badge."

A thing would have to be very remarkable indeed to seem so to Mackay. School and all its associations had apparently slipped from his mind until the sight of Emmie only yesterday had brought them back.

"He'd seen me coming and had it ready. It's such a lonely place. I was the first person from Kinning he'd seen since the end of term, apart from John Rokeby, who was up there one day. You can't get past the farm without being seen."

"She must have been up there. Celia." I tried to fit her into this new setting. "If people are so conspicuous, it's a wonder no one saw her."

Emmie made no reply.

"I don't suppose we shall ever know what happened," I

said, when after a short silence a summing-up seemed called for.

"Things have a way of being found out." Again she seemed to hesitate. Indeed her manner throughout this uneasy conversation had been hesitant. She wasn't used to letting on about things.

"Then your walks haven't only been for pleasure—lately, I mean."

It was an observation rather than a question. Questioning Emmie was on the whole a waste of breath. She still hadn't explained why she had not told me about yesterday's discovery until I had found it out for myself. But now she appeared to be considering my remark and presently said:

"Not entirely for pleasure, but mainly. It's been interesting to have an object: something to look for. But walking gives me a chance to be alone, to think my own thoughts—and be happy. I've been intending to tell you, Kate. I'm going to be married."

As if in response to this explosion, a tiny apple dropped on my head. I disentangled it from my hair and held it in my palm: a scarcely formed abortive thing which had given up trying to be a fruit.

"Married! Emmie! That's wonderful. So you've . . ." On the brink I stopped, half lost in wild surmise. They must have patched things up. "You didn't say . . ." With relief I found the safe way out. "Is it anyone I know?"

"No. How could it be? He's Stephen Brent." Had her thin lips taken a faint upward curve, grown a trifle fuller even? "We were friends a long time ago in our student days. We met by chance in the Christmas holidays and then again at Easter."

And then at the weekend of the conference, I silently interpolated, twirling the infant apple.

"But it was only this last time, ten days ago to be precise, that we made up our minds. He's a captain in the Royal Engineers and almost certain to be going overseas again."

"So you'll be married soon?"

"The last week in August."

"Well!" With a feeling that our lives were falling apart, I groped for the right thing to say. "What sort of a person is he?"

"He isn't a sort of person." She smiled and picked up her boots. A wise answer to a silly question! She was right in not trying to describe him. Who, for that matter, could accurately describe her? Presumably Stephen Brent knew what he was taking on. I had not been mistaken about the complexity of her baffling personality, though I certainly had been about so much else.

"I'm going to put the kettle on," she said after I had continued to exclaim for a minute or two. "You need a cup of tea and something to eat."

"Emmie! There's one thing I must ask you." It was surely safe to do so now that the arrival of Captain Brent had cut through all earlier entanglements. She had gone as far as the path but turned and came back a little when I spoke her name. "Do you think Celia's disappearance had anything to do with Westmain? She was having an affair with him, you know."

Her response quite stunned me. For the second time I saw her face unguarded and totally revealing. What it revealed this time was pure astonishment, heartfelt and unmistakably sincere.

"Westmain! Celia Mond!" She was almost breathless. "Affair? Where on earth did you pick up such a far-fetched idea? As if he would . . ." Her light hazel eyes had grown brilliant. With indignation? They fascinated me and as I stared up at them their expression changed. Her voice softened. "No, Kate. You must put any such idea out of your mind. It just isn't true."

"But she did . . . There was a man . . ."

"Not Westmain," Emmie said. "Never."

She turned her back on me and went slowly across the grass.

"Emmie!" I half got up but a sudden languor overcame me and I sank down again. "I haven't said . . . I haven't told you how very happy I hope you'll be, both of you."

"Thank you." She gave a backward glance and smiled.

The lassitude that kept me motionless under the apple tree was of mind and spirit as well as of body. What had I been doing, apart from making a fool of myself? The past months, so ardently experienced, seemed in retrospect to have taken on a hopeless stagnation, no more responsive to my efforts than a weed-infested pool is stirred by the skimming of a water beetle. Mystery, I discovered, is a snare, a temptation to the busy mind.

It was time to give my mind to other things and extricate myself from the unrealistic mood into which the deceptive airs of Kinning had lured me. As a private investigator I had relied entirely on imagination. The very foundation of my case was false. No one, it seemed, was in love with Westmain: Westmain had never been in love with Celia. I was sick to death of the man; tired of doing his job for him; wished the war would end immediately so that he could come home and release me.

As for Celia, she remained a phantom, a girl I had never known, in love with a stranger as unreal as herself. I must pluck her from my mind; root out the mystical notion that our paths had ever converged and that her disaster was in some way my disaster too. Forgetting her (if I could) would leave a dangerous emptiness. Without her, there would be nothing to distract me from the growing anxiety about my own future.

Dropping the apple, I saw it join a small lost harvest of others of its kind, doomed never to swell and sweeten, never to ripen and be enjoyed. It could only be dread of that emptiness that drove me to make one last effort to find out what had happened to the girl who throughout the strange disturbing summer had been my close though always invisible companion.

20

It was farther than I had thought; another half-hour's walk from the road before a turn in the bridle-path brought me within sight of Moor Edge Farm.

Once having made up my mind, I had left in a rush, staying just long enough to swallow a hasty meal. At the door I remembered that James would be calling for me, scribbled a note to tell him where I was going and left it on the kitchen table. It was about two o'clock when I set off, with no clear idea of my destination except that the farm was somewhere between Aldernole and Bardslow Moor.

The sensible thing—as I realised when no more than half-way up the first hill—would have been to wait for Miller's bus, which would leave the market cross at half past three. But it was always late and I was in no mood for waiting. There was nothing for it but to toil on.

It was a stroke of luck when an army truck overtook me and pulled up.

"I could be court-martialed for this," the driver said. "Hop in. Moor Edge? That's the Fardels' place, isn't it?"

He was delivering supplies to the camp at High Bardslow and dropped me at the end of the farm lane. It was uphill all the way until I came out of a belt of trees into the open where the path ran level between tall bracken stems. Away to the left rose the naked cliff of the Edge; and there at last, below the high shoulder of the moor, lay the farm, its stone roof tiles greenish-grey against the green hillside.

The farmyard was deserted, drowsing between hay-time and harvest. Then a dog stirred and dragged its chain; and before I could knock at the open door, a voice called my name. A young man was striding down the hill to a side gate. Two sheep dogs leapt the wall ahead of him and bustled up to me.

"Mackay!"

"Miss Borrow! Well, this is a surprise."

We beamed at each other like long-lost friends and actually shook hands. I had never noticed how good-looking he was: black-haired and grey-eyed. My view of him had been chiefly of the top of his head. Until now he had been no more to me than an animated pencil. But here, in the brief spell of freedom between school and call-up, he was happily at ease and genuinely pleased to see me.

"Shall you come in, Miss Borrow? I'll tell Marian."

"May I sit here for a while?"

It was cool on the stone steps leading to the hayloft. Pigeons preened and shuffled on their landing place on the granary wall. In its shade speckled hens picked their way through the straw.

Marian came out, wiping a floury hand on her apron before she offered it.

"I've heard plenty about you, Miss Borrow," she said to my surprise. "You'll have had a time with them if they're all as thick as our Alec here. Come into the front room. It's over-hot in the kitchen."

But I begged to stay outside and presently they brought a tray of tea and scones straight from the oven.

"We've our own lard, you see." Marian spoke apologetically, as we had all got into the habit of doing, whether producing or failing to produce food. "I don't know how people manage with just the ration."

She joined me on the steps. Mackay seated himself on an upturned crate.

"You're just out for a walk then?"

There was no need for me to turn the conversation in the direction I wanted. Mackay did it for me.

"All by yourself, like Miss Emmot. She was up here yesterday. I've never known her so chatty."

"We got talking about Celia Mond," Marian explained. "You wouldn't know her, the girl that disappeared. She used to go to the grammar school."

"I only met her once."

"I can't say I knew her either. Living up here, you don't get to know Kinning folk. But it's funny how you see people and think nothing of it until you stop seeing them and then you begin to wonder. But if somebody asks you, you don't like to make more of it than what it was."

"Do you mean that you used to see Celia here?"

"Three or four times. Well, I think it must have been her, but I couldn't be sure when I never knew the girl. Like when the police came asking questions. Seemingly somebody had reported seeing her round about Kinning. I couldn't tell them anything definite—and it was the same with Miss Emmot. Except"—Marian looked puzzled—"it did seem to come back to me more when I was talking to her."

"She's used to getting answers out of people," her brother reminded her. "And I must say she seemed really keen to know."

"It's natural—when a girl disappears nobody knows where."

We sipped our tea, safe in the sunny farmyard. The sky was cloudless. On the green hillside sheep were grazing. When one of them moved, it seemed an event.

"It's all very well"—Marian turned to me confidentially when Alec had gone to fetch hot water—"but when they start going with men . . . The girls are a bit too free these days, with going to the University and that."

"Was Celia with a man when you used to see her?"

"Oh, yes." She lowered her voice still further. "Earlier

on. Not lately, of course. I've seen them first thing in the morning. They must have been there all night." The tilt of her head indicated the open country beyond the gate.

"But where could they have been?"

"Well, there are places. There's the old shooting lodge. Fred thought it was an escaped prisoner that had been using it, but you never know. Ee, a cup of tea does you good. Mind you, I'm not saying definitely there was anything wrong, especially if the poor girl's dead and gone. If she did anything amiss, she's paid for it. 'Tall and fair,' Miss Emmot said. Yes, it must have been her. I've watched her. The path goes round the yard there. She made nothing of the hill. It knocks the wind out of me but she went up like a bird."

Each gorse bush on the hill bore on its eastern side a pocket of shade; otherwise all lay open to the light. I thought how conspicuous a person would be, especially in early summer, before the bracken grew; and pictured her walking quickly and confidently up the steep path, singing perhaps, to meet her lover; then coming down encircled by his arm. I had at least been right about that. A lover there had certainly been, whoever he was.

"I would never have known who she was—only, with Alec having seen her as well . . ."

"Alec! He saw Celia?"

"Well, you know Alec. It wasn't till yesterday when we were talking to Miss Emmot, both of us together, that he mentioned it."

"When would it be? Was it since he left school?"

"No, it was when he was up here swotting for his exams. He was in the loft over the stable. He could have slept in the house but he seemed to think he'd get on better if he was really uncomfortable. All I saw of him was when he came over for his meals."

"You can't say I didn't try, Miss Borrow." Mackay put down the hot-water jug on the tray. "By the way, there's something wants looking at in the oven, judging by the smell of burning."

"My pasties! 'By the way' he says, as if all day would do. Give Miss Borrow another cup of tea. I'll be back in a minute."

"Your sister was telling me," I said when she had gone hastily indoors, "that you saw Celia up here once. If that was in June, it can't have been long before she disappeared. You don't remember exactly when it was?"

"Couldn't say for sure. It must have been a Thursday when I came because I got a lift in the egg van. And it might have been a couple of days later when I saw this girl running down from the moor."

"What time of day would it be?"

"That's what Miss Emmot asked. I'm not sure. About this time or earlier, I would think. It was warm, I know that. I was up there in the loft, books all round. No, honestly, Miss Borrow, I know what you're thinking, but I wasn't. I was definitely reading; working to a system; history one day, English the next. I'd done Shakespeare. That wasn't too bad. Oh, I know, it must have been Saturday. It was Milton that was worrying me and I thought Saturday would give me the longest stretch because that's always my day off from milking.

"I was sitting with my back against a sack of meal facing the window. It's just an opening, no glass. You can't see anything but the hill, not even the sky. I must have dozed off. Anyway I remember waking up and finding the place on the page again—and then . . ."

"You saw her."

"I looked straight out onto the hill and there she was."

"Running?"

"Belting down as fast as she could go, with her feet turned sideways. It's steep, as you can see. Blow me, I thought, what's Delphine been up to?"

"Delphine? But it can't have been."

"No, it wasn't, but I was half asleep, remember, and at first sight it looked like Delphine. In fact I jumped up to catch her at the gate, but she didn't come this way. She went straight over the wall." He pointed to a spot some distance from the farmyard. "She was over in a jiffy."

"So you didn't see her close to."

"Close enough to see that it wasn't Delphine; so I didn't think any more about it until I found the badge with her name on it."

"And you thought you must have been mistaken."

"No, it definitely wasn't Delphine. But I did think she must have been up here sometime, until Miss Emmot came asking questions about the sister."

"It's a wonder you didn't recognise Celia. She was quite an outstanding person at school."

The news of her disappearance, like a good many things, had washed over his unconscious head. In a way it was a relief to find that his abstracted state of mind was habitual and not induced by the study of English Literature. In this case there was some excuse: the news had not filtered up to the farm while he was there and by the time he had got himself back to school to start his exams, the talk had largely died down. Moreover, he now reminded me of a circumstance I had forgotten if I had ever known it, one which partly explained his detachment. He had not grown up in the school but had come there only a year ago. When his father went into the army, Alec and his mother had moved from Derby to Kinning to be near Marian.

He had heard vaguely that something was up with one of Delphine's sisters. He didn't know how many sisters Delphine had. I was surprised to find that Celia herself had made little impression on him.

"I did see her once. She came into a lesson," he reminded me. "You probably don't remember. I thought at the time"—with pencil in hand, no doubt—"that her head was the same shape as Delphine's."

"They are very much alike."

Or should I have said "were"? I emerged from a short reverie to find that Mackay was disagreeing.

"No, not very much, if you don't mind me saying so, Miss Borrow. Similar, I grant you. But she couldn't hold a candle to Delphine."

Since there could be no suitable answer to this interesting observation, I attempted none but gave my mind instead to a question that troubled me.

"When you saw her, did you have the feeling that she was running because she was late"—still intending to get back in time for Monday's examination—"or was she running away? Towards, or from?"

And immediately I saw the futility of the question. How could one possibly know? Mackay's response was unexpected.

"That's it." If only it had been my happy lot on earlier occasions to kindle in his eyes the light of intelligent interest that shone in them now! "You've hit on something that did just flash through my mind at the time. Seeing her wasn't quite—ordinary."

"You mean it's unusual to see people coming down from the moor, especially a girl on her own?"

"You're right up to a point, but it's not exactly the Wild West, you know. We do see people going for walks. Mr. Rokeby went past the other day, and yesterday there was Miss Emmot. No, I meant there was something unusual about the girl, the way she was behaving. At first I was on the wrong track, as I said, and I thought it didn't seem like Delphine to . . . I'd never thought of her—like that." The imprecise phrase was oddly significant. "But even when I realised it wasn't Delphine, it still struck me as a bit peculiar."

"How do you mean?"

"Well, for one thing, you have to be in a terrific hurry to

go crashing into a gorse bush and rush on as if you'd hardly noticed."

Skin torn, dress ripped? The gorse needles could have done that, but they were not responsible for the panic. That must have been there already.

"She was distressed?"

"Before she fell down? Could have been. But if she'd been running to fetch help she'd have come to the farm."

"She might have been running for a train—or a bus."

"From here to Kinning station—or even to the bus stop at Aldernole? At that pace? Nobody in their senses would start a long-distance run at a sprint, Miss Borrow."

"So you think she was running away from something."

"There's nothing much to frighten anybody that I know of, not even a bull for miles." His eyes narrowed as he looked up the steep hill, as if visualising the lines of her body tilted backward against the sunlit grass. "When you're running away from something you tend to look back now and again to see if it's catching you up. Queer, isn't it?" He consulted his mental picture again. "If she was running away and there was no one following her . . ."

"It must have been from something that had happened."

"Then judging by the way she got herself down the hill and over that wall and along the track into the trees, whatever it was must have scared the living daylights out of her."

So that her eyes could still dilate with shock and the blood drench from her face at the sight of Mrs Buckle emanating from the shade. But that was miles away and goodness knows how many hours later. Come to think of it, it was a wonder she had got so far; impossible to guess what, at the limit of her strength, she had done next.

"What's your mother going to say?" Mrs Buckle had jeered. For her there could be only one explanation of torn clothes and nervous distress.

"Your sister mentioned a man. I suppose you never saw him."

"Not with her. I only saw her that once, by herself. But yes, I have seen a man on the moor."

"In the distance?"

The light was changing more rapidly now. Patches of shade cast by the gorse bushes on the cropped turf had lengthened; the line of the moor had deepened to purple.

"No, I saw him close to. It was once when I went up after the sheep, late on. I wouldn't have seen him; it was the dog that sniffed him out. He was lying in the heather. . . ."

"No one you knew? There's been talk of a deserter—or an escaped internee."

"Yes, Marian told me. There's a camp over at High Bardslow. But this chap wasn't a foreigner. He could have been a deserter, I suppose, only he was more like . . ." Mackay had difficulty in placing him. "A shabby-looking chap in a sleeping bag, but from the way he spoke . . . Well, I should say it was an upper-class sort of voice."

I smiled to myself. It was like coming upon a familiar and beloved face in a bad dream.

"You woke him?"

I pictured him at peace in the cool of the evening after the heat and shattering noise of the forges and realised, not for the first time, that peace, for James, was not easy to find.

"He was lying with his hands behind his head, staring up at the sky, and when Tess went shoving up to him, he just rubbed her neck. 'Hullo,' he said to me, 'you'll be the Good Shepherd, I imagine, come after the lost sheep. Well, here I am.' He never turned a hair. You'd have thought the moor belonged to him. An educated sort of bloke. I've seen him again since then, once in town walking down to Pond Street and once talking to those tinkers in the quarry at Kinning. I'd gone there to do some sketching."

I got up to go. As it happened, that was to be the last time I saw Mackay. He would be flattered perhaps to know that I have remembered him, in spite of everything, with affection—and gratitude. He cannot know how I have treasured in my heart his vignette of James lying at peace under the first stars.

"Are you going, Miss Borrow? I'll tell Marian."

Black-and-white cows were ambling home from the bottom field. I walked to the gate opening onto the hill. The lengthening shadows touched the scene with that melancholy sense of loss that haunts the evening of a summer day. It was a beautiful secluded place, its peace marred only by the thought of Celia hurling herself down the hill and over the wall as if demented. Without the serenity I had so much admired she would be a different girl altogether. What catastrophic change in her world could have wrought such a change in her?

For all the pastoral charm of Moor Edge, I regretted having come. I had found out nothing except that James was not the only one to frequent Bardslow Moor. Celia had been here too, a fact which, far from solving the mystery of her disappearance, merely opened up new vistas of uncertainty.

And yet it must have been then that the scene changed, with a sudden shift, as if in one of the strange transitions of a dream I had been wafted to a high point where I could look down with altered vision on the farm, the moor, a girl, a man. . . .

A red-crested cock lifted a foot and paused, as if putting it down would change the world. Then one of the sleeping dogs got up and stretched. I turned. Mackay was crossing the yard and behind him Marian. She had called out to me. She held a piece of paper and, coming up to me, stood looking at it.

". . . if it hadn't been for Alec." I had missed the first part of the sentence. "He's really clever at it. We had an uncle the same. He could draw anything, like lightning. It's a gift, say what you like."

"It was Miss Emmot's idea." Mackay sounded apologetic. "She asked me to."

I took the paper. There was no doubt about it: Mackay had a touch of genius. The likeness couldn't be perfect: it had been dashed off from memory, and he had seen his subject only three times and for a few minutes. His style was crude, even cruel, so that there was nothing in this face of the gentleness I loved. The teasing mouth had been exaggerated into harsher curves; the full lips were coarsened, the brows so resolutely outlined that they frowned. That was a fault Mackay must overcome: a tendency to impose his own style on every face he drew, so that his subjects looked more like each other than individuals should.

All the same, the countenance I stared at was alive—and so much like another sketch by the same hand that the paper trembled in mine. The cruelty of the style had transferred itself to the face and there was some other quality I didn't like. Mackay had made James far too much like the actor he had drawn—the one who played Comus, the evil enchanter.

"We wouldn't have known"—Marian was looking over my shoulder with pride—"if it hadn't been for the drawing."

"Known what?"

"That Alec and I had seen the same man. This was the man I used to see with Celia Mond."

21

From up there on Bardslow Edge I would be able to see him when he came out of the belt of trees. That would give me time to prepare myself, to think what I must say, if words could be found. The blow had been so entirely unforeseen that only one thought survived its crushing impact: I must never again allow myself to be caught unawares.

The grey cliff filled my view, the sheer line of its summit knife-edged against a sky from which the blue had faded. Still stupefied by shock, I must have stared up at it for a long time before there crept into my mind some notion of its living force, its absolute reality. Based in the earth, holding up the sky, it demonstrated beyond doubt that the external world was still there. Its silent disregard of my wretchedness could bring no comfort, only the reminder that I too was still there, though shrunk in its vast shadow to the smallness of an insect; so that it was an enormous effort even to think of crawling up the rock face from earth to sky, out of the shadow into the light. But from the top I would be able to see James before he saw me. The advantage would be mine. Nothing unexpected must happen ever again.

Pride had somehow got me away from Marian and Alec without loss of face.

"You look tired, Miss Borrow," Marian said with some concern as I handed back the paper.

"It was Miss Emmot's idea, for me to draw him." Mackay glared at his sketch as if sensing that something was wrong.

I nodded, trying to believe that when we talked under the apple tree, Emmie had already identified Celia's lover and had not warned me. Very likely she had known all along. Was that possible? Was such cruelty possible?

"I must go home," I said—and seeing that Mackay intended to come with me, I added quickly, "there'll be someone coming to meet me."

From the bridle-path, walking steadily, head erect, I actually turned to wave to them with a pitiful attempt at a comradely flourish. Only when a curve took me out of their sight and the bracken closed me in, could I submit to the anguish. Its onslaught was physical; the pain was in my heart and lungs and head. With the instinct of a sick animal I hauled myself through a gap in the drystone wall, lay face down and, with eyes closed, was lost in despair as if entering a dark tunnel with no light at the end: no end.

After another measureless stretch of time I remembered again that James would have found my note and would have set off at once to follow me to Moor Edge. He must already be near. The dread of meeting him brought me to my hands and knees.

On my right the green slope rose steeply until it became submerged in thick-strewn boulders and fallen stones. Above them soared the massive bulk of Bardslow Edge, a vantage point commanding a wide sweep of countryside for miles to the east and north. From there I would be able to see James the moment he left the shelter of the trees. Meanwhile no one must see me in such a state. When I did force myself to move, it was to creep up the hill, crouching close to the wall until my feet slithered on the first loose stones under the Edge.

So far the sinking sun had shone on my face, but as I stepped into the shadow of the cliff it was as if a light went out and I found myself among tumbled grey boulders in a region of stone as mournful as Golgotha.

Seen at close range, the layered rock was thinly patched with bramble and heather. An occasional sapling of birch or elder offered a dubious hold. Lost to all sense of reality, I thought nothing of physical danger, and indeed the climb is easier than it looks. Having scrambled up the treacherous belt of scree, I came on a track winding upwards in wide curves and it was no more than a steep walk to the top and into the sudden glare of sunset.

The stretch of moor was familiar. At once I found my bearings: the dragon-shaped boulder, the towerlike shooting lodge. The white tufts of cotton grass were gone, leaving a dull stretch of bog where they had made a mirage of pale water; but ling was coming into rose-purple bloom. I remembered the gushing spring and took a few steps towards finding it, but the memory of the last time I had drunk there brought so sharp a pang of disillusionment that all power of decision left me. It would be easier just to die of thirst up here alone and be found after a long time. "Her heart was broken," people would say as the moorland wind lifted the tattered garments from my bleached skeleton. Someone would tell my parents.

Tears welled. Through them I saw the purple moor swell and fall and, wiping them away, was aware of a real movement. Less than a quarter of a mile away, between me and the sunset, two figures moved: two men with rucksacks. It was surprising how quickly their steady walk brought them nearer. Perhaps they had seen me. They would think it odd—a girl alone in such a place.

Remembering my reason for being there, I went quickly back to the Edge and sat down on a boulder, with another at my back to conceal me from the open moor. With the light behind me I couldn't easily be seen from below either. But I could command the entire view, softened by lengthening shadows: the trees, the bracken-fringed path, the patches of gorse and spikes of thistle on the green slope between stone walls.

And as I waited, my mind grew clearer, unconsciously sifting out for me the one aspect of the affair it was possible to be clear about; so banishing to the margins of consciousness other, less definable, aspects, chief among them a question too dangerous to be put to myself, though at the earliest opportunity it must be put to James. It hovered, ready to swoop in my first unguarded moment, to rend the breast with merciless claws and beak and expose the heart of the matter. The disturbing image brought with it a memory of James's violent reaction to the sight of the hawk tearing its victim apart. He had always had an abnormal fear of violence and death. Always? Or only since . . . ?

Meanwhile it was more than enough to know that he had deceived me. He was not the person I had thought him to be. Some vestige of mental discipline lingering at the core of my pain and bringing no respite from it prompted me to sort out relentlessly all the mistakes I had made. The effect was to induce yet another form of torture, such as one might experience in looking up the answers after an examination on the subject of one's life—and finding out what a mess one had made of the paper.

The philanderer, the breaker of hearts was not Westmain—but James. The acute sensitivity I had so carefully respected was no more than an inability to be honest with me. His reluctance to talk for talking's sake was reasonable enough, considering all he had to conceal. His changes of mood, his erratic comings and goings, which I had accepted as the shortcomings of a highly strung temperament, could now be seen as the devious manoeuvres arising from a double life: excuses, evasions, lies.

Craning my neck I could see, topping the nearest rise, the mock battlements of the shooting lodge. It lurked there almost out of sight, a forbidden place: forbidden, that is, to me. "There isn't time," he'd said when I wanted to explore it. Had there been some other reason for keeping away?

Every word he had spoken was now suspect. Every minute spent in his company had been tainted with falsehood. The happiness—it had been more than that—the rapture had been to me fresh, unique, exclusive to the two of us; and on his part it had been a fake, its intimacy stale, the warmed-up leavings from another love affair. At this point my mind slid away in disbelief. He would be able to explain.

Immediately, with a glow of thankfulness—it was like reviving after an anaesthetic—I understood how it had happened. He had known her before he had even seen me. Was it likely—I had barely thought of this before—that a man of James's attractions would have escaped all such attachments until I chose to arrive in Kinning? After all, he was twenty-six years old. From the moment we met, I told myself, he had shaken her off. His love for me had been as true as mine for him.

The moment we met . . . The whole complex problem of James was suddenly reduced to the figure of a man holding back a door curtain and looking out at me. In the most poignant sense we had met, alone together on a threshold of time. But behind him in the blacked-out house there had been someone else. She was with him when I knocked. I was sure of it. Ahead of me on Foley Bank she must have turned right into the lane I was to take, the one leading to the Hall—not left as I had, mistakenly as usual, supposed. And Emmie, waiting and listening in the dark, had recognised her voice. "There was only one place she could have been going," she had said, knowing it all.

Still, until then there had been nothing wrong in the affair, no double-dealing at any rate. That something had not been right I had felt at my first glimpse of James's face; but for my precious intuitions I now felt nothing but contempt—not to mention far-fetched theories about searching for the other half of one's psyche. There was simply nothing in it, with all due respect to Plato.

And yet how true it was that Celia had gone ahead of me—and found her way before me into James's heart; or perhaps only into his arms; there was a difference, all the difference in the world, and after all, that was before he knew me.

Only—on that evening in April in the twilight under the trees when she had clung to him as if she would never let him go, he certainly knew me then. It was no use pretending that once he had met me, James had severed all connection with Celia. How many times had she stolen away from her studies before that last time on June 13? And after that last fatal time—silence. But James had grown calmer. His moods of nervous irritation had been less frequent. His spirits had improved as if . . . a burden had been . . . got rid of.

The tendency to shiver, which had troubled me for some time, became a violent shuddering. It took an effort of will to get up and plant my feet firmly on the ground, crushing the inoffensive yellow flowers of tormentil that starred the thin turf; then to stamp a few paces in an attempt to control the shaking of my limbs; with some success. Impelled by the need to survive and be normal again, I rubbed my cheeks and arms and felt some warming of the blood.

It was while performing these antics that I again saw the two men with rucksacks at the same distance as before; but by this time they had crossed the moor and were standing, as I was, on the edge of the escarpment. They were looking my way. I dodged back to my boulder, knelt down and eyed them warily from behind the stone that had formed my backrest.

The taller man had turned to look down on the scene which had become so familiar to me in the past half-hour that I see it still: the trees under their heavy foliage, the bare slope open to the light between its downright stone walls. He was pointing downward with the stem of a pipe, I thought. They both glanced in my direction, seemed to confer, then, to my relief, turned their backs and followed some path invisible to me which led them downhill, for in a few minutes their heads had sunk below my line of vision.

The interlude had been a diversion; not that I had paid any attention to their appearance beyond forming a vague impression of rolled-up shirt-sleeves and shorts, and on the head of the shorter man with a pith helmet such as a colonial district officer might wear, pulled well down over the eyes. But there had been a reassuring normality about the two figures: a reminder of happier ways of spending a summer day. When they had gone the feeling of nightmare came back.

Then, venturing to the extreme edge of the cliff, I saw what they must have seen. It was James. He was walking quickly along the bridle-path. In a quarter of an hour he would reach the farm. They would tell him that I had set off for home.

But he had stopped. Face upturned, he was scanning the whole length of the Edge and with the quick glance by which he had so often picked out a bird, a flower, a hare, he picked out me. Without a pause he stepped through the bracken, over the wall, and came straight up the hill.

I could have called or waved; but how misleading any greeting must be! There was nothing I could say to him; nor could I bear to wait there until we came face to face. Turning to the open moor, I stumbled through tufts of heather, followed the first sheep track—and presently found that it was leading me over the brow of the hill towards the shooting lodge. I saw it as a haven: somewhere to hide until I could think what to say.

There were upright slabs of stone forming gateposts but the gate was gone. The house itself, three stories high, was like another narrow slab of the same colour as the boulders that rose less starkly from the encroaching heather. Its weathered walls blotted out the sunset, but a nimbus of gold softened their harsh edges so that the place seemed to smoulder with a sinister glow.

Inside the dilapidated garden walls, nettles grew high. Jackdaws fled squawking from the chimney-pots. When they had gone there was no sound, no one there. It wasn't likely that there would be, I reminded myself, half-convinced.

I picked my way to the back of the house through a litter of iron bars and rotting wood and came into the warmth of a sunny terrace. There were sunflowers, their yellow heads lying askew; clumps of valerian; the smell of herbs. An extension had been built out and here the roof was lower. A window looked out on a wide stretch of heather and beyond to distant hills humped against a luminous sky.

And this—I was almost sure—was where they had come: where they had met. The place was theirs. A glimpse through the window of chairs, cushions, a table suggested a home of sorts and accused me of trespassing, not only here but in their lives. Sometimes, because I had thought of her with such intense interest, Celia had seemed to come between James and me when I should have thought only of him. I had never told him, never dreamed of any connection between them. And all the time it had been I who had been the intruder.

When I returned to the front of the house, James was already quite near—no more than two hundred yards away. He came quickly. All at once I realised with panic that he didn't yet know that I knew; and yet his expression, when he was near enough to have smiled a greeting, was grave. For all his ruthless speed in trampling down the heather, he was walking without zest. His whole demeanour was sombre. I saw him as an older man than he had appeared even yesterday: a different man; so that it no longer seemed necessary, even if I could have achieved it, to approach him carefully, mindful of the ease with which he could be hurt. It was not, to say the least—my mood flared into anger—an occasion for tact. The moment had come. Now at once I must ask him. The question, unconsciously rehearsed, sprang to my lips—no more than half a dozen words.

I didn't wait until he came up to me. He was still a few yards from the gatepost. His face, despite the energetic climb and rapid walk, was colourless. And although it was more than a personal need—it was a duty to ask: "Where is she? What have you done with her?"—in the event I could not say those words. They formed not only a question but an accusation I couldn't bear to make.

The question that actually passed my lips took a different form: a feeler feebly extended, not without hope.

"How well did you know Celia Mond?"

He had stopped half-way up the path. His answer took my breath away.

"Well enough to marry her," he said.

And if my life had ended then—as everything else seemed to have ended—my last impression would have been of the misery in his face; a misery far more bitter than my own.

22

So much for my determination never to be taken unawares. Married! It had never occurred to me that they might have taken so irrevocable a step; that they were legally and morally bound together: man and wife, one flesh. It was as if he had undergone some visible change and I saw him transformed into Celia Mond's husband.

"I thought"—he spoke at last. I watched his lips move, knowing how stiff they felt, how hard it was to say anything at all—"I thought it would be a relief when you knew. You've always been able to make me . . . not happy—I've given up hope of that—but somehow I imagined you putting your arms round me and finding some way out of the mess I've made of things."

Instead, as he came closer, I shrank back against the door.

"It was a pipe-dream. No one, not even you, can work miracles. I've known all along that I must lose you. It's been just a question of time. Sometimes I've almost got to the point of telling you; but being with you was always so . . ." His voice was unsteady. ". . . you know how it was—that I could never bring myself to spoil it. And I was right, in my rotten senseless way, to keep it from you, because now that you know, it's worse than ever. There's nothing left for either of us."

Actually he was wrong about that. My anger and jealousy had been momentary, a primitive reaction. The pain that stirred in my heart as he spoke was one of sympathy. Our suffering united us; no one else could help; we needed each other more than ever.

"How did you find out that I knew?"

"I saw Emmie. She gave me the note and more or less made it clear that the game was up."

She would know exactly how to do it, with no more than a word or two, a shrug, a lift of the eyebrows.

"I got the impression that she'd had me pretty well summed up all along. That shook me, as if I'd been found out cheating—by someone who didn't care, not just whether I cheated or not, but whether or not you were cheated."

She had given me no hint of friendly warning. There had been, it is true, a shade of pity in the way she had looked at me—no more than a few hours ago, not a lifetime as it seemed. Hating the world, I hated her, and her pity most of all.

"She just said that Mrs Fardel at Moor Edge had shown her a sketch of a man she had seen with . . ." It was to be some time before either of us could speak Celia's name— " 'They'll probably show it to Kate,' she said and went to put the kettle on or something. I didn't know how quickly to get to you."

All the same, having rushed home for the car, he had driven only as far as Aldernole and left it there.

"I might have missed you by going round by the road. But that wasn't the real reason. I'd have found you all right, but it would have been too quick. I wasn't ready to face you."

Yet perversely he had taken every short cut as if to convince himself that he was doing everything in his power, now that it was too late, to put things right. The craziness of these contradictions I well understood. My own behaviour had been just as irrational.

We had been talking with long pauses between each

painful remark, as if we were trying out a new language, when some slight movement, a returning jackdaw or a sheep lurching out of the heather, recalled me to the physical world. It was cool on this sunless side of the house.

"If only we could go inside and sit down!"

"Of course." He produced a key. "The place is mine. I wish to God I'd never bought it. If I hadn't, none of this would have happened."

It was here, in this isolated spot, where one might come a hundred times and never see a living soul, that they had met, and by sheer chance. The bare fact was all he told me then; the rest I heard later. As the heavy door closed behind us and we stood in an empty stone-flagged hall, a new experience absorbed my attention. James must have felt it even more strongly than I did. Oh, it was over-fanciful to feel that we were not alone; that the silence was active; that in every sense but the physical she was there. Standing breathlessly still, I waited for the idea to take on substance, as if the dank air might thicken into the shape of a girl, her eyes alight with the elation of being in love.

James opened an inner door. A dusty shaft of sunlight slanted towards the lower treads of the staircase. There, in the shadow of the newel-post, a figure might stand, its outline blurred in the interplay of light and shade. But already the remembered image was yielding to other images. If she were there, the expression in her eyes would not be as I had seen it. Even when I first saw her she had not been the Virgin Lady of Milton's masque whom no evil could harm. Even then she had been James's wife. The thought diminished her.

"James!" I called out abruptly. "What did you do to her? Why did she . . . ? Where is she?"

I saw only his silhouette against the sunlit windows and not his expression. His head was raised as if he were looking past me so that I too looked quickly over my shoulder towards the dim recess under the stairs; and having followed him into the room, I instinctively went back and closed the door between us and the unpredictable shadows in the hall.

The shabby room was filled with yellow light. Beyond the window lay the quiet moor, the immense sky. My mood changed.

"I'm sorry. I shouldn't have spoken like that. You would never harm anyone. It's just . . ."

"You're wrong, Kate."

"You've always hated violence, more than most people."

"That's because I know what it's like. I'm afraid of it because I know what it is to be violent."

Half an hour ago, from my viewpoint on the Edge, I had seen with an all-embracing vision how inevitably each detail of the scene merged with the whole; how obvious it was that James had done some dreadful thing. But now that we stood once more face to face and I could see nothing else but James . . .

"I don't believe it." The idea was preposterous. He was exaggerating.

"It's true. I kept on warning you not to think too highly of me. You don't know me." The haggard face he turned to me might indeed have been the face of a stranger. "Do you know what I can't get out of my mind? The marks of my hands on her throat. If she hadn't got away, I would have murdered her."

The confession appalled me. At the same time my very bones melted in relief. He had not murdered her. When Mackay had seen her she was escaping from something that had scared the living daylights out of her but the crude description now conveyed a situation infinitely less awful than it might have been.

But after that? Once again I felt the strange duality of our lives, Celia's and mine. I knew how she must have felt. If James had tried to murder me, I too would have resisted but afterwards I wouldn't have wanted to go on living. I would have behaved exactly as she did, fled right off the face of the earth. Even the discovery that he had loved someone else had brought me to the brink of despair. But if he . . .

I glanced across at him. It was like him to have withdrawn deliberately as though such intense emotional pressure was too much for him. He was kneeling on the hearth with his back to me as he raked out the grate with a kind of nervous dedication, as if there weren't a moment to lose. A smell of wood ash filled the air together with a thin veil of dust through which I saw him, not as the being to whom our shared unhappiness had seemed to unite me more closely than ever, but, for a disquieting moment, as a man with a heavy poker in his hand.

He put it down, crumpled up sheets of newspaper, and rummaged in a box of sticks. He had exaggerated. A gentle person would remember even the slightest lurch towards violence as an act of savagery. His remorse would be disproportionately keen.

"Can you keep this going while I fetch some water?" He applied a match and waited until the paper was alight. "When it's going, put on those two pieces of wood." The sticks began to crackle. He pushed a sagging armchair up to the hearth. "Sit down. You're dead tired. But for heaven's sake don't fall asleep and let the fire go out."

He took an enamel jug from the dresser, then put it down again and, taking me gently by the shoulders, guided me to the chair.

"You'll stay there till I come back? You won't run away?"

Odd that he should put it like that! When he had gone, I knelt by the fire, a log of wood in each hand. There could be circumstances when one had to run away and never come back. How far would Celia's tragic love for him take her? Having lost all that made life worth living, would she hesitate to bring it to an end? He had not killed her; but there was no reason to think that she was still alive; every reason for believing her to be dead. It was only her ghost we had to reckon with.

The sticks reddened and dissolved into flame. The logs began to glow. I stretched out my hands and felt a faint but growing warmth; and bowed my head, ashamed.

23

Against all probability the evening was not an entirely wretched one. Time, no doubt, has blotted out its bitterest moments. Perhaps I see it still suffused by the pure unearthly light that for a time flooded the room. It was impossible to ignore the spectacle in the western sky. I remember feeling, as we thrashed things out, that something important was going on outside to which we ought to have been attending: a pageant of gilded clouds massing about a lake of flawless emerald as if in celebration of some cosmic event. It was not long before the gold melted and the light dimmed; but their afterglow has lingered over the years in compensation for the too-sudden darkening of our own affairs.

Meanwhile, fortified by tea and tinned food, we revived and talked for the first time with an openness that seemed, though it was not, complete.

"Nobody wanted a place that couldn't be got at. No road, no water or electricity." James piled wood on the fire. "Nobody but me."

Bardslow Lodge had been on the market for years and remained unsold even when the threat of air raids stimulated a rush for country cottages. James had bought it with its musty contents for a hundred pounds in the autumn of 1940, not as a bolt-hole from the enemy but as an escape into solitude. He had always spent much of his spare time on the moor and it had seemed a good idea to have more substantial shelter than a tent or sleeping bag, though he greatly preferred sleeping out of doors.

"You asked if it was a folly. Remember? On my part it certainly was, but I was as pleased as Punch—and came straight up here the day I got the keys. A Saturday afternoon." For the first time he smiled. "It was an adventure. No one knew I'd bought it. No, I didn't tell Mother."

He had never before confessed to the frustration he felt in living at home, though I had guessed at the stifling effect of Mrs Conrad's constant fussing.

It was on that first visit, on a mild September day, that he had met Celia. He had walked round the house to admire the view and there she was, sitting on the wall. Her apparently magical appearance had a prosaic explanation: she had been walking with friends; an argument had developed and become serious, hers the one dissentient voice; she had suddenly outgrown their company and marched off alone.

I glanced out at the low wall cushioned with green stonecrop. An adventure indeed to have acquired the house, with a beautiful bride thrown in for good measure! How lovely she must have looked! No man could resist her; and they were both heart-whole. The time and place were right. Had there been reluctance on either side, the deliberate manipulation of Fate in bringing them together would surely have overcome it. But there was no reluctance. They had explored the house together, almost, I thought, like a newly married couple who had escaped all the tiresome preliminaries.

Only the word "bride" did not at first apply. It was not as a potential wife that Celia saw herself. The argument that had driven her to leave her friends, despairing of their callow and parochial outlook, had been on the very subject of love and marriage. For Celia love was a creative force: an ecstatic response to the promptings of blood and senses, a liberation of the spirit, a sublimation of the soul. It was an irresistible tide in whose current were purified and then dissolved the small restricting differences that separate one individual from another. In love there could be no conventions. Love need have nothing to do with marriage.

"Something like that." James had done his best but felt its inadequacy.

"She couldn't know all that, not from experience."

"It was mostly, in fact all, second-hand. She'd been reading . . ."

"Lawrence, for one."

"And Lord knows who else. I thought it quaintly attractive—at first. She was eloquent, and convincing in a way. I was surprised by her confidence. It was as if she had found the clue to successful living and needed no one's guidance and support apart from a few favoured authors'. That is, the surprise came when she told me who she was."

"Who she was?"

"Well, a village girl. One didn't expect . . ."

"That's the first snobbish remark I've ever heard you make. Old-fashioned, too."

The reproof was mechanical. It was beyond my power to be large-minded, just, or fair. Anything to her detriment would have been music to my ears. If only she had been coarse, thick-ankled, had spoken with a strong local accent! But she was refined in speech, soft-eyed as a gazelle, quiet in spirit as a solitary candle flame.

For all his liberal views it was as a village girl that James had thought of her, and to do him justice, the effect was to arouse a sense of obligation he might have been less conscious of if she had been a girl of his own set. Left to him, the affair might never have flourished. The initiative had not been his.

"The responsibility—yes, that was mine, of course—and I would never have tried to avoid it if . . ." He hesitated. "But the determination to keep nothing back, that was hers. She was always talking about commitment."

" 'Experience must include all that the world has to give'?"

"Is that a quotation? It's exactly the sort of thing she used to say."

I got up abruptly and went to the window. Deep clouds were filling the sky, their leisurely drift inexorably shutting out the light. 'Then came slow evening on . . .' That was a quotation too, I acknowledged resentfully. There was no doubt that one could read too much: become too familiar with other people's words so that every thought came formally clothed in the language of a greater mind instead of springing, untidy but spontaneous, from one's own experience. We had been exposed to the same intellectual risks, Celia and I. It occurred to me that she might have taken the infection more dangerously.

"Her talk was always theoretical." James confirmed the conclusion I had silently reached. He had followed me to the window and was running a none too clean finger up and down the moulding of the shutter. "I mean, most of us generalise far too much but she generalised about every mortal thing. It was as if she was working out some lofty system of human relationships. Experience would supply the necessary data. I sometimes felt like a proposition in an argument or a symbol in a formula."

As time went on, the constantly alternating impulses of attraction and irritation had bewildered and exhausted him.

"But not at first," I said, being careful to remember that I was hearing his side of the story. There was no need to ask how it had been at first when he came into the sunshine and found her on the wall, divinely poised as if waiting for him. He was lonely, frustrated by the uncongenial life he was leading and, for all his apparent assurance, shy. She was by nature self-possessed, physically alluring, not to mention the rare quality I had felt at once: some indefinable grace that touched the imagination. That was it. Suddenly I could define it. To those who were susceptible to it, she communicated the spark which sets alight the visionary faculty.

"There was a radiance about her. No wonder you loved her," I managed to say, determined in this unequal contest not to sink to the level of petty jealousy.

James didn't answer. He had been unusually communicative. Words had flowed from him as if to express them made things easier: as if at last he was talking for talking's sake. His expression puzzled me. For much of the time as we stood together by the window, I had looked not at him but at the darkening moor and changing sky. Now, facing him directly, I felt again a touch of alarm.

Surely I should have noticed it before, a strangeness in his manner quite apart from his unusually rapid speech. At first I had thought him distressingly pale, as if the course of his blood had been diverted to serve some other purpose than to give warmth and colour to the skin. But now his whole face, even the forehead, was coloured by a darkish-pink flush. A quick pulse beat in his temple. I should have recognised these as danger signals. In a way I did; I could no more overlook them than I could forget, during this whole conversation, the dreadful confession which had started it. But to my everlasting regret I lacked wisdom to find the means of lowering the nervous tension which—I looked away uncomfortably—had quite altered his appearance.

"The radiance, as you put it? Yes, it was there."

"I only saw her once, you know, but we talked and I felt it strongly. I can quite understand how you—"

"You'll never understand. God, how it irritated me!" He raised his voice so suddenly that I jumped. "That everlasting brightness. Nothing in her whole life had ever dulled it, not for a second. Nothing had ever shaken her confidence. She had no doubts about herself, no perception of other people's doubts, no inner conflict—and absolutely no sense of humour."

At this last remark he grimaced, acknowledging its banality.

"Well, really," I said, "you can't have everything."

"Everything was not what I wanted. The total commitment was her idea. She bestowed herself upon me. There and then, more or less, taking it for granted that I would be delighted—and grateful—and so I was—then. I was dazzled and went on being dazzled for a while. It was rather superb, her calm assumption that she was conferring an immense favour in loving me; and she was right, I suppose, to rate herself so highly. Otherwise what she offered would have seemed—casual; and it certainly wasn't that."

It was almost always here that they had met. The absolute privacy of the affair had helped. There had been no observers to make them conscious of differences in background; no friends in common; no shared social life.

"Nothing led up to it. It was a new life. No, not a life. I never thought of it as more than an interlude, exhilarating but temporary; with no past and definitely, quite definitely, no future."

As one might find oneself afloat for a while on a shining cloud, blissfully untroubled by the problem of how to get off?

The floating had continued for some months, during which time Celia went up again for the Michaelmas term. It was then that she began to slip away. A note or telegram would announce the time of her arrival.

"She came here. I would find her waiting. Or I would pick her up somewhere and we would come together. Once I came here not expecting her and she suddenly—turned up."

"Has she . . . ?" I stopped, confronted by the momentous differences involved in a mere matter of tense. I had meant to say: "Has she a key?" He had only to nod and so lay us open to the possibility that she could turn up again. A turn of the lock, a whine of hinges, and she could walk in at any time—now, for instance. But how much worse the implications of "Had she a key?" How much more disturbing in that case would be her return if she chose to come back! My conviction that she would come and go as she pleased, dead or alive, was, for a wild moment, absolute.

I pulled myself together. In any case the door was unlocked. But I could understand how the utter privacy of this rendezvous could strain the nerves and intensify a relationship until it became explosive. Already I was becoming oppressively aware that a thousand acres of moorland were silently closing us in: or, worse still, closing in on us. We were extraordinarily isolated.

Had James been listening too? He seemed all at once unable to keep still. Having lifted and lowered the catch of the shutter until it came away in his hand, he lunged across the room, sat down, put his feet up on another chair, and immediately got up again.

"Unfortunately"—his attempt at a half-humorous detachment was not successful—"the more we saw of each other, the more obvious it was that we were heading for trouble. Obvious to me, that is. 'Radiance,' you said. That's the wrong word. It was an air of unfailing enlightenment. Once I'd noticed it, it got more and more irksome. Light without warmth or depth, like the beam of a lighthouse. You know—there's no variation in it. It revolves steadily, forcing you to look at it. There's nothing you can do, only accept it as a warning and go away. That's what I should have done while it was still possible."

But if the brightness remained constant, in other ways Celia changed. To his dismay she began to appear as what she had always been but didn't at first show herself as being: the innocent country girl seduced; the dependent female turning as her only hope of security to the ravishing male.

"I don't know that she specifically said anything of the kind but I began to see myself in that light—and to hate myself. And she did make her requirements absolutely clear."

"It was marriage then that she wanted after all?"

"Kate." He came close to me and again I moved away. "Can you believe that I married her not because I loved her (I knew nothing about love then, although I found out soon after) but because I would have despised myself if I hadn't. When she came up with the suggestion—that was in November—I didn't take it seriously. The prospect of her lifelong companionship was unthinkable."

"You would be assuming that her life would be long."

He winced as if stung and no wonder. But the cruel reminder of the brevity of their marriage had not been intended as a taunt: I was simply trying to understand the state of mind that led him to behave as he did, then and later.

"Yes, naturally I did. What's more, for very good reasons I had decided years ago that I would never marry. When she made it clear that marriage was what she expected and felt entitled to, I resented her high-handed way of ignoring all the stuff she had preached at first; but I knew very well that in justice I owed it to her. She—if it had been anyone else I would have said she persisted—but persistence admits the possibility of failure. She didn't need to persist about anything. She had a way of imposing her views on others: in this case me. Not a tap dripping but a bland bright inability to imagine that any man could fail to appreciate his good luck in having her as a lover—and eventually as a wife."

He was still undecided when an unexpected event influenced him as strongly as Celia's claims on him: namely the blitz on Sheffield on December 12.

"God certainly moves in a mysterious way," he said grimly. "That night brought home to me the real facts of life—and death—and disgusted me with my own special knack of sitting on the fence. For once I was in the thick of the slaughter; not for long, but long enough to see myself as committed to nothing, neither a CO nor an active serviceman; letting my useful job serve as an excuse for avoiding decisions. To be fair to her, she must have convinced me with her theory of headlong involvement. At any rate I saw the moral necessity of taking a firm decision. There was no dodging the fact that I must marry her."

In the very moment of making it he recognised the decision as a disaster and relapsed wretchedly into the habitual state of uncertainty and self-doubt which must have tormented him increasingly the whole time I had known him.

"I see now. The last time I saw your mother, I believe she almost told me. She seemed to be warning me."

"How could she? She doesn't know. No one knows. I couldn't face telling people and having them talk about us, much less all the ballyhoo that goes with a wedding. Luckily she felt the same about keeping it to ourselves, at least for the time being."

Celia's reasons were more practical. Her father would be furious: he had made sacrifices to send her to the University. She was subsidised by the Board of Education on condition that she underwent a year's professional training as a teacher after taking her degree. A State Scholar couldn't just throw everything up in order to marry, especially to marry a civilian. Though things were to change rapidly during the war, it was a time when most women still had to choose between marriage and a career.

Fortunately the secret meetings satisfied Celia's taste for romance, which was less irritating to James than her tendency to lecture him on literature and moral philosophy. They were married in London by special license.

"You'll think it ridiculous, Kate: you're such an honest

thinker; but at the back of my mind was a crazy notion that by marrying her, I had settled my account with her. There need be nothing more."

No sharing of plans? No settled way of life? The absurdity of this fancy was soon evident. Throughout the autumn they had met, not without inconvenience, here at the Lodge. With the onset of winter it became inaccessible. When Celia came home at Christmas they had met haphazardly in furnished rooms in town. During Mrs Conrad's illness the Hall was closed until the beginning of January, when James went home to air the house for her return.

"It was then that it dawned on me what I was in for."

"But surely you knew already."

"No. I mean it hadn't occurred to me that she would turn up at the Hall; just calmly walk in as if she had a right, which of course she had."

The jerk of his head was probably a nervous gesture but it seemed like a quick glance at the door. I mustn't have closed it properly. It had swung half open.

"There's something else I haven't told you." He reached for my hand. I snatched it away. "The root of all the trouble. It's an obsession I have. About death; sudden death. I have nightmares about it."

He was appealing to me for help. I could at the very least have taken his hand in mine but I made no move.

"I dream that there's a suffocating weight pressing me down: or sometimes it's a vague shape, and then it moves as if it had tentacles. I struggle madly to get away and wake in absolute terror. Then, when my mind begins to work again, I think about death and every way of dying: bayonets, bombs, bullets, suffocation. More than once I've thought that if I ever did actually kill someone"—he spoke so low that I could hardly hear—"it would put an end to the nightmares. Then in the morning I'd be all right again."

"Don't talk about it."

"I have to tell you because . . ." With an effort he controlled the trembling of his lips. "To make you understand."

He went to the table and lit the lamp. It took a little time.

"When she walked in that night she was glowing with life, confident that I would be delighted to see her. There was snow on her hair. 'You didn't expect me' she said. And suddenly I wanted to strangle her. For a few seconds—or minutes—I couldn't see her. All I could see was a column of grey mist, and I had the most peculiar feeling in my arms, as if they had turned into tentacles with a life of their own, like the ones I dream about. It took all my strength to stop them from reaching out . . ."

"James!" I cried out. "You mustn't. It wasn't real. You imagined it."

"I have to tell you because this is where you come into it. You came to the rescue. You knocked at the door and saved her. Saved me too. I couldn't believe it. If you hadn't come just then, God knows what I might have done."

He gave a shuddering sigh. The lamp made deep shadows under his eyes. Every detail of his stricken face comes back to me—and is gone again.

"She must have realised—how you felt."

"When I went back, she was looking along the bookshelves, and humming. Believe me, she wasn't capable of grasping that she could ever be unwanted, much less in danger of driving me mad. That's what it was, Kate, madness. It was finding her unruffled without the slightest inkling of what we had been on the brink of—it was then that I felt the hopelessness of ever finding a chink in that gleaming glassy surface. You understand that none of this was her fault. It was just her misfortune to marry a man it wasn't safe to be with. Ever since then I've lived in dread of actually doing it the next time."

It took me a little while to recover from this last revelation.

"There can't have been many more times," I said at last.

"The next day she went back and I didn't see her for weeks. But I was always on edge, always expecting her to turn up at the Hall or even at the works. This place was more or less snow-bound from January to March. There was only one place where I felt safe."

"You needn't tell me. It might spoil it for you."

"There's nothing left to spoil. Besides, you must admit I'm pretty good at spoiling things for myself—and everybody else, including you, especially you." The ill effects seemed to have been equally shared out between the three of us, but I was too dispirited to contradict. "You won't know Sarah Buckle. She used to be our laundry maid. She has one of our cottages in Foley Lane. There's a room there I can use. Strictly speaking, it's let to that fellow you're standing in for. I started dropping in there for a night or two in desperation when I couldn't settle anywhere else. Sarah likes it. She's absolutely loyal to the family and would never breathe a word."

So much that I had never known or dreamed of: so much that I had misinterpreted. The ghostly sheets on the line, the two dressing-gowns, the armoury of razors, too many for one man!

". . . a good sort, Sarah, although it's tedious having to put up with the endless anecdotes in praise of her official lodger. Well deserved, I'm sure. He must be a fine chap, with all the qualities I haven't got. Not the sort to mind my sleeping in his bed while he risks his life on my behalf."

"Oh, James!"

"At any rate, for three months she didn't turn up. On the other hand"—his eyes were full of sadness—"you did."

During the Easter vacation he had tried to avoid her. Pressure of work had provided a legitimate excuse. They had met only three or four times. When I saw them together she had begged for a last walk before he put her on the overnight train for Chesterfield. Though it was not a thing to discuss, I gathered that Celia had been more in love than ever.

"It showed," I said. "Even when you weren't there."

It had also made her more demanding; made him more resentful, more dangerous.

"You should have told me." I went and crouched by the fire.

"Yes, I should have told you." The fidgeting ceased. His voice was steady. "Instead I deceived you, broke your loving little heart—and loved you, love you, Kate."

"You said nothing could shake her confidence, but you must be wrong." I forbore to mention the most striking example of Celia's distress. "Wasn't it a sign that she was shaken, to come rushing up here to find you in the middle of Finals?"

"Yes, it was."

"Something must suddenly have upset her—at last. A letter from her sister . . ."

"From Delphine?"

". . . mentioning as an interesting item of local news that her beloved Miss Borrow was more or less engaged to Mr Conrad at the Hall."

"Oh, no! She had no right. I never said . . . You know how they talk."

"It was bound to happen. It was only a question of how soon she would find out."

Uncharacteristically, Celia had apparently lost her head. Having despatched a telegram to James's working address, she had made the sudden decision to break her journey and come to Kinning on the off chance of finding him there; had deduced from the absence of his car that he was in town—and must have found herself in a quandary. I never did discover where she spent the night, but she had made her own way to the Lodge. James had not received the telegram until the Saturday morning. It was mid-day before he could leave work. He had found her here—asleep.

Waking, she heard the cruel truth: that their marriage was hateful to him, that she exasperated him beyond control, that he did indeed love someone else. Nerving himself to tell her all this, he had told it brutally, and when she protested . . . The rest I already knew. The physical violence he loathed could scarcely have been more ruthless than the disillusionment he thrust upon her; but when she fled, weeping, it was not only a sad retreat but a desperate escape.

I became aware of the profound silence and didn't know how long it had lasted or how to break it. The air pulsated with dangers of every kind, not one of which I knew how to face.

"And you've never seen her since?"

"Never."

"Nor heard from her?"

He shook his head, almost, I thought, with indifference. But he must have felt my unspoken reproach.

"I felt nothing but relief that she had gone."

I pushed open the window. The night air smelt of heather and late-summer flowers; but for all its fragrance it was cool and bracingly sharp. It went to my head. My mind became perfectly clear. How long this conversation had gone on, in whispers, half-formed statements, hints, agitated questions, I have no idea. But some demon inspired me to choose that ungentle hour of the night to make a clear exposition of the hopelessness of our plight.

"James! Do you think she's still alive?"

He had lain on the divan, his head on a rolled-up sleeping bag. He didn't answer.

"Because if she is, there's no hope for us. You're her husband. I couldn't . . . Do you realise—this is probably the last time we shall ever be together?"

He still didn't answer and I moved relentlessly to the other alternative.

"And if she's dead . . ."

"Then there is hope for us?" The ironic question suggested that his mind too was working clearly.

"No. None. If she's dead, we drove her to her death—between us." Dedicated as she was to experiencing all that life could offer, would she stop short of the last thing, the most challenging experience of all? "How could we ever be happy, knowing that? We would never forgive ourselves, or each other."

"I could forgive you. It's hard to see how you are in any way to blame. The point is—could you forgive me?"

"We'd never forget that we had driven her to take her own life."

"It's the only life one has any right to take, one's own. And she wasn't driven to taking hers; only to the point of choosing whether to take it or not." There was no pity in his voice. "If she's dead, I envy her."

Even then, though my heart responded to his despair, I failed to interpret his mood as one of self-torturing regret; was as far removed from the ordeal he was suffering as if I had been blind and deaf.

"You haven't understood what I've been trying to tell you." He had got up again and was sitting on the edge of the divan, head in hands. "Two narrow escapes. There could be a third time."

"How could there be when she's gone?"

"I'm not thinking of Celia."

But I was. As so often before, it was on Celia that my mind was fixed. Until she met James, her life had been one unbroken success; for her nothing had gone wrong. That was no longer true; and yet in spite of the horrible circumstances in which she had been put to flight, she had been successful again: triumphantly so. We were at her mercy.

She had the upper hand. She would haunt us both for the rest of our lives.

Lying back on the moth-eaten cushions of the dusty armchair, my eyes on the black window panes, I forgot James's failures and thought only of Celia's success. If she had wanted to avenge herself (supposing her to be capable of stratagem), no plan however intricate could have been more effective than the simple act of disappearing. Whereas her presence might have driven us furtively and dishonourably into each other's arms, and even news of her would have drawn us together like conspirators, her absence and silence would always keep us guiltily apart.

It might be years before we knew whether James was free to marry again. Though my love for him might last and his for me, there could be no ease, no rest when at any moment she might come back. Even now the whisper of a breeze, the creak of old timbers could sound like the rustle of a dress, a footfall. Without subtlety or harmful intent she had taken possession of our lives with a completeness that witchcraft could not rival. The spell was binding. There was no solution: no sprinkling of pure fountain drops to break the evil charm.

"There's no future for us. None at all."

I said it aloud, staring into the darkness like an oracle. It came as no more than a half-regarded interruption when James spoke:

"I think I'd feel better if I could see the stars."

He came over, bent down and kissed me.

"Forgive me, my love," he said, "forgive me . . ." — and went out.

I heard the outer door close, the sound of the big key turning, followed by a scraping sound. He had locked me in.

"James! What are you doing?"

I picked up the lamp and crossed the hall. The light fell on an object lying on the floor. It was the key. He had pushed it under the door through a hollow worn in the step. I stared at it stupidly. A funny thing to do!

But I was too tired to think about it: to think or care about anything; too tired even to stand up. I lay on the divan and fell instantly into a deep sleep.

24

It was probably the reek of paraffin that woke me. The lamp had gone out. I had no idea of the time but there was light enough from the window to show a network of cracks in the discoloured ceiling. Staring up at them, barely awake, I could not at first distinguish their crazy twists and turns from the grey convolutions of my dream in which spectral shapes had come and gone, bent over me and dissolved, leaving a residue of distress. The last and most persistent of them had been that of an older woman whose anxious hovering I recognised.

So that my first waking thought was of Mrs Conrad and the need to comfort her. Yet she had seemed to feel a similar obligation towards me. She had been warning me. Her thin, lined face above the long neck and nervously swallowing throat—these features came to me not from my dream but from the last time I had seen her; and from other times, unregarded and half-forgotten.

"I wouldn't for the world have you hurt. Nor would James. Only . . ."

It was the sort of thing she might have said if she had known of his marriage and was screwing up courage to tell me. But she didn't know that he was married. She had been warning me of something else.

Seen in the cool grey of morning, the shabby room had become a different place, its ceiling higher, its corners sharper, its mystery gone. And as the events of the previous night came drifting back, they too had undergone a change of stress. This time the emphasis lay not on Celia but on James: not on what he had told me but on himself. He filled my mind.

There had been something about him that I ought to have given all my attention to. His constant changes of mood from restlessness to abstraction had seemed to differ only in degree from similar moods I had seen in him before. But there had been a new anxiety. One would have thought he was filling in time before some expected event: like a man bent on catching a train but not quite ready to start—not needing to start just yet. Part of his mind had been concentrated elsewhere. As we talked, sometimes whispering, in the darkening room, the situation—which for me had been one of absolute crisis engaging all my attention—had not involved him fully. To him it was part of a bigger catastrophe. He had not told me everything, as if my time for helping him was past: a conclusion no sooner reached than rejected and replaced by another, more disturbing. He had been trying to tell me and I had not been listening.

Already uneasy, I raised myself on one elbow. My neck ached from hours of contact with a peculiarly uncomfortable pillow. Only then did I discover that it was not a pillow at all but James's rolled-up sleeping bag. Until then I had supposed him to be sleeping out of doors and had drawn some comfort from the thought. A few hours' rest under the stars he loved to watch would do him a world of good. But now . . . If he had wanted the sleeping bag, he would have taken it or come back for it; and having pushed the key under the door, he would have had to wake me to let him in.

He had not locked me in: he had locked himself out; he had gone out with some other purpose than to sleep. The effect of these discoveries was electric. It was as if I awoke fully at last not only to the steady advance of sunrise but to the full blaze of understanding. I understood his inability to worry anymore about Celia. (From then on I too ceased to think of her.) He was the very last person to survive the emotional tangle of being loved by two women and the conflict involving his responsibility to both. Worse than that, with a pang of remorse for not having done so before, I understood the magnitude of his ordeal.

"There could be a third time . . . I wasn't thinking of Celia." Celia had escaped. He was afraid of what he might do to me. His nightmares were becoming real. He knew that he was going mad.

It was as if the sky darkened and I lay cowering under the threat of some monstrous disaster, an enormity of nature beyond my understanding. Was it possible that even in the few hours since we parted, James had been changed by it? The idea might have been someone else's: it held no meaning for me; but a wave of distress afflicted me like an illness and I turned away from the light to face the blank wall, feeling sick and cold.

It comforts me to remember how soon a stronger impulse than fear restored me. I lay thinking of James and could think of him only as he had been when he stooped to kiss me and ask me to forgive him. In his extremity of despair he had tried to protect me. A passionate longing to help him warmed me into life. All the resources of mind and body revived, united in a single purpose: to reach him if it wasn't too late; to help and comfort him; but first to find him.

I leapt off the divan and, without washing or eating or combing my hair, ran to unlock the door, fled down the path and into the unwelcome light of early morning. The openness struck me like a blow in the face. I stopped, overwhelmed by an impression of distance: of acres of heather unfolding in endless undulations to meet an immensity of sky. A grouse rose almost at my feet startling me with its harsh threat: *Go-back, Go-back.* Another followed. The shallow arc of their flight was no more than a tiny gesture in the vastness of space.

"James!" I called, my voice faint and thin after the raucous bird-call. There was just a chance that he might have stayed near the lodge. He might have dropped into an exhausted sleep as I had done and be lying in the heather.

There was nothing in any direction except ground to be covered. Every minute as the light grew, the plateau of moorland grew with it, the horizon receded. I called again and again, urgently at first, then hopelessly. To this day I cannot set foot on moor or fell, cannot smell the early sweetness of heather, without hearing the forlorn echo of my voice or seeing his name imprinted on the air; without waiting for an answer that never comes; never came.

I might call and search all day. It was useless. Yet the need to find him was more compelling than ever—or, if not James, then his mother. The absolute necessity of choosing a direction drove me at last to remember the farm. The Fardels were probably up and might take me part of the way home. After one or two false starts I found the path down the Edge, slithered over the scree, and raced headlong down the green slope, feeling almost weightless and strangely disembodied, as if I were someone else. In the thin violet light nothing had substance; the walls had not yet become solid; the gorse bushes had the air of never having been there before. Presently in the same light-headed way I could see the gap in the wall, the bracken fronds, the belt of trees.

My heart leapt. He was there—at the gate—amazingly —in the right place at exactly the right time.

"James! Wait!" I kept on running, feet turned sideways, skirting thistles, swerving round bushes until I came to the wall and scrambled through the gap. "I'm so relieved—that you're here." Green sprays of bracken brushed my forehead and hid him from me. I pushed through the stiff stalks. He had seen me, had come nearer and was waiting.

Something caught my hair. I tore it free and came out into the path. "Oh, James!" I sobbed, falling into his arms.

But they were not his arms. The man was not James. In an agony of disappointment I drew back to look at him, unseeingly. Whoever he was, he went on holding me as if holding me up: as if he thought I might fall down.

"You must be the girl I'm looking for," he said. "Thank God I've found you."

The words didn't make sense. I ignored them. What I did notice was something in his voice: an inexplicable kindness. It was in his eyes too and in his way of holding me by the arms, as if he knew how much I needed help; knew better than I did how very much I needed it. That frightened me.

"I wanted to go back to Kinning. There's someone . . . It's about James—James Conrad. He might . . ."

"That's why I was looking for you." He hesitated. I watched his lips tighten and then part—and dared not breathe. "You needn't be afraid for him. Not now."

"You've seen him?"

He nodded.

"He's all right?"

There was a momentary flinching.

"James has found his own way of putting things right." His grip on my arms tightened. "There's something I have to tell you. You're going to be hurt, more than you've ever been hurt before. But he won't suffer anymore. For him it's all over, Kate."

And he told me what James had done. It didn't take long. It needed no more than a few words. It didn't take long for me to grow old, for my heart to die.

"Like his father," I said. "Exactly the same." And it was as if in the dungeon to which James had been doomed from birth, a door had clanged shut.

* * *

The neck of the flask struck painfully against my chattering teeth but the brandy must have helped a little. I was sitting with my back against a tree, a jacket round my shoulders.

"It wasn't cowardice," I heard my voice say. It had a peculiar overbearing sound, unsuited to its quiet audience. "People say that about—suicide. But with James it was different. It was courage. He did it"—why had he done it? —"to set me free. He loved me." The awful voice quavered but became recognisably my own. I said it again, looking earnestly into the stranger's kind eyes but addressing myself, convincing myself.

"That certainly doesn't surprise me," he said. "It's very much what I would have expected."

"You see he felt himself going mad."

"That was how Virginia Woolf felt," he said.

"Yes, yes." For some reason it helped, to be reminded that only a few months ago she had been driven to do the same thing: so rare and brilliant a person. "He felt responsible for—everything. I didn't realise. I didn't help him enough."

"You made him love you. What more could you do? Loving you must have helped him enormously."

"It didn't make him happy."

My eyes came to rest on the bottom of the gate. I did not know why they lingered there in fascination until it presented itself to my weary gaze as a band of light: a bar of gold. The sun had fully risen. Colour had come back: green to the grass and bracken, purple to the fringe of moor, an innocent blue to the sky. With it the pain, too, came back—and James. I felt him everywhere: in the green shade, in every curve of the path and contour of the hills, in every sunlit clearing; not yet a memory but a presence; no longer alive but not yet dead.

"The happiness was all mine," I said and wept for his

lack of it, for love of him, for the terrible loneliness of his end.

"I don't believe that, you know."

My companion had waited with no sign of waiting patiently, rather with the air of being there only for my sake if I needed him. I had forgotten him, had scarcely thought of him as a person distinct from the situation that united us in so sudden an intimacy. But now some extraordinary quality in this heart-to-heart conversation with a stranger roused in me a dull wonder. In his concern, his involvement in James's tragedy—and mine, in his protective understanding, he could have been—though how could he be?—a friend.

"You were looking for me?"

"We thought, as you hadn't turned up, that you might still be about here somewhere. We saw you yesterday. You were on the Edge—and we saw him, too, coming to meet you."

"Oh, yes. You were walking."

The two men with rucksacks! Even so, that didn't explain how he had found out about James or why he was out so very early in the morning looking for me, a complete stranger.

"You haven't told me—where it happened."

"I'm going to take you home," he said. "I have a car along there."

"You're very kind to me." It was hard to get up, difficult to stand. "Your jacket . . ." He put out a hand to help me. "But I don't know you." It had seemed entirely natural to put my hand in his. "You called me Kate."

"I didn't think you'd mind."

"Who are you?"

He smiled.

"My name's Westmain," he said. "Edmund Westmain."

25

I must have responded with something more than a stupefied stare. I certainly hope so. The name did penetrate my befogged senses and arouse a startled recognition; but it was recognition of some distant circumstance far removed from the man at my side. To grasp how he came to be there was, for the time being, beyond me.

Nevertheless I did try.

"It must have been a terrible shock to you," I remember saying, "when you found . . . when you found what had happened in your room."

"Terrible things happen all the time," he said.

His unexpected return to his lodgings at some time after midnight was all that I had so far taken in; as to how he chanced to be in Kinning at all, the details emerged as we walked slowly to the car to join John Rokeby, who had been wrong about the sudden posting in June.

"So you never went to Suez?"

He had been sent instead to one of the newly built corvettes on the Clyde. As soon as she was commissioned they were ordered to northern waters for exercises and were shortly to go into service with a convoy escort in the Atlantic. His leave ended at midnight tomorrow.

"We couldn't fit in the usual climbing holiday in Langdale, but these moors are the next best thing."

"And now your leave is spoiled and Rokeby will be disappointed again."

I said it as one says things at such a time, in a remote and mindless way; and I listened with the same numbness of perception as he told me that they had set off for Bardslow Edge from Rokeby's home in Sheffield, planning to return by way of Kinning and spend the evening with Miss Butler at her home in Pottergate. It had not been their intention to go to Foley Lane; but having talked too long and missed the last bus to town, they had no alternative.

On her return from the pictures Mrs Buckle had had her supper and gone to bed, knowing nothing of what had happened in the bedroom at the back, until she was roused by the rightful tenant and bustled in to turn down the sheets.

"Poor Mrs Buckle!" I overcame a wave of nausea. The thing must be talked of and it had been so much worse for them. "She'll never get over it."

Never can double-dealing have been more cruelly exposed. From dismay on seeing Westmain, she had passed to horrified distress on finding James, had run out of the house in a frenzy and refused to go back—ever.

Meanwhile . . .

"You won't feel like going back either."

"That isn't a problem. I was only keeping the rooms on because I could never summon up courage to give notice."

Between them, with Miss Butler's help, the two men had taken charge: summoned the doctor; fetched Mrs Conrad's sister from Hammer to comfort her; gone to Bennets to break the news; learned from Emmie that I had gone to Moor Edge and had not come back.

They had all doubtless drawn their own conclusions, the wrong ones as it happened, as to how I was spending the night, but this did not occur to me as I struggled against a growing physical discomfort. My head felt thick and yet tender, my skin hot and dry, and a pain in my chest troubled me when I breathed at all deeply. Sights and sound kept on fading and then surging back with almost painful vividness.

"I'll get Chris to pack your things." He was talking with unhurried ease, as if this were the most natural way to spend a precious day's leave after being up all night and having taken on the responsibility of dealing with the ghastly situation into which he had been thrust. "And we'll telephone your parents. The sooner we get you home, the better."

"You don't mean—to Chardon? Today?"

"We could be off in an hour."

He didn't explain, nor did I think of asking, his reasons for hustling me away. It saved me from questioning by the police and from local gossip, which would certainly have fastened on the fact that James and I had been together on the night before his death. As it was, no one but Westmain, Rokeby, and Emmie ever knew of my escapade on the moor.

Afterwards I was better able to appreciate the smoothness of the operation; and to marvel at my good fortune in falling into the hands of a man whose reputation for efficiency I had been mean-spirited enough to resent.

The details of my last morning at Kinning have never been clear to me, apart from one or two impressions that isolated themselves from the confusion and remain sharply etched by the onset of fever.

I remember as we drove to Bennets how the car lurched to a stop. Someone said, "Damn! It's a cat. Right in the middle of the road. You'd think it was waiting for somebody."

I remember meeting Emmie face to face at the door.

"I'm sorry, Kate." Her hazel eyes were brilliant for a moment, with genuine sympathy, I dare say. "Desperately sorry."

I passed her without a word and went blindly to my room.

It couldn't have been more than half an hour before we left. Butler was there—where had she come from?—to say goodbye.

"Keep your chin up." She waved us off, her ruddy face sagging a little, her brown eyes red-rimmed after a late night and an early rise. "See you in September."

She didn't know that she would never see me again: that I was never going back.

Other people were leaving too. We slowed down in Mafeking Terrace to steer carefully past a furniture van drawn up at the Monds' house. Delphine with a laundry basket in her arms was coming through the gate and saw me, I'm sure. I gave no sign and my last glimpse of her was of an anxious face, eyes wide, lips parted in an unspoken message as they had been once before when she had something to tell and I had turned a deaf ear.

John Rokeby left us at the station.

"You've had a bad time, Kate. Try not to let it get you down. Wish I was coming with you but you'll be all right with Edmund. All the best till we meet again."

I followed Westmain to the booking office and felt obliged to make one more protest.

"Really, I can manage now. You mustn't come any further. It worries me to inflict myself on you like this."

"As a matter of fact it suits me very well. I'd have been travelling in this direction tomorrow anyway—and this gives me a chance to look up friends in Edinburgh. It's the least I can do, to keep an eye on you as far as Newcastle."

There was one further source of embarrassment.

"I've just realised. I haven't enough money with me so I can't . . . But I'll . . ."

"All the more reason for not letting you go about on your own."

I could only thank him meekly. He was obviously not a man to whom one could send a postal order—and I never did.

We had to stand a good deal of the way or sit on our bags in the corridor. An increasing muzziness in my head blurred the passing landscape of small terraces, pit-heads, slag-heaps, and stagnant pools into a sequence of shapes without meaning; the journey had no recognisable purpose; the man beside me was sometimes a stranger, sometimes a close friend, and once as I jerked out of a doze with my head on my knees, it was James and I dared not look at him.

At York we were lucky enough to find seats and could look out in comfort at the red-tiled farms in the Vale and the blue hills to the east. We talked a little and after that I must have slept more soundly.

"Wake up!" I had the window-seat. My companion was leaning past me to look out. "You mustn't miss this."

We were coming into Durham where the city obligingly sinks out of sight to leave a splendid view over its roof-tops of the cathedral rising from the foliage of riverside trees: firm as the rock it stands on, unearthly as the clouds above its twin towers. We watched it silently as we steamed north and, turning to each other, nodded approval.

"Reassuring," I said.

"One never knows these days when it may be the last time."

"It must make a perfect target," I said and then remembered that even if the cathedral was spared, this might be the last time he would see it. U-boats, mines, bombs, the sea itself would do their best to stop him from coming back.

The train was slowing down. The air held a familiar sharpness. The sky was high and clear. A callous light laid bare every soot-grimed brick of the industrial wasteland on either side: every broken slate and boarded window of its disused sheds and warehouses; every treeless patch of ravaged earth. On the bridge we had to wait. The Tyne was crammed with shipping. Barrage balloons hovered like air-borne whales. Gulls shrieked and wheeled. I came to life.

"It always felt strange. Kinning, I mean. I loved it but it wasn't right for me. The place."

"What was wrong with it?"

"There was always the feeling that there was more there than I could see." How could one describe the mysterious shifts of light and shade, the interchanging shapes of hills and clouds, the elusive human figures who could change their very nature from one moment to the next and even disappear altogether? "That's what makes it so beautiful, but it clouded my judgement and made me imagine too much. I didn't see things—or people—as they really were."

"I'm all for imagination," he said. "If it weren't for other people's imagination, you and I would be out of a job, the same job as it happens. But—yes, I do believe there is such a thing as the spirit of a place and that you were affected by it."

"Wonderful—and terrible."

"Like all enchantment."

The train lurched forward. He got up to take my bag from the rack.

"It would have been better for everybody if I'd never gone there."

"You could be wrong about that."

He slid open the door and we went out into the corridor.

"I don't suppose we shall meet again," I said. "I won't be going back to Kinning. But I'm very glad—and grateful—that we met even for such a short time, especially . . . and I hope you won't . . . I mean I hope you will . . ."

He cut short my stammering attempt to say something suitable by offering his hand.

"Goodbye, Kate," he said.

My parents were waiting on the platform. There was

just time for introductions, handshakes, warm thanks and farewells before his train pulled out.

After my brief revival I relapsed again, stunned by the noise and stench of locomotives and by the jostling crowds. All initiative left me. I was put like a dummy into a taxi and taken out of it at our own gate.

"It could have been much worse," my father said.

The remark roused me. I stared at him in disbelief. How could it have been worse? He was pointing at the garage. A land-mine dropped in the nearest field the week before had blown the door off.

"Thank God you're home," my mother said later in my bedroom. "No, don't talk, not yet. Mr. Westmain told us all about it on the phone. Mind your feet." She thrust into my bed a stone hot-water bottle wrapped in a vest. "Drink this and go to sleep. It's got something in it." She paused at the door. "There's so much kindness in the world. And really, I must say that was the handsomest man I've ever seen in my life."

I could not contradict, not only from lack of energy but because I had barely noticed his physical attributes. In an otherwise total bleakness he had been—the word occurred to me again—reassuring. But his was not the face I strove to rediscover as with eyes closed I strained imagination to its limits to bring back the form and features that could never live again except in memory.

26

My abrupt departure from Kinning culminated in an attack of pneumonia sharp enough to threaten a more permanent departure: a touch-and-go situation in which I would not have minded going but somehow contrived to remain in touch. Nothing good can be said of the illness except that it provided a respectable excuse for not going back. As soon as I could control a pen, I sent in my resignation.

I had been too much absorbed in other things to make any close friends on the staff. Emmie had left Bennets. Butler was the only one who wrote, declaring that she was no letter-writer but was anxious to know how I was. Her two or three notes contained nothing but small items of school news: nothing remotely connected with the Conrads, a subject she was evidently determined to steer clear of. I composed several letters to Mrs Conrad and posted none of them, persuading myself that too much time had passed and that a letter from me would only revive unhappy memories: a weakness I now deeply regret. Soon after I left, John Rokeby was seconded to an atomic-research unit, its whereabouts highly secret; and so another link with Kinning was broken.

Strange that an experience which had involved me so intensely should sink into the past almost without trace. But my time at Kinning had been short, no more than two terms in the steady succession of academic years on which I had left little imprint.

"My name was writ in water," I wrote to Cressida. "It will be as if I had never been."

"You're obviously getting better," she wrote in reply.

Her letter was as usual a comfort: such comfort, that is, as a single girl derives from the news that her best friend is engaged to be married.

The weeks of my convalescence were divided between my bedroom and the air-raid shelter, a grim apartment formerly a fuel store leading off the scullery. It had been cleaned up, white-washed, and reinforced with concrete to give protection against shrapnel and blast. The bombing was less severe than in the previous year, but from September to the end of December there were a good many raids, sometimes in daylight, more often at night.

Our daily maid left early in October to work in a munition factory, and it was one afternoon in that same month that Mrs Conch, who came in once a week to do the heavy work, appeared at my door to announce a visitor.

"For me?"

"I told her Mrs Borrow was out. 'It's Miss Borrow I've called to see,' she says. Very smart! But a southerner, you can tell. No, I didn't think to ask her name."

The visitor paused in the doorway. Smart indeed! Discreet make-up under a little velvet hat tilted over one eyebrow: a waisted camel-and-mohair coat; slim-fitting brown court shoes and—a lightning glance identified them—the sheerest of silk stockings.

"Emmie!"

There had been time to forget that I would never forgive her. Besides, the grudge I bore had been against another woman, not this elegant creature who bent over and actually kissed me, her eyes glowing with life and warmth.

"Kate! It's good to see you—and looking better than I

expected. I've been so worried. I heard from Butler and Dr Rooke."

"I should have written but . . ." It would have been a prevarication to say that I didn't know her address: I would not have written in any case.

"How could you? Besides, we parted—not quite friends. There was a cloud."

"I didn't know what I was doing. It was such a ghastly time. But this is wonderful. Where have you come from?" I assumed that her husband must be stationed somewhere near.

"From London. Stephen left yesterday for North Africa, we think. I had made up my mind that as soon as he went I would come and see you."

"You came all this way just to see me?"

"Indeed I did. How are you, Kate?"

"Oh, better. Except that you've taken my breath away. How long can you stay? Mother is out visiting but she'll be so pleased. Do take off your things. That hat!"—as she removed it. "You look marvellous."

"I wanted to impress you."

"And the stockings!"

"I brought you a pair. It's easier in London."

It was at that gratifying moment that the air-raid siren sounded an alert and was followed almost at once by the crackle of gun-fire.

"It may be nothing much."

We waited, ears cocked. The gun-fire continued; then came the ominous crump of a distant bomb—and another.

"We'd better go down. It's a good thing you got here before it started."

Mrs Conch had gone. We were alone in the house. There was no light or heat in the shelter. A candle under an inverted plant pot provided a little warmth, in time, and another in a jam jar gave a wan and dismal light. We wrapped ourselves in quilts and eiderdowns and sat on low bunks facing each other. The circumstances were not conducive to idle chat, as Emmie clearly felt.

"I had two reasons for wanting to see you," she said, coming accurately to the point. The hat had concealed the frown between her brows but it was still there. "It was obvious when you left without saying goodbye that I had offended you, even allowing for your being very upset about James. At first I couldn't understand it. It was only gradually that I worked it out."

I listened from the depths of my eiderdown and imagined her working it out. Seated in the wicker chair with Herbert in her lap, she would ponder, analyse my wayward goings-on and unaccountable attitudes, reduce the intractable material to a series of tenable propositions, draw suitable conclusions. . . .

"You weren't angry when you left Bennets to go to the farm. Did you resent my letting you go without warning you of what you would find out about James?"

"Yes. I thought it—" The bomb was still a comfortable distance away but near enough for us to hear the whine of its descent. I took the opportunity of an understandable pause to reject the word "cruel." "I thought it unfriendly of you not to tell me. You had known all the time, hadn't you, about James?"

"Suppose I had told you, right at the beginning, one or two things that might have influenced you: that there was mental instability in the family and that his father had committed suicide. Incidentally, I wasn't alone in knowing that."

"As a matter of fact, Butler told me."

I saw her pop this insignificant fact into a neat mental file before she went on:

"Did it make any difference to your feelings or put you on your guard?"

"You know it didn't."

"Then what would have been the point in my telling you? It must have been common knowledge years ago, when Mrs Conrad came back to the Hall, but Kinning takes that sort of thing in its stride. There's hardly a family that hasn't had some such tragedy to live down and, for most of the time, forget. In an inbred community the silences are inbred too."

She hadn't changed after all. On the sun-warmed flagstones at Bennets, its front wall draped with roses, by the first light of a rising moon, in one of her rare expansive moments, she had talked in just this way, pausing to resolve a problem in her knitting as now with no more than a lift of the eyebrows she paused to calculate the approximate distance of an occasional bomb.

"As for the other thing I knew, that he had been involved with Celia Mond, I had assumed that once he met you that affair was over—and a good thing too. It wasn't until she disappeared that I began to wonder what was going on. But if I'd told you that he hadn't been honest with you, what would you have done? Would you have stopped seeing him? Aren't you glad now that you went on being deceived? You surely don't begrudge him the happiness you had together. It didn't last long. He might not have had even that if I had interfered."

An air-raid shelter is not unlike a condemned cell. It too concentrates the mind wonderfully. A heavier raid would have made this conversation impossible even for Emmie: a lighter one would have left us elsewhere in an atmosphere less stark. Short of a direct hit we were safe, but there was just sufficient risk of total annihilation to clear the mind of cant. The rattle of gun-fire from coastal defences, the intermittent drone of an aircraft unmistakably "one of theirs," and the flat thud of bomb or land-mine—these sharpened the edge of awareness and at the same time set at a comfortable distance the subject of our talk.

It was as if all our previous encounters had been a preparation for this one. Stripped of the cosiness, the cocoa, and the cat, it had the utter simplicity of a meeting between two souls. Embedded in our quilts and eiderdowns, we had lost shape, become formless. Two faces regarded each other. Hers was pale. The candle made nonsense of her discreet make-up; but the eyes blazed, brilliant instruments of communication. This time she was the one who talked.

"No one can interfere in a love affair. It's useless to try. You have to find out for yourself, be hurt—and recover. Besides, in a thoroughly irrational situation like being in love, good advice can easily turn out to be the wrong advice. If I had warned you, you might have suffered less; but I do know that suffering makes you appreciate your happiness all the more when it comes back; when you're given another chance. That's really what I came to tell you." She broke off. "There it goes."

The long steady note of the siren confirmed her message. Life was never sweeter than at the first sound of the all-clear.

"I came to tell you that first love, however, deep, is no more than a foretaste of the happiness one finds in the second."

Did we really end on this high note? Dazed, blinking, we bundled ourselves out into the scullery, through the kitchen, and into the hall to find that the afternoon had gone. It would soon be dusk.

"You must have some tea."

"No, I must get to the station before the black-out. I'm sorry it isn't a longer visit."

In a few minutes she had left. It seemed probable that having made a careful study of timetables, she would arrive at whatever destination she had in mind. She had said what she came to say. It had not been an apology: she would have thought that a waste of time; she had offered what she valued more highly, an explanation; and—more convincingly—a demonstration of the transforming effect of happiness in a second love.

"Well!" My mother had lost no time in escaping from wherever she had been sheltering and must have met Emmie at the gate. "Mrs Brent! I do wish I'd been in. She isn't at all as you described her. I hadn't expected anyone so young and pretty." She looked me up and down. "As soon as you're fit to go shopping, you'll have to have something to wear. That second-hand woman in Shipley Street will give coupons for clothes in good condition, especially men's. Your father won't even notice. Of course it isn't legal but you're only young once. All the way from London! That's true friendship."

Whatever it was, it marked a turning-point. All was not lost. Emmie had spoken from experience. One could be happy again, though not for years, of course. The bitterness that had marred my memories of Bennets had gone. I began to get well and was soon strong enough to enjoy walking through autumn leaves along our quiet roads or on the hill overlooking the sea. Concrete posts and barbed wire sealed off the beaches, but from the cliff one could look down on the little pirate cove where sea-gulls nested —and smell seaweed.

Sometimes I dropped into a news theatre in town to watch Ministry of Information films and was particularly struck by the gallantry of our sailors manning the little corvettes in the Atlantic. There was always the possibility of catching a glimpse—under a peaked cap or behind a beard—of a face one knew.

By the New Year I was well enough to go back to work —to a post in a Senior School in a dingy part of our nearest town. It began as a challenge and soon became a crusade. Stopping occasionally to draw breath, I was surprised to find how much I loved it.

The Japanese attack on Pearl Harbor had changed the climate of the war. With the United States and Russia as our allies we were now sure of ultimate victory; but the huge expansion of hostilities made an early end impossible. It was not until the second half of 1942 that the tide turned in our favour. By that time the war had become a familiar way of life and seemed likely to go on until those of us who were left had grown old and grey: a prospect that might have depressed me had not an unexpected phone call given me something else to think about.

"It's for you." My mother handed me the receiver, mouthing something incomprehensible, and backed rather meaningfully out of earshot.

The voice, a man's, was faintly familiar, the call a short one.

"He's coming on the two twenty-eight and asked if he could call for an hour or two," I told my mother.

"You did say yes? He was wonderfully kind to you. Your father wanted to write and thank him but we had no address and you were so ill. They must have put in somewhere on the Tyne."

I met him at the station. It was over a year since he had rescued me from the catastrophe of James's death. We met without awkwardness, as friends who had shared an important experience; and even before that we had been acquainted, in an odd kind of way.

"I had always looked forward to meeting you," he said as we walked home, "though hardly under those circumstances. Actually I almost did once—at school."

"I remember. You left me a note."

"Sorry to have missed you, Miss Borrow." It had been a simple friendly message but by that time I had already cast him as the villain of the piece, sinister in every word and deed.

"I'd heard so much about you. People wrote to me, you

know: John, Miss Butler, not to mention the faithful pupils. It was Carole Mercer who kept me up to date until she left school. And you cropped up in most of the letters."

"I do hope . . ."

"The reports were favourable. In fact they made me uneasy. You sounded too good to be true. I'd almost got to the stage of hoping to hear that you had one or two small failings."

"Oh, if you only knew! There were plenty of those. And that was exactly the way I thought of you, a kind of paragon I could never live up to."

I was ashamed, having much more to conceal than envy of a successful rival; and it was doubly shameful that the resentment had apparently been all on my side.

We had stopped to let a convoy of army trucks go by and I could look at him. He must still have been the handsomest man my mother had ever seen. The past year, so far as I knew, had not greatly enlarged her experience of handsome men. But I thought the Battle of the Atlantic had probably left its mark on him. There was something about his eyes—they were of a deep blue and unexpectedly pensive—the eyes of a man who had seen other men drowning, dying of cold or in the heat of burning oil, or so fearfully mutilated that death would have been merciful. The bleakness of such memories and the knowledge that his own life might be short may have sharpened his natural inclination to put time to good use.

"Carole sent me a photograph of you taken on some outing or other. So you see, even when we met at Bardslow Edge you were no stranger to me." The last of the trucks had passed but he did not move. "You won't remember what I said. But it was perfectly true."

With some embarrassment I remembered my dramatic rush into his arms but not what he had said; and he didn't enlighten me. It was after he had left, during an unusually wakeful night, that the words came back to me, and with a new significance that set me smiling in the dark:

"You must be the girl I've been looking for."

That first visit was a short one. Far from being docked in the Tyne, his ship was at Liverpool. The trip to Chardon had been carefully timed with no margin for delay.

"You didn't think I would let you slip through my fingers," he said as I saw him off. "I wanted to give you time."

"That's a man who knows what he wants," my father said when I had drifted absent-mindedly home.

"And so good-looking," my mother sighed.

He came again—and again, whenever he had leave. We went dancing, walked on the cliffs, then went home to idle by the fire or in the garden. Above all we talked, and gradually it all came out. With him there were no forbidden areas; no fear of giving offence or inflicting unintentional wounds. I told him everything, much as I have told it here. Some of my wilder flights surprised and amused him; but sometimes I felt that my confidences and soul-searching revelations were no more than confirmation of what he already understood, so thorough and sound was his insight, so sympathetic his capacity for listening.

"I won't ask you to make any promises, Kate," he said, "until this is all over. Anything could happen, and you've already had to come to terms with one violent death. You must stay absolutely free."

It was clear from his manner that he hoped to be told this was nonsense, as indeed it was. If he was killed, what consolation would there be in not having exchanged vows? It was not his scruples that convinced me of the wisdom of waiting but my own caution. Old wounds were healed but their scars remained. I had learned that the brighter the prospect, the more relentlessly the sky can change.

But we did make plans. As Emmie had predicted, Edmund would not be going back to Kinning Grammar School. He had already been offered and had accepted a more promising post in Oxfordshire, and that was where we would make our home when he was demobbed. With all my hopes fixed on the future, I rarely thought of Kinning. Time and activity and natural resilience had successfully buried the past when in the summer of 1945 news from Cressida made me realise how shallow was the grave.

There were two letters in the morning post. The other was from Edmund. I took them up to my room and on the principle of keeping the best till last, opened Cressida's. It was written from her new home. She had enclosed a newspaper cutting and something that felt like a photograph.

> . . . Taking over Robert's father's house as well as the practice has certainly solved a lot of problems, but now that we're settled I feel at a loose end. Any chance of a visit before you get too much involved in wedding preparations? We're only about eight miles from Sheffield and the shops there are very good.
>
> And now, speaking of weddings, I always meant you to have this photograph but I've been doubtful about sending it in case—well, you've been so determined not to talk about that dreadful time at Kinning that I didn't want to upset you by bringing it up again. So I bided my time. But now that things are going so well for you, here it is. I happened to see it in a newspaper office in Plymouth a year ago, an enlargement right in the middle of the window. Then I caught sight of the name . . . knew you'd be interested . . . persuaded them to let me have a print. They weren't going to but the editor's daughter was a WREN and that helped. The groom, by

> the way, is a GI from a fabulously wealthy family . . . a chain of drugstores.

Mystified, I unwrapped the tissue paper with one hand.

> Isn't she lovely? Spiritual-looking, wouldn't you say? Or is that what all those yards of tulle are supposed to make you look? And what about the dress? Her in-laws must have sent it over. Talk about Bundles for Britain! We always said we wouldn't offer ourselves up in sacrificial white, but if one could look like this! Ah well, I suppose like me you'll have to make do with something that can be worn to shreds afterwards. . . .

I stared at the photograph in disbelief. Alive! And lovelier than ever. The fair oval face, innocently youthful in its cloud of white tulle, was serious. The delicate eyebrows, soft eyes, and slender neck were touching in their girlish purity. She looked not a day older for all she had suffered. I looked away and back again, as one would look incredulously at a vision rising in radiant white from the ruins of blitzed Plymouth.

Would one in such a situation experience this niggling sense of something having gone wrong: that this was the wrong sort of apparition to float serenely upward from the wreckage of an earlier tragic love? The feeling was unjust. But it was not the first time I had been saddened by a discrepancy between the ideal and the actual. I was making the same mistake again. Having endowed an unknown girl with a wealth of irreconcilable virtues—serenity and strength, innocence and charm, the entire range of femininity at its best—what on earth could I expect? There was nothing left for her to do except to fall short of the standard I had set her: nothing that would not disappoint me

—except to die. That was it. She could only satisfy me by remaining lifeless like a work of art.

And what was more—descending with unhappy speed from the sublime to the mundane, from the archetypal girl to the one in my hand, I was aware of an imperfection I could actually put my finger on. She had made a false step. It was surely, and especially in wartime, an error in taste to dress like that for one's *second* wedding.

As for the reappearance of the Monds in this new setting, they must have settled there when they left Kinning. I remembered that Mrs Mond had had a sister in Devon with whom she sometimes stayed.

In a world of bewildering changes one thing remained unaltered: my capacity for being wrong. Unfolding the cutting, I read the brief account of the wedding twelve months ago and discovered with rapidly alternating feelings of relief, pleasure, disappointment, and anxiety that the GI bride was Delphine.

The small incident affected me to quite an extraordinary degree. It taught me that my strange entanglement with Celia Mond had never ended. The absence of any reference to her in the newspaper need not be significant; there was no list of guests, little more than an announcement of the wedding with the names of the bride, groom, and parents, all that the shortage of newsprint allowed. But even to recall her name, to think of her at all, threatened my peace of mind and revived the morbid feelings of guilt I had only seemed to forget.

I had escaped from tragedy into a happiness far greater than any I had known before. But what about her? Her flight from Kinning had been more headlong even than mine. Where had it taken her? Into what depths of suffering? I was amazed at my own heartlessness in having allowed years to pass without trying to find out.

By this time someone, somewhere, must have had news

of her. She could not have vanished forever without trace. I owed it to her at least to make a few enquiries, even if it was as useless as to put flowers on a grave.

Besides, an unfinished story disturbs the mind with the disharmony that mars all unfinished things. A missing fragment confuses the pattern and frustrates the design so that no meaning can be seen in it, no purpose.

Edmund would help. He would know exactly what to do. Sure enough, as if he had known my need of guidance, his letter pointed the way. He was coming to Chardon but would break his journey at Kinning to arrange for the removal of his things.

"But there are far more important things to arrange," he wrote. "We've waited so long. . . ."

The thrilling nearness of my own marriage made me all the more keenly aware of the other marriage I had—though unintentionally—been instrumental in bringing to an end. Someone at Kinning must know the Monds' address: Sadie Peller perhaps, if she was still there. I telephoned Cressida and arranged to spend the weekend with her; then sent a wire to Edmund.

"Will meet you at Kinning about noon Saturday."

27

I lingered on the soft grass, my back against the sun-warmed milestone. The air was heavy with the scent of honeysuckle, the day so nearly perfect as to need only its crowning touch. Presently it came, heralded by the sound of quiet footsteps. My eyes on the last curve of the dusty road, I waited.

"Edmund! I'm sorry. You must have thought I wasn't coming."

"I must admit my heart sank when you weren't on the bus. Then I guessed that you wanted to come back gradually—on your own. No, don't get up. Just let me look at you."

We looked at each other, smiling as lovers do. I was aware that the green dress had been noted and approved. Cressida had been right.

"A milestone! What could be more appropriate to this stage in our affairs." He sat down beside me. "So—you've changed your mind. You don't feel that Kinning is the wrong place for you after all?"

"Not now. With you I could be happy anywhere."

"Then it's to be a ghost-laying exercise," he said when I had told him my reason for coming. "Let's see what we can do."

We sauntered arm-in-arm past the church and market cross to Butler's little house in Pottergate which he occasionally made use of while she was away on holiday.

"I shall have to see Dr Rooke," he said when we had finished our cold lunch, "and collect a few things. You'll come with me?"

"If you want me to. But wouldn't this be a good opportunity for me to have a chat with Sadie? You'll be quicker if you know I'm waiting for you, and we don't want to get involved with Mrs Rooke." On this, as on more important matters, we were in complete agreement.

"If you're not here in an hour, I'll come and find you."

"Only—if Sadie's not at home, I may wander about a little."

"Wherever you are," he said, "I'll find you."

When he had gone, I cleared away the remains of lunch, locked the door and stepped out into the sunny street. At the market cross, three or four people were waiting for a bus which was already in sight at the end of Pottergate. There was no one else about except a young man hurrying down Station Road, his gait a curious mixture between limping and loping. He recognised me and stopped.

"Parkinson! Denis!"

"You remember me, after all this time? Well, I'm blessed." He was in a dilemma, keeping an eye on the bus yet obviously wanting to talk. I asked about his leg.

"Could be worse. I was invalided out. Went into insurance. Are you staying long?"

"Only a short visit. I'm going to be married—to Mr Westmain."

"Hey, that's wonderful. He's a lucky man. As a matter of fact I'm married too. And what do you think, I'm a proud father. We've got a lovely little girl, Eve. I wish you could see her, Miss Borrow. Talk about intelligent. She's as bright as a button."

The last passenger to board the bus was beckoning.

"You'd better go."

"Why don't you walk along and see the baby, Miss Borrow. We're living in Mafeking Terrace, Number 12. You will?" He was delighted. "I'll be seeing you."

There would still be time to drop in on Sadie. I could make the acquaintance of the intelligent Eve and incidentally of Denis' wife, take the field path leading to the wood, and come back to Bennets by way of Foley Lane.

The long row of houses had kept its air of quiet respectability, with perhaps a slight falling off on the part of Number 12. Not that its condition was too discreditable to young Mrs Parkinson, who had after all a baby on her hands; but it certainly fell short of the spruceness of Number 11. My knock brought no reply, but the next-door neighbour appeared and came half-way down her path to tell me:

"She's out. She'll have taken the children for a walk. It's hard to find her in on a fine day."

With a critical glance at Number 12, followed by a sigh and a tightening of the lips, she went indoors.

Absolved for the time being from my promise to Denis, I skirted his house and took the path that led past the meadow, through a copse and eventually to the river. It was the way, in reverse, that James and I had walked home after the incident of the sparrow-hawk. It had been our last walk together. We had come up from the river to join this very path and there below—I came out of the copse and stopped to look down—we had lain on the thyme-scented bank, seen sun on a dragon-fly's wings, watched the hawk tearing apart its prey, seen death. Its effect on James had been a warning signal I should have recognised.

A new sound dispelled the memory: a child's voice raised in anxious appeal. On the farther bank a small boy was trying to attract my attention.

"She's there. I've found her." He was pointing to a red-and-white object lying on the last of the stepping stones, the one nearest to him but separated from him by two feet of rushing water. "But I can't reach her. Mummy won't let me go there by myself." He took a nervous step or two towards the water, ran back and positively danced with frustration. "She's in the water. Nearly in."

"Stay there. I'm coming." I ran down and across the stones to pick her up, a handsomely dressed cloth doll lying on her back, her two fair pigtails dangling in the stream, her painted eyes under their flaring lashes wide open in permanent astonishment. "She's all right. Just wet. You'll have to put her in the sun to dry."

His face too was wet but he had stopped crying. He was a slimly built little boy of between three and four years old, I judged. His eyes, upturned to me, were dark with concern. He took the doll hesitantly, as one might handle a dead thing, shivered, and was all at once transfigured with relief. Colour flooded to his face; his eyes shone blue; he became genial and informative.

"It's Eve's dolly," he said confidentially. "I came back to find her. Mummy and Eve are coming, but they're very slow."

The engaging friendliness with which he took my hand and pulled me gently towards the wood seemed to include me in the family circle. A charming child. Denis had not mentioned him, only Eve. Besides . . .

"She's called Flossie." My companion gave her a paternal shaking.

"And what's your name?" I asked, allowing myself to be led and totally unprepared for the answer. It came with the careful distinctness of a child still young enough to be proud of knowing it.

"James Conrad," he said.

I saw her first in the shade as she came towards us out of the wood, walking slowly with the baby in her arms: a dignified young country woman in a blue dress, her strong bare feet in brown sandals, her fair hair tied loosely at the back of her neck. Having opened and closed the gate with one hand, she came on in the same unhurried way and I saw her in full sunlight.

She was less slender than when I last saw her: her skin less delicate, her manner less responsive.

"Did you say thank you to the lady?"

Her glance included Flossie and me without distinguishing between us. If her smile lacked lightness and warmth, their absence was remarkable only because they were the qualities I remembered. Neither, on this occasion, was required.

"Thank you, thank you." James overdid it as he pranced round us, holding the doll by its arms and planting an occasional kiss on its surprised wet face. "Thank you very much."

"It's Eve's doll," his mother said, "but James loves it best."

She had not recognised me. A good deal had happened to her since our first meeting: much more—I took in as if they represented the whole spectrum of her experience the darker shades in her fair hair, the shadows that deepened her eyes, the stain of spilt baby food on her dress—much more than had happened to me. Moreover, she had known the disastrous part I played in her life but she had never known me. It didn't occur to me at that moment that our opportunities for knowing each other had been exactly equal.

"It's the best-dressed doll I've seen for years."

Indeed Flossie's red velvet skirt and white voile blouse were almost too smart for the life she was leading.

"I have a sister in America. She sent it."

This was my cue to make myself known by asking after Delphine. Why did I fail to take it? It must have been from a conviction that the resulting situation would be one I couldn't quite deal with. Such was my mental state that when James held out Flossie so that she, too, could say thank you, her look of vacant astonishment could well have been my own. After all, it must be a rare thing to see a ghost warm into life.

Celia put down the striped bag she was carrying over her arm and stooped to take out a shawl. The bag held a book too.

"Let me hold the baby while you do that."

Eve would be sandy-haired like the Parkinsons: a calm, chubby infant. When her mother had spread the shawl on the grass, I put her down to crawl.

"Thank you, thank you very much," James chanted in a passion of gratitude.

Celia wiped his tear-stained face and sent him to pick flowers, then seated herself between two sinuous tree roots, leaned back against the trunk, and took out her book.

"You can't have much time for reading," I observed, "with two small children."

"I make time," she said.

Though dismissed, I could not bring myself to leave. One does not lightly quit the scene where a resurrection has just taken place. She who had been lost was found. The various guises in which she had haunted me for so long—pale corpse, lost soul, reproachful ghost—were suddenly and disconcertingly obsolete.

There she sat quietly reading under a tree a few yards away: James's wife, James's widow, and now James's mother. With her had been exhumed much more that had been buried, much that we had shared. So I stayed, feeling that there was more to be shared, more to be said. Yet to sit down would have been too deliberate an act. It would have prolonged uncomfortably an encounter comprising too many omissions. The discomfort, I dare say, would have been entirely mine. If Celia's enviable poise had ever been at risk, she had retained it.

I took refuge in helping to pick daisies. Eve cooed and crawled; her mother turned a page; James and I ranged the grassy slope together. And as we plucked and exclaimed over each new find, in getting to know the younger James, I advanced in knowledge of the elder.

I was fairly sure (it dismayed me to acknowledge some element of doubt) that if he had known of Celia's pregnancy, he would have told me. Very likely when they had last met, neither of them had known: or perhaps she had intended to tell him and had been silenced by all that he had to tell her, not to mention the silencing effect of his hands on her throat.

After their long separation in the winter it must have been in the Easter vacation that Celia had conceived. Before or after James had allegedly fallen in love with me? Amid all that there was to forgive it seemed the supreme act of treachery to have remained so very positively the husband of a wife he no longer loved. If his relationship with her was as he had described it, if he was already tired of her as he professed, there had been no need for *that,* I told myself with a coolness I had not felt before.

And with a surge of relief I knew that I had broken free of him. Until now, even after all this time, the obligation to keep faith with him had troubled me. It had modified my happiness in Edmund's deeper, more selfless love. But now —the sensation was as distinct as if I had taken a physical step—I left him behind. It was over.

"There! Those are all for you."

Young James was scattering daisies in his mother's lap. She hugged him, removed a dandelion from Eve's mouth, and returned to her book. The curves of her cheeks and mouth had lost their girlish prettiness and taken on a less fragile beauty. Her downward-tilted profile expressed a self-contained gravity. With her attention fixed once more on the printed page, her withdrawal was complete.

My mind slid in amazement to Parkinson, who had mentioned his lovely intelligent daughter but not his lovely intelligent wife. "Celia would never look at me," he had once said ruefully. I thought it unlikely that she ever had looked at him as she had looked at James. But looking at Parkinson might be one of the things she hadn't needed to do: he had always been there. Like the tree, the stream, the long dark nights of winter, he was part of the natural environment to which she was now committed. She was, after all, a village girl.

Her concentration on the book impressed me. Seeing it as a pathetic attempt to hold on to the intellectual life once within her grasp, I edged near enough to read the title. It was not what I expected. With her left hand Celia groped in her bag, found a bar of chocolate, and bit confidently into it without taking her eyes from the book, a popular romance of the lighter kind.

"No more daisies!" My small companion was staring dismally at what must have seemed to him a vast stretch of flowerless grass. "We've picked them all." His abrupt descent into melancholy was familiar. He gazed mournfully at his two fistfuls of white-faced flowers. "No more hands."

"Bring them to me, love." Celia laid aside her book, face down. "There are plenty for a daisy chain." She spread the flowers over her skirt. "Now then . . ."

His features lost their sharpness. He flushed with pleasure, quivering with eagerness for her to begin.

"With James it's all sunshine and showers," Celia said, remembering that I was still there.

"Like his father."

The remark slipped out. I had not meant to say it. She turned her head slowly. Our eyes met. Now that we were at last, unbelievably, face to face, how would she respond to so momentous a meeting?

"I'm Kate Borrow." I bowed my head, not knowing what to expect—reproach . . . or forgiveness?

"Oh, yes." Looking up, I saw her dredge my name from the depths of memory and consider it dubiously like a drowned relic that could once have had significance. "You used to be . . ."

It was not a response I had expected but I was still too much concerned with what must be said to take on its implications.

"I've thought of you," I said, "a great deal." Even if words could convey those thoughts and the extent to which they had influenced me, this was no time for anything but simplicity. "I never thought there would be an opportunity to tell you, to explain that if I caused you unhappiness, it really wasn't my fault. I didn't know about you and James until right at the end. Otherwise I would never have . . ."

The explanation petered out. She had given no sign of the kind of flurry I was feeling. Had her eyes clouded? When she spoke, did her voice tremble? I thought not—and soon discovered why.

"Do you know, I'm afraid I'd forgotten all about you," she said.

The appalling remark might have been redeemed by the air of bright sweet candour with which she made it if I had not felt (recovering myself as from a slap in the face) that an air was all it was! The manner that had once charmed me had become—if it had not always been—a mannerism.

Could she have forgotten that Delphine had told her James and I were engaged: that James had told her that he loved me? Was it possible that while I, constant to her memory, had refined and elevated her into pure spirit, she had barely noted my existence before erasing it altogether from her mind?

"In any case it doesn't matter now," she said.

Still speechless but less dazzled now by the serene beauty of the face turned towards me, I wondered if what didn't matter now had ever mattered; or whether harsh truths had simply glanced off that gleaming glassy surface. Forgotten phrases, other people's, came back to me:

"smugly enclosed in her own bright self, . . . a kind of obtuseness, . . . a coarsening of the sensibilities . . ." phrases I felt under no obligation to repress.

"There had been no news of you," I said at last, and was aware of some justifiable coarsening in my own sensibility, "when I left Kinning."

She looked away from me and spoke into the blue scented air, not so much letting me into her confidence as addressing some other audience. Herself? Yet however marginal my involvement in her life, she did seem to acknowledge my right at least to talk about it.

"I had written to my husband but the letter didn't arrive until after . . . until it was too late. It was returned to me."

"So he never knew"—I guessed the contents of the letter —"about the baby."

"No. But he had provided for me in his will. There will be plenty of money."

"James loved children," I said, feeling the need to strike a different note. As a reproof for what I thought a lack of taste, it missed its target. Celia was pursuing another line.

"I ought to have come back sooner." The brightness had grown brighter, the sweetness sweeter, as if—I would once have thought—in response to an inner light. Now I wondered if it had ever seemed like that to Parkinson, and if so, for how long.

"James would still have been alive if I hadn't left him as I did. You see, he couldn't face life without me." The lovely eyes were clear as an unclouded summer sky and as empty of sorrow. She spoke with the same limpid enthusiasm as in the classroom when she had talked of poetry and virtue and experience, and with the same groundless confidence. "That's why he killed himself. He loved me too much and couldn't bear to think that he had hurt me. It was wrong of me to leave him without a word. Afterwards

I realised he must have thought he had driven me to suicide—and wanted to join me."

"It must be a comfort to you," I said but not immediately, "to feel that he loved you like that."

"It's not just a feeling. I know. His love for me never changed."

"Then why did you run away?"

The blunt question may have forced her errant memory back to the scene in the shooting lodge. She had involuntarily raised her hand to her throat.

"It seemed the only thing to do. I don't talk about it. But the last time I saw him, James was upset. He didn't know what he was doing—or saying. He was suffering from delusions, I knew that. It must have been the beginning of his breakdown. Perhaps you know that when people are in a disturbed state, they usually turn against the person they love best. It seemed the only thing to do—to go away. I have never blamed him. . . ."

The sweetly patient smile, the brave lift of the head may still have been the outward signs of inward grace; but as she spoke of James I could only think that his anguish had washed over her: that tragedy was beyond her scope.

My eyes came to rest on their son, so like his father. There was one comfort. Whatever hazards lay ahead of him, his mother's heart would not be broken by them.

"Yes," Celia said, her eyes following mine, "he is like his father. I'll show you something." She drew a locket from inside her dress and opened it. "Mrs Conrad gave it to me."

It was a tinted photograph of a child's face, the resemblance so strong that it could have been young James. It roused in me no memory of the James I had known. What did interest me was the other half of the locket.

"It is strange," Celia was saying, "meeting you like this. And of course I do remember now." Some faintly tactful impulse must have stirred in her. "You were attracted to

James yourself. As you said, you didn't know that he was married." She became aware of my interest. "Oh yes, it's very precious to me."

It was a lock of hair of a pale brown streaked with gold.

"Before she went away, Mrs Conrad asked me to see to James's personal things. Naturally I had been upset about everything," she said with smiling composure. "Then when I found this . . . It was in the breast pocket of his jacket, the one he always wore. I didn't even know that he had a lock of my hair. He must have treasured it and it proved to me that he always felt me near him, no matter what happened." She closed the locket. "When I found that he had kept it next to his heart, I knew that nothing had ever come between us."

It cost me an effort, beset as I was by a variety of emotions, most of them unworthy, but I could afford to be generous; and the words when they came were perfectly true:

"I know just how you felt. It was very touching."

And briefly, from far away and long ago, there came back to me the feel of a March day with flying clouds . . . a glimpse of Gipsies in the hollow.

As for the hair, Celia's was less fair than it had been but still fairer than mine. She had seen in the curl, as she had seen in the whole affair, what she wanted to see. Not that she was alone in being able to turn things into other things. I had been something of an expert in the field myself, though the faculty seemed to be deserting me now. I had never seen Celia as she really was, but neither had she; and a great many other things she had not seen at all.

Especially me. The flimsiness of my existence did at least make it easy for me to melt away.

"Do give my love to Delphine when you write."

She licked a smear of chocolate from her fingers and put the locket away.

"We don't write." And when I proffered the lame suggestion that families drift apart, she added: "She took offence for some reason and hasn't forgiven me."

"But surely—"

What on earth could there be that Delphine would not forgive—except the rebuff of not being wanted, not being told, of waiting in distress for news that did not come?

"I don't know why. But she does send presents to the children." Celia's smile was only slightly tinged with regret for her sister's disengagement.

"Shall we start now?" James thrust the first overheated daisy into his mother's hand. She split the stem with her thumb-nail and did not look up as we exchanged goodbyes.

I backed away, then turned and took to my heels, splashed across the stream and ran up the slope on the other side. Arriving breathless on the path, I saw Edmund coming to meet me as he had promised.

"I've got news for you," he called. "You'll never guess." And coming closer. "What's happened? You look—subdued."

I pointed.

"Celia! Yes, I was going to tell you. I heard about it from Rooke. So—you found what you were looking for." I thought he seemed amused. "And now you're satisfied."

The missing fragment was in place; had suffered no noticeable damage; was safely provided for and in perfect health. But I shook my head and told him why.

"She's got it all wrong," I concluded. "And she's become so . . ." Impossible to describe what she had become. "When I remember the girl she used to be . . ."

"The girl you gave so much thought to never existed, Kate. You invented her." He put his hands on my shoulders and gave me a gentle shake. "You saw Celia in the light that never was on sea or land and turned her into a poem. That's your special gift and one of the things I love you for. What's more, you created her in your own image."

While I considered this extraordinary theory, he went on:

"The qualities you saw in Celia were your own. Remember I know you both. No doubt you added a few more that you would like to have, but the light and warmth, the charm and loveliness are yours, my love."

"Now who's inventing?"

I wasn't so misguided as to believe him. All the same I was gratified, to say the least; and if he could think of me like that, it certainly seemed to show how much in love he was.

"There must be something about this place," I conceded modestly, "if it can make you see me as I once saw Celia."

He was looking thoughtfully at the little group on the other side of the stream.

"I can well believe," he said, "that her account of things would be different from yours."

I too looked down again at the blue figure under the wide-spreading branches. I knew her now: shallow, insensitive . . .

Imperceptibly the leaves moved. A changed light wavered upon her hair, leaving the rest of her in deeper shade. The judgement was harsh: too harsh. It made no allowance for the cunning distortions of memory or the ease with which the mind can falsify; and surely there had also been something more: some grace, some glimmer of beauty to transcend those lesser things and set the visionary flame alight in me if not in others.

The daisy chain was finished. The children had fallen asleep. To the beautiful stillness of the afternoon the seated figure seemed to bring a matching stillness, an equal beauty. If there were imperfections, from this distance I could not see them; could not, in the pattern of light and shade under the boughs, make out the details. For a moment, before the shadows moved again, the composition was complete, the picture flawless.

If Edmund was right and it was my own blurred vision that transformed the commonplace and made it dreamlike —well, he had no room to speak. Turning quickly, I caught the expression in his eyes and knew that he had been looking at me in the same deluded way. It was a discovery in which I found no cause for complaint.

"Shall we go?" He drew my arm through his.

"Listen!"

The sound was indistinct, low-pitched and soft. I thought she was singing. But it was only the murmur of the stream I heard as countless lovers must have heard it: some who loitered in the wood and escaped unscathed from its enchanted glades; and others less fortunate; none of them able to remember exactly how it all happened; each one telling a different story.

FREE FROM DELL

with purchase plus postage and handling

Congratulations! You have just purchased one or more titles featured in Dell's Romance 1990 Promotion. Our goal is to provide you with quality reading and entertainment, so we are pleased to extend to you a limited offer to receive a selected Dell romance title(s) *free* (plus $1.00 postage and handling per title) for each romance title purchased. Please read and follow all instructions carefully to avoid delays in your order.

1) Fill in your name and address on the coupon printed below. No facsimiles or copies of the coupon allowed.
2) The Dell Romance books are the only books featured in Dell's Romance 1990 Promotion. Any other Dell titles are not eligible for this offer.
3) Enclose your original cash register receipt with the price of the book(s) circled plus $1.00 **per book** for postage and handling, payable in check or money order to: Dell Romance 1990 Offer. Please do not send cash in the mail.
   Canadian customers: Enclose your original cash register receipt with the price of the book(s) circled plus $1.00 **per book** for postage and handling in U.S. funds.
4) This offer is only in effect until March 29, 1991. Free Dell Romance requests postmarked after March 22, 1991 will not be honored, but your check for postage and handling will be returned.
5) Please allow 6-8 weeks for processing. Void where taxed or prohibited.

Mail to: Dell Romance 1990 Offer
P.O. Box 2088
Young America, MN 55399-2088

Dell

NAME____________________

ADDRESS____________________

CITY__________ STATE__________ ZIP__________

BOOKS PURCHASED AT____________________

AGE____________________

(Continued)

Book(s) purchased: ______________________________

____

____

I understand I may choose one free book for each Dell Romance book purchased (plus applicable postage and handling). Please send me the following:

(Write the number of copies of each title selected next to that title.)

☐ **MY ENEMY, MY LOVE**
Elaine Coffman
From an award-winning author comes this compelling historical novel that pits a spirited beauty against a hard-nosed gunslinger hired to forcibly bring her home to her father. But the gunslinger finds himself unable to resist his captive.

☐ **AVENGING ANGEL**
Lori Copeland
Jilted by her thieving fiancé, a woman rides west seeking revenge, only to wind up in the arms of her enemy's brother.

☐ **A WOMAN'S ESTATE**
Roberta Gellis
An American woman in the early 1800s finds herself ensnared in a web of family intrigue and dangerous passions when her English nobleman husband passes away.

☐ **THE RAVEN AND THE ROSE**
Virginia Henley
A fast-paced, sexy novel of the 15th century that tells a tale of royal intrigue, spirited love, and reckless abandon.

☐ **THE WINDFLOWER**
Laura London
She longed for a pirate's kisses. . . even though she was kidnapped in error and forced to sail the seas on his pirate ship, forever a prisoner of her own reckless desire.

☐ **TO LOVE AN EAGLE**
Joanna Redd
Winner of the 1987 *Romantic Times* Reviewer's Choice Award for Best Western Romance by a New Author.

☐ **SAVAGE HEAT**
Nan Ryan
The spoiled young daughter of a U.S. Army General is kidnapped by a Sioux chieftain out of revenge and is at first terrified, then infuriated, and finally hopelessly aroused by him.

☐ **BLIND CHANCE**
Meryl Sawyer
Every woman wants to be a star, but what happens when the one nude scene she'd performed in front of the cameras haunts her, turning her into an underground sex symbol?

☐ **DIAMOND FIRE**
Helen Mittermeyer
A gorgeous and stubborn young woman must choose between protecting the dangerous secrets of her past or trusting and loving a mysterious millionaire who has secrets of his own.

☐ **LOVERS AND LIARS**
Brenda Joyce
She loved him for love's sake, he seduced her for the sake of sweet revenge. This is a story set in Hollywood, where there are two types of people—lovers and liars.

☐ **MY WICKED ENCHANTRESS**
Meagan McKinney
Set in 18th-century Louisiana, this is the tempestuous and sensuous story of an impoverished Scottish heiress and the handsome American plantation owner who saves her life, then uses her in a dangerous game of revenge.

☐ **EVERY TIME I LOVE YOU**
Heather Graham
A bestselling romance of a rebel Colonist and a beautiful Tory loyalist who reincarnate their fiery affair 200 years later through the lives of two lovers.

Dell

TOTAL NUMBER OF FREE BOOKS SELECTED ____ X $1.00 = $______ (Amount Enclosed)

Dell has other great books in print by these authors. If you enjoy them, check your local book outlets for other titles.